BLACK
HEART

Also by Holly Black from Gollancz:

White Cat
Red Glove
Black Heart

BLACK HEART

HOLLY BLACK

The Curse Workers
Book Three

The right of Holly Black to be identified as the author
of this work has been asserted by her in accordance with
the Copyright, Designs and Patents Act 1988.

First published in Great Britain in 2012
by Gollancz
An imprint of the Orion Publishing Group
Orion House, 5 Upper St Martin's Lane,
London WC2H 9EA
An Hachette UK Company

This edition published in Great Britain in 2013
by Gollancz

1 3 5 7 9 10 8 6 4 2

A CIP catalogue record for this book
is available from the British Library

ISBN 978 0 575 09681 3

Printed in Great Britain by
Clays Ltd, St Ives plc

The Orion Publishing Group's policy is to use papers
that are natural, renewable and recyclable products and
made from wood grown in sustainable forests. The logging
and manufacturing processes are expected to conform to
the environmental regulations of the country of origin.

www.blackholly.com
www.orionbooks.co.uk
www.gollancz.co.uk

To Fizzgig, my long-haired gray moppet of a cat, who was patient and friendly despite always appearing enraged.

CHAPTER ONE

MY BROTHER BARRON sits next to me, sucking the last dregs of milk tea slush noisily through a wide yellow straw. He's got the seat of my Benz pushed all the way back and his feet up on the dash, the heels of his pointy black shoes scratching the plastic. With his hair slicked back and his mirrored sunglasses covering his eyes, he looks like a study in villainy.

He's actually a junior federal agent, still in training, sure, but with a key card and an ID badge and everything.

To be fair, he's also a villain.

I tap my gloved fingers impatiently against the curve of the wheel and bring a pair of binoculars to my eyes for about the millionth time. All I see is a boarded-up building on the wrong side of Queens. "What is she *doing* in there? It's been forty minutes."

"What do you think?" he asks me. "Bad things. That's her after-school job now. Taking care of shady business so Zacharov's gloves stay clean."

"Her dad won't put her in any real danger," I say, but the tone of my voice makes it pretty obvious I'm trying to convince myself more than I'm trying to convince my brother.

Barron snorts. "She's a new soldier. Got to prove herself. Zacharov couldn't keep her out of danger if he tried—and he's not going to be trying real hard. The other laborers are watching, waiting for her to be weak. Waiting for her to screw up. He knows that. So should you."

I think of her at twelve, a skinny girl with eyes too large for her face and a nimbus of tangled blond hair. In my memory she's sitting on the branch of a tree, eating a rope of red licorice. Her lips are sticky with it. Her flip-flops are hanging off her toes. She's cutting her initials into the bark, high up, so her cousin can't claim she's lying when she tells him she got higher than he ever will.

Boys never believe I can beat them, she told me back then. *But I always win in the end.*

"Maybe she spotted the car and went out the back," I say finally.

"No way she made us." He sucks on the straw again. It makes that rattling empty-cup sound, echoing through the car. "We're like ninjas."

"Somebody's cocky," I say. After all, tailing someone isn't easy, and Barron and I aren't that good at it yet, no matter what he says. My handler at the agency, Yulikova, has been encouraging me to shadow Barron, so I can learn second-hand and can keep myself safe until she figures out how to tell her bosses that she's got hold of a teenage transformation worker with a bad attitude and a criminal record. And since Yulikova's in charge, Barron's stuck teaching me. It's supposed to be just for a few months, until I graduate from Wallingford. Let's see if we can stand each other that long.

Of course, I'm pretty sure this isn't the kind of lesson Yulikova's been imagining.

Barron grins, white teeth flashing like dropped dice. "What do you think Lila Zacharov would do if she knew you were tailing her?"

I grin back. "Probably she'd kill me."

He nods. "Probably she would. Probably she'd kill me twice for helping you."

"Probably you deserve it," I say. He snorts.

Over the last few months I got every last thing I ever wanted—and then I threw it all away. Everything I thought I could never have was offered up on a silver platter—the girl, the power, a job at the right hand of Zacharov, the most formidable man I know. It wouldn't even have been that hard to work for him. It probably would have been fun. And if I didn't care who I hurt, it would still all be mine.

I lift the binoculars and study the door again—the worn paint striping the boards and crumbling like bread crumbs, the chewed-up bottom edge as ragged as if it had been gnawed on by rats.

Lila would still be mine.

Mine. The language of love is like that, possessive. That should be the first warning that it's not going to encourage anyone's betterment.

Barron groans and throws his cup into the backseat. "I can't believe that you blackmailed me into becoming Johnny Law and now I have to sweat it out five days a week with the other recruits while you use my experience to stalk your girlfriend. How is that fair?"

"*One*, I think you mean the extremely dubious benefit of your experience. *Two*, Lila's not my girlfriend. *Three*, I just wanted to make sure she was okay." I count off these points on my leather-covered fingers. "And *four*, the last thing you should want is *fairness*."

"Stalk her at school," Barron says, ignoring everything I've just said. "Come on. I have to make a phone call. Let's pack in this lesson and get a couple of slices. I'll even buy."

I sigh. The car is stuffy and smells like old coffee. I'd like to stretch my legs. And Barron is probably right—we should give this up. Not for the reason he's saying but for the one that's implied. The one about it not being okay to lurk around outside buildings, spying on girls you like.

My fingers are reaching reluctantly for my keys when she walks out of the worn door, as though my giving up summoned her. She's got on tall black riding boots and a steel gray trench. I study the quicksilver gestures of her gloved hands, the sway of her earrings, the slap of her heels on the steps, and the lash of her hair. She's so beautiful, I can barely breathe. Behind her follows a boy with his hair braided into the shape of two antelope horns. His skin is darker than mine. He's got on baggy jeans and a hoodie. He's shoving a folded-up wad of something that looks like cash into an inside pocket.

Outside of school Lila doesn't bother wearing a scarf. I can see the grim necklace of marks on her throat, scars black where ash was rubbed into them. That's part of the ceremony when you join her father's crime family, slicing your skin and swearing that you're dead to your old life and reborn into wickedness. Not even Zacharov's daughter was spared it.

She's one of them now. No turning back.

"Well, now," says Barron, gleeful. "I bet you're thinking we just observed the end of a very naughty transaction. But let's consider the possibility that actually we caught her doing something totally innocent yet embarrassing."

I look at him absently. "Embarrassing?"

"Like meeting up to play one of those card games where you have to collect everything. Pokémon. Magic the Gathering. Maybe they're training for a tournament. With all that money she just handed him, I'm guessing he won."

"Funny."

"Maybe he's tutoring her in Latin. Or they were painting miniatures together. Or he's teaching her shadow puppetry." He makes a duck-like gesture with one gloved hand.

I punch Barron's shoulder, but not really hard. Just hard enough to make him shut up. He laughs and adjusts his sunglasses, pushing them higher on his nose.

The boy with the braids crosses the street, head down,

hood pulled up to shadow his face. Lila walks to the corner and raises her hand to hail a cab. The wind whips at her hair, making it a nimbus of blown gold.

I wonder if she's done her homework for Monday.

I wonder if she could ever love me again.

I wonder just how mad she'd be if she knew I was here, watching her. Probably really, really mad.

Cold October air floods into the car suddenly, tossing around the empty cup in the backseat.

"Come on," Barron says, leaning on the door, grinning down at me. I didn't even notice him getting out. "Grab some quarters for the meter, and your stuff." He jerks his head in the direction of the boy with the braids. "We're going to follow him."

"What about that phone call?" I shiver in my thin green T-shirt. My leather jacket is wadded up in the backseat of my car. I reach for it and shrug it on.

"I was bored," Barron says. "Now I'm not."

This morning when he told me we were going to practice tailing people, I picked Lila as my target half as a joke, half out of sick desire. I didn't think that Barron would agree. I didn't think that we'd actually see her leaving her apartment building and getting into a town car. I for sure didn't think that I would wind up here, close to actually finding out what she's been doing when she's not in school.

I get out of the car and slam the door behind me.

That's the problem with temptation. It's so damn tempting.

"Feels almost like real agent work, doesn't it?" Barron says as we walk down the street, heads bowed against the wind. "You know, if we caught your girlfriend committing a crime, I bet Yulikova would give us a bonus or something for being prize pupils."

"Except that we're not going to do that," I say.

"I thought you wanted us to be good guys." He grins a too-wide grin. He's enjoying needling me, and my reacting only makes it worse, but I can't stop.

"Not if it means hurting her," I say, my voice as deadly as I can make it. "Never her."

"Got it. Hurting, bad. But how do you excuse stalking her and her friends, little brother?"

"I'm not excusing it," I say. "I'm just doing it."

Following—*stalking*—someone isn't easy. You try not to stare too hard at the back of his head, keep your distance, and act like you're just another person freezing your ass off in late October on the streets of Queens. Above all you try not to seem like a badly trained federal agent wannabe.

"Stop worrying," Barron says, strolling along beside me. "Even if we get made, this guy will probably be flattered. He'd think he was moving up in the world if he had a government tail."

Barron is better at acting casual than I am. I guess he should be. He's got nothing to lose if we're spotted. Lila couldn't possibly hate him more than she does. Plus, he probably trains for this all day, while I'm at Wallingford studying to get into the kind of college there is no way I am ever going to attend.

It still annoys me. Since I was a kid, we've competed over lots of things. Mostly, all those competitions were ones I lost.

We were the two youngest, and when Philip would be off with his friends on the weekends, Barron and I would be stuck doing whatever errands Dad needed doing, or practicing whatever skill he thought we needed to learn.

He particularly wanted us to be better at pickpocketing and lock-picking than we were.

Two kids are the perfect pickpocket team, he'd say. *One to do the lift, the other one to distract or to take the handoff.*

We both practiced dips. First identifying where Dad kept his wallet by looking for a bulge in a back pocket or the way one side of his coat swung heavily because something was inside. Then the lift. I was pretty good; Barron was better.

Then we practiced distraction. Crying. Asking for directions. Giving the mark a quarter that you claim they dropped.

It's like stage magic, Dad said. *You've got to make me look over there so I won't notice what's happening right in front of my face.*

When Dad didn't feel like fending off our clumsy attempts at lifts, he'd bring us to the barn and show us his collection: He had an old metal tackle box with locks on all the sides, so you had to run the gauntlet of seven different locks to get into it. Neither Barron nor I ever managed.

Once we learned how to open a lock with a tool, we'd have to learn to pick it with a bobby pin, with a hanger, then with a stick or some other found object. I kept hoping that I'd be naturally great at locks, since I was pretty sure I wasn't a worker back then, and since I already felt like an outsider in my family. I thought that if there was one thing I was better at than all of them, that would make up for everything else.

It sucks to be the youngest.

If you get into the supersecure box, we'll sneak into the movie of your choice, Dad would say. Or, *I put candy in there.* Or, *If you really want that video game, just open the box and I'll get it for you.* But it didn't matter what he promised. What did matter was that I only ever managed to pick three locks; Barron managed five.

And here we are again, learning a bunch of new skills. I can't help feeling a little bit competitive and a little bit disappointed in myself that I'm already so far behind. After all, Yulikova thinks Barron has a real future with the Bureau. She told me so. I told her that sociopaths are relentlessly charming.

I think she figured I was joking.

"What other stuff do they teach you at federal agent school?" I ask. It shouldn't bother me that he's fitting in so well. So what if he's faking it? Good for him.

I guess what bothers me is him faking it better than I am.

He rolls his eyes. "Nothing much. Obvious stuff— getting people to trust you with mirroring behavior. You know, doing whatever the other person's doing." He laughs. "Honestly, undercover's just like being a con man. Same techniques. Identify the target. Befriend. Then betray."

Mirroring behavior. When a mark takes a drink from his water glass, so should you. When he smiles, so should you. Keep it subtle, rather than creepy, and it's a good technique.

Mom taught it to me when I was ten. *Cassel,* she said, *you want to know how to be the most charming guy anyone's ever met? Remind them of their favorite person. Everyone's favorite person is their own damn self.*

"Except now you're the good guy," I say, and laugh.

He laughs too, like I just told the best joke in the world.

But now that I'm thinking about Mom, I can't help worrying about her. She's been missing since she got caught using her worker talent—emotion—to manipulate Governor Patton, a guy who hated curse workers to begin with and now is on national news every night with a vein popping out of his forehead, calling for her blood. I hope she stays hidden. I just wish I knew where she was.

"Barron," I say, about to start up a conversation we've already had about a million times, the one where we tell each other that she's fine and she'll contact us soon. "Do you think—"

Up ahead the boy with the braids steps into a pool hall.

"In here," Barron says, with a jerk of his head. We duck into a deli across the street. I'm grateful for the warmth. Barron orders us two coffees, and we stand near the window, waiting.

"You ever going to get over this thing with Lila?" he asks me, breaking the silence, making me wish I'd been the one to do it, so that I could have picked another subject. Any other subject. "It's like some kind of illness with you. How long have you been into her? Since you were what, eleven?"

I don't say anything.

"That's why you really wanted to follow her and her new hire, right? Because you don't think that you're worthy of her, but you're hoping that if she does something awful enough, maybe you'll deserve each other after all."

"That's not how it works," I say, under my breath. "That's not how love works."

He snorts. "You sure?"

I bite my tongue, swallowing every obnoxious taunt that comes into my mind. If he doesn't get a rise out of me, maybe he'll stop, and then maybe I can distract him. We stand like that for several minutes, until he sighs.

"Bored again. I'm going to make that phone call."

"What if he comes out?" I ask, annoyed. "How am I going to—"

He widens his eyes in mock distress. "Improvise."

The bell rings as he steps out the door, and the guy at the counter shouts his customary "Thanksforcomingcome-again."

On the sidewalk in front of the deli, Barron is flirting like crazy as he paces back and forth, dropping the names of French restaurants like he eats off a tablecloth every night. He's got his phone cradled against his cheek, smiling like he's buying the line of romantic nonsense he's selling. I feel sorry for the girl, whoever she is, but I am gleeful.

When he gets off the phone I will never stop making fun of him. Biting my tongue won't be enough to keep me from it. I would have to bite off my whole face.

He notices me grinning out the window at him, turns his back and stalks to the entranceway of a closed pawnshop half a block away. I made sure to waggle my eyebrows while he was looking in my direction.

With nothing else to do, I stay put. I drink more coffee. I play a game on my phone that involves shooting pixelated zombies.

Even though I've been waiting, I'm not really prepared when the boy with the braids walks out of the pool hall. He's got a man with him, a tall guy with hollow cheekbones and greasy hair. The boy lights a cigarette inside his cupped palm, leaning against the wall. This is one of those moments when a little more training would help. Obviously running out of the deli and waving my arms at Barron is the wrong move, but I don't know the right one if the boy starts moving again. I have no idea how to signal my brother.

Improvise, he said.

I walk out of the deli as nonchalantly as I can manage. Maybe the kid's just hit the street for a smoke. Maybe Barron will notice me and come back over on his own.

I spot a bus stop bench and lean against it, trying to get a better look at the boy.

This isn't a real assignment, I remind myself. It doesn't matter if he gets away. There's probably nothing to see. Whatever he's doing for Lila, there's no reason to think that he's doing it now.

That's when I notice the way that the boy is gesturing grandly, his cigarette trailing smoke. Misdirection, a classic of magic tricks and cons. *Look over here,* one hand says. He must be telling a joke too, because the man is laughing. But I can see his other hand, worming out of his glove.

I jump up, but I'm too late. I see a flash of bare wrist and thumb.

I start toward him, not thinking—crossing the street, barely noticing the screech of a car's brakes until I'm past it. People turn toward me, but no one is watching the boy. Even the idiot guy from the pool hall is looking in my direction.

"Run," I yell.

The hollow-cheeked man is still staring at me when the boy's hand clamps around the front of his throat.

I grab for the boy's shoulder, too late. The man, whoever he was, collapses like a sack of flour. The boy spins toward me, bare fingers reaching for skin. I catch his wrist and twist his arm as hard as I can.

He groans and punches me in the face with his gloved hand.

I stumble back. For a moment we just regard each other. I see his face up close for the first time and am surprised to notice that his eyebrows are carefully tweezed into perfect arches. His eyes are wide and brown beneath them. He narrows those eyes at me. Then he turns and runs.

I chase after him. It's automatic—instinct—and I'm wondering what I think I'm doing as I race down the sidewalk. I risk a look back at Barron, but he's turned away, bent over the phone, so that all I see is his back.

Figures.

The boy is fast, but I've been running track for the last three years. I know how to pace myself, allowing him to get ahead of me at first when he starts sprinting, but catching up once he's winded. We go down block after block, me getting closer and closer.

This is what I'm supposed to do once I'm a federal agent, right? Chase bad guys.

But that's not why I'm after him. I feel like I am hunting my own shadow. I feel like I can't stop.

He glances back at me, and I guess he sees that I'm gaining on him, because he tries a new strategy. He veers abruptly into an alley.

I take the corner in time to see him reaching for something under his hoodie. I go for the nearest weapon I can find. A plank of wood, lying near a stack of garbage.

Swinging it, I catch him just as he gets out the gun. I feel the burn of my muscles and hear the crack as wood hits metal. I knock the pistol against the brick wall like it's a baseball and I'm in the World Series.

I think I'm as surprised as he is.

Taking slow steps, I hold up the plank, which is split now, a big chunk of the top hanging off by a splinter, the remainder jagged and pointed like a spear. He watches me, every part of him tense. He doesn't look much older than I am. He might even be younger.

"Who the hell are you?" When he speaks, I can see that some of his teeth are gold, flashing in the fading sun. Three on the bottom. One on top. He's breathing hard. We both are.

I bend down and lift the gun in one shaking hand. My thumb flicks off the safety. I drop the plank.

I have no idea who I am right now.

"Why?" I say, between breaths. "Why did she pay you to kill him?"

"Hey," he says, holding up both his hands, the gloved and ungloved one, in a gesture of surrender. Despite that, he seems more stunned than scared. "If he was your friend, then—"

"He wasn't my friend."

He lowers his hands slowly until they rest at his sides, like he has made a decision about me. Maybe that I'm not a cop. Maybe that it's okay to relax. "I don't ask why anyone wants anything. I don't know, okay? It was just a job."

I nod. "Let me see your throat."

"No marks." He pulls the neck of his shirt wide, but there's no scarring there. "I freelance. I'm too pretty for all that bullshit. No one puts a collar on Gage."

"Okay," I say.

"That girl—if you know her, you know what she's about." He reaches into his mouth, pulling out a loose tooth—a real one—black with rot at the top. It sits like a flawed pearl in the palm of his glove. Then he grins. "Good thing murder pays so well, right? Gold's expensive."

I try to hide my surprise. A death worker who loses only a single tooth with each hit is a very dangerous guy. Every curse—physical, luck, memory, emotion, dream, death, and even transformation—causes some kind of blowback. As my grandfather says, all work works the worker. Blowback can be crippling, even lethal. Death curses rot a part of the worker's body, anything from a lung to a finger. Or, apparently, something as minor as a tooth.

"What's a death worker need a gun for anyway?" I ask.

"That gun's real sentimental. Belonged to my gran." Gage clears his throat. "Look, you're not going to shoot. You would have done it already. So can we just—"

"You sure you want to double-dog-dare me?" I say. "You sure?"

That seems to rattle him. He sucks on his teeth. "Okay, all I know is what I heard—and not from . . . *her*. She never said anything, except where I could find him. But there's rumors that the guy—he goes by Charlie West—bungled a job. Killed a family in what was supposed to be a simple smash and grab. He's a drunk coward—"

My phone starts to ring.

I reach down and tug it out of my pocket with one hand, then glance down. It's Barron, probably just having realized that I ditched him. At that moment Gage vaults himself at the chain-link fence.

I look at him go, and my vision blurs. I don't know who I'm seeing. My grandfather. My brother. Myself. Any of us could be him, could have been him, coming from a hit, scrambling to get over a fence before getting shot in the back.

I don't yell for him to get down. I don't fire a warning shot or any of the stuff that I could do—that a federal agent trainee watching a murderer escape should do. I just let him go. But if he's got the role that I was supposed to have, then I have no idea how to be the person left in the alley. The good guy.

I wipe off the gun on my green shirt, then tuck it in the

waistband of my jeans, against the small of my back, where my jacket will cover it. After I'm done, I walk to the mouth of the alley and call Barron.

When he arrives, he's with a bunch of guys in suits.

He grabs me by the shoulders. "What the hell were you doing?" his voice is low, but he sounds honestly shaken. "I had no idea where you were! You didn't answer your phone."

Except for that last time, I hadn't even heard it ring.

"I was *improvising*," I say smugly. "And you would have seen me if you hadn't been busy hitting on some girl."

If his expression is any indication, only the presence of other people keeps him from strangling me. "These guys showed up at the murder scene right after the cops," he says, giving me a loaded look. As mad as he is, I understand what he's trying to communicate. *I didn't call them,* his expression says. *I didn't tell them anything about Lila. I didn't betray you. I didn't betray you yet.*

The agents take down my statement. I tell them that I followed the hit man, but he got ahead of me and over the fence. I didn't see where he went from there. I didn't get that good of a look at him. His hood was up. No, he didn't say anything. No, he didn't have a weapon—or at least nothing other than his bare hand. Yes, I shouldn't have followed him. Yes, I know Agent Yulikova. Yes, she will vouch for me.

She does. They let me go without patting me down. The gun remains tucked in the back of my jeans, rubbing against the base of my spine as Barron and I walk back to the car.

"What really happened?" Barron asks me.

I shake my head.

"So, what are you going to do?" he asks, like he's challenging me. Like there's even a question. "Lila ordered that hit."

"Nothing," I say. "What do you think? And you're not doing anything either."

Girls like her, my grandfather once warned me, girls like her turn into women with eyes like bullet holes and mouths made of knives. They are always restless. They are always hungry. They are bad news. They will drink you down like a shot of whisky. Falling in love with them is like falling down a flight of stairs.

What no one told me, with all those warnings, is that even after you've fallen, even after you know how painful it is, you'd still get in line to do it again.

CHAPTER TWO

WALLINGFORD PREPARA-tory on a Sunday night is full of exhausted students trying to do the homework we were sure would be easy, back on Friday when the weekend stretched before us, full of lazy hours. I yawn as I walk in, as guilty as anyone. I still have a paper to write and a big chunk of *Les Misérables* to translate.

My roommate, Sam Yu, is lying on his stomach on his bed, headphones covering his ears, head nodding in time with music I can't hear. He's a big guy, tall and heavy, and the springs of his bed groan when he turns over to look at me. The dorms are full of cheap cots with frames threaten-ing to break every time we sit on them, chipboard dressers, and cracked walls. It's not like the Wallingford campus doesn't have beautiful wood-paneled chambers with soaring ceilings and leaded glass windows. It's just that those spaces are for professors and donors. We might be allowed in them, but they're not for us.

I shoulder my way into our closet and step up onto a sagging box. Then, reaching under my jacket, I pull out the gun, and tape it with a roll of duct tape high on the back wall, above my clothes. I arrange a jumble of old books on the shelf just below it to block it from view.

"You've got to be kidding me," Sam says.

He clearly watched the whole thing. I didn't even hear him get up. I must be losing my touch.

"It's not mine," I say. "I didn't know what to do with it."

"How about *getting rid of it?*" he says, his voice dropping to a harsh whisper. "That's a *gun*. A gun, Cassel. A guuuuuuuun."

"Yeah." I climb down, hopping off the box and landing with a thud. "I know. I will. I just didn't have time. Tomorrow, I promise."

"How much time does it take to throw a *gun* in a *dumpster?*"

"I really wish you would stop saying the word 'gun,'" I say, low, flopping down onto my own bed and reaching for my laptop. "There's nothing I can do about it now, unless I want to chuck it out the window. I'll deal with it tomorrow."

He groans and goes back to his side of the room, picking up his headphones. He looks annoyed, but nothing worse. I guess he's used to me acting like a criminal.

"Whose?" he asks finally, nodding toward the closet.

"Some guy. He dropped it."

Sam frowns. "That sounds likely—and by 'likely' I mean '*not at all likely*.' And by the way, did you know that if someone found that thing in here, not only would you be thrown out of school, you would be, like, stricken from school memory. They would burn your face out of the Wallingford yearbooks. They would get a team of memory workers to come in and make it so that no one even recalled they'd ever gone to school with you. This is exactly the kind of thing they promise parents will never happen at Wallingford Preparatory."

A shudder runs across my shoulders at the mention of memory workers. Barron is one. He used his power to make me forget a lot of things—that I am a transformation worker, that he pushed me into becoming a disturbingly efficient assassin, even that I transformed Lila into an animal and he kept her in a cage for years. My sociopathic big brother, who stole chunks of my life. The only brother I have left. The one who's training me.

That's family for you. Can't live with them; can't murder them. Unless Barron rats me out to Yulikova. Then I really might.

"Yeah," I say, trying to regain the thread of the conversation. "I'll get rid of it. I promise. No, wait, I already promised. How about I pinkie swear?"

"Unbelievable," Sam says, but I can tell he's not really mad. As I am busy determining this, watching the play of emotions cross his face, I notice he's got about a dozen pens piled on the navy blanket next to him and he's marking a pad with each one.

"What are you doing over there?"

He grins. "I got these on eBay. A whole case of disappearing-ink pens. Nice, right? They were used by the KGB. These are serious spy tools."

"What are you going to do with them?"

"Two choices, really. Awesome prank or potentially actually useful for our bookmaking operation."

"Sam, we've already talked about this. It's yours now, if you want it, but I'm out." I've been the bookie for ridiculous school stuff for as long as I've been at Wallingford. If you wanted to put money down on the football game, you came to me. If you wanted to put down money on whether or not there was Salisbury steak for lunch three times a week or whether Headmistress Northcutt and Dean Wharton were having an affair or whether Harvey Silverman would die of alcohol poisoning before he graduated, you also came to me. I would calculate the odds, hold the cash, and charge a commission for my trouble. In a school with lots of bored rich kids, it was a good way to line my pockets. It was pretty harmless, until it wasn't. Until kids started taking bets on which students were curse workers. Until those students were targets.

Then it felt a lot like I was taking blood money.

Sam sighs. "Well, there are still endless pranks we could pull. Imagine a whole room full of test takers, and then *nothing* on any of the tests twenty-four to forty-eight hours later. Or what if you slipped one of these into a teacher's grade book? Chaos."

I grin. Chaos, beautiful chaos. "So, which one will you choose? My pickpocketing skills are at your service."

He chucks a pen in my direction. "Be careful you don't do your homework with that," he says.

I snatch it out of the air a moment before it crashes into my lamp. "Hey!" I say, turning back to him. "Watch it. What's with the wild pitch?"

He's looking at me with a strange expression on his face. "Cassel." His voice has gone low and earnest. "Do you think you could talk to Daneca for me?"

I hesitate, glancing down at the pen in my hands, turning it over in my gloved fingers, then looking back up at him. "About what?"

"I apologized," he says. "I keep apologizing. I don't know what she wants."

"Did something happen?"

"We met up for coffee, but then it turned into the same old argument." He shakes his head. "I don't understand. She's the one who lied. She's the one who never told me she was a worker. She probably never would have told me either, if her brother hadn't blurted it out. How come I'm the one who has to keep apologizing?"

In all relationships there's a balance of power. Some relationships are a constant fight for the upper hand. In others one person is in charge—although not always the person who thinks they are. Then, I guess there are relationships so equal that no one has to think about it. I don't know anything about those. What I do know is that power can shift in a moment. Way back at the beginning of their relationship, Sam was always deferring to Daneca. But once he got mad, he couldn't seem to stop being angry.

By the time he was ready to hear her apology, she no longer wanted to give it. And so they've somersaulted back and forth these past few weeks, neither one sorry enough to placate the other, neither of them sorry at the right time, both sure the other is in the wrong.

I can't tell if that means they're broken up or not. Neither can Sam.

"If you don't know why you're apologizing, your apology probably sucks," I say.

He shakes his head. "I know. But I just want things to go back to the way they were."

I know that feeling all too well. "What do you want me to say to her?"

"Just find out what I can do to fix things."

There's so much desperation in his voice that I agree. I'll try. He's got to know he's already in a pretty bad way if he's coming to me for help in matters of the heart. There's no point rubbing it in.

In the morning I am crossing the quad, hoping the coffee I drank in the common room will kick in soon, when I pass my ex-girlfriend, Audrey Dolan, in a clump of her friends. Her copper hair gleams like a new penny in the sunlight, and her eyes follow me reproachfully. One of her friends says something just low enough for me not to hear, and the rest laugh.

"Hey, Cassel," one of them calls, so that I have to turn around. "Still taking bets?"

"Nope," I say.

See, I'm *trying* to go legit. I'm trying.

"Too bad," the girl shouts, "because I want to put down a hundred bucks that you'll die alone."

Sometimes I don't know why I am fighting so hard to stay here at Wallingford. My grades, always determinedly and consistently mediocre, have really taken a dive in the last year. It's not like I'm going to college. I think about Yulikova and the training my brother is getting. All I would have to do is drop out. I'm just delaying the inevitable.

The girl laughs again, and Audrey and the others laugh with her.

I just keep walking.

In Developing World Ethics we talk a little bit about journalistic bias in reporting and how it influences what we think. When asked to give an example, Kevin Brown brings up an article about my mother. He thinks that too many reporters blame Patton for being an easy dupe.

"She's a criminal," says Kevin. "Why try to act like Governor Patton was supposed to be prepared for his girlfriend to try to curse him? It's an obvious example of a reporter trying to discredit the victim. I wouldn't be surprised if that Shandra Singer had gotten to him, too."

Someone snickers.

I stare at my desk, focusing on the pen in my hand, and the sound of chalk scraping across the board as Mr. Lewis quickly launches into an example from a recent news story about Bosnia. I feel that strange hyper-focus that occurs when everything narrows to the present. The past and the future fade away. There is only now and the ticking moments, until the bell rings and we hustle out into the hall.

"Kevin?" I say softly.

He turns, smirking. People rush around us, clutching bags and books. They look like streaks of color in my peripheral vision.

I hit Kevin's jaw so hard that I feel the impact right down to my bones.

"Fight!" a couple of kids yell, but teachers come and drag me back from Kevin before he can get up.

I let them pull me away. I feel numb all over, the adrenaline still coursing through my veins, nerves sparking with the desire to do something more. To do something to someone.

They take me to the dean's office and leave me with a slip of paper pressed into my hand. I crumple it up and throw it against the wall as I am shown inside.

Dean Wharton's room is stacked with papers. He looks surprised to see me, getting up and lifting a pile of folders and crossword puzzles out of the chair in front of his desk and indicating that I should sit. Usually whatever trouble I'm in is so bad I get sent straight to the headmistress.

"Fighting?" he says, looking at the slip. "That's two demerits if you're the one who started it."

I nod. I don't trust myself to speak.

"Do you want to tell me what happened?"

"Not really, sir," I say. "I hit him. I just—I wasn't thinking straight."

He nods like he's considering what I said. "Do you understand that if you get one more demerit for any reason, you'll get expelled? You won't graduate from high school, Mr. Sharpe."

"Yes, sir."

"Mr. Brown will be here in a moment. He's going to be telling me his side of the story. Are you sure you don't have anything more to say?"

"No, sir."

"Fine," Dean Wharton says, pushing up his glasses so that he can massage the bridge of his nose with brown-gloved fingers. "Go wait outside."

I go and sit in one of the chairs in front of the school secretary. Kevin walks past me with a grunt, on his way into Wharton's office. The skin along Kevin's cheek is turning an interesting greenish color. He's going to have a hell of a bruise.

He's going to tell Wharton, *I don't know what came over Cassel. He just went nuts. I didn't provoke him.*

A few minutes later Kevin leaves. He smirks at me as he walks out into the hall. I smirk right back.

"Mr. Sharpe, can you come in here, please?"

I do. I sit back in the chair, looking at the piles of paper. Just one push would send a stack crashing into all the others.

"You angry about something?" Dean Wharton asks me, as though he can read my thoughts.

I open my mouth to deny it, but I can't. It's like I have

been carrying this feeling around with me for so long that I didn't even know what it was. Wharton, of all people, has put his finger on what's wrong with me.

I'm *furious*.

I think of not knowing what compelled me to strike a gun out of the hand of a killer. Of how satisfying it was to hit Kevin. Of how I want to do it again and again, want to feel bones snap and blood smear. Of how it felt to stand over him, my skin on fire with rage.

"No, sir," I manage to get out. I swallow hard because I don't know when I became so distanced from myself. I knew Sam was angry when he talked about Daneca. How come I didn't know that I was mad too?

Wharton clears his throat. "You've been through a lot, between the death of your brother Philip and your mother's current . . . legal woes."

Legal woes. Nice. I nod.

"I don't want to see you head down a path you can't come back from, Cassel."

"Understood," I say. "Can I go back to class now?"

"Go on. But remember, you have two demerits and the year isn't even half over. One more and you're out. Dismissed."

I get up, sling my backpack over my shoulder, and slink back to the Academic Center in time for the next bell. I don't see Lila in the halls, although my gaze pauses on any blond-haired girl who passes me. I have no idea what I will say to her if I do see her. *So, I hear you ordered your first murder. How was that?* seems a little on the nose.

Besides, who says it was her first?

I duck into the bathroom, turn on the faucets, and splash my face with cold water.

It's a shock, liquid streaming over my cheeks and collecting in the hollow of my throat, splashing my white shirt. Darkening my gloves. Stupidly, I forgot to take them off.

Wake up, I tell myself. *Snap out of it.*

Reflected in the mirror, my dark eyes look more shadowed than ever. My cheekbones stand out, like my skin is too tight.

Really fitting in, I tell myself. *Dad would be so proud. You're a real charmer, Cassel Sharpe.*

I still make it to physics before Daneca does, which is good. Theoretically she and I are still friends, but she's been avoiding me since she started fighting with Sam. If I want to talk to her, I'm going to have to corner her.

We don't have assigned seats, which means it's easy for me to find a desk near where Daneca usually sits and dump my stuff on the chair. Then I get up and talk to someone on the other side of the room. Willow Davis. She seems suspicious when I ask her a question about the homework, but answers without too much hesitation. She's telling me something about how there are ten different dimensions of space and one of time, all curled around one another, when Daneca comes in.

"Understand?" Willow asks. "So there could be other versions of us living in other worlds—like maybe there's a world where ghosts and monsters are real. Or where no one is hyperbathygammic. Or where we all have snake heads."

I shake my head. "That can't be real. That *cannot* be real science. It's too awesome."

"You didn't do the reading, did you?" she asks, and I decide that this is the moment to retreat to my new desk.

When I walk back, I see my plan has worked. Daneca is sitting where she always does. I move my backpack and flop into its place. She looks up, surprised. It's too late for her to get up without it being really obvious that she doesn't want to sit next to me. She scans the room like she's racking her brain for some excuse to move, but the seats are mostly full.

"Hey," I say, forcing a smile. "Long time, no see."

She sighs, like she's resigned herself to something. "I heard you got into a fight." Daneca's wearing her Wallingford blazer and pleated skirt with neon purple tights and even brighter purple gloves. The color of them more or less matches the faded purple streaks in her wooly brown hair. She kicks clunky Mary Janes against the brace of the desk.

"So you're still mad at Sam, huh?" I realize this probably isn't how he'd want me to broach the subject, but I want information and class is about to start.

She makes a face. "He told you that?"

"I'm his roommate. His moping told me that."

She sighs again. "I don't want to hurt him."

"So don't," I say.

Daneca leans toward me and lowers her voice. "Let me ask you something."

"Yes, he's really, really sorry," I say. "He knows he overreacted. How about you guys forgive each other and start—"

"Not about Sam," she says, just as Dr. Jonahdab walks

into the room. The teacher picks up a piece of chalk and starts sketching Ohm's law on the board. I know what it is because of the words "Ohm's law" above it.

I open my notebook. "What, then?" I write, and turn the pad so that Daneca can see it.

She shakes her head and doesn't say anything else.

I am not really sure I understand the relationship between current and resistance and distance any better by the end of class, but it turns out Willow Davis was right about the whole snake-head dimension thing being possible.

When the bell rings, Daneca takes my arm, her gloved fingers digging in just above my elbow.

"Who killed Philip?" she asks suddenly.

"I—," I start. I can't answer without lying, and I don't want to lie to her.

Daneca's voice is low, an urgent whisper. "My mother was your lawyer. She did your immunity deal for you, the one that got the Feds off your back, right? You made a deal to tell them who killed those people in the files. And Philip. For *immunity*. Why did you need immunity? What did you do?"

When the Feds dumped a bunch of files onto my lap and told me Philip had promised to name the killer, I didn't really stop Daneca from looking at them. I knew that was a mistake, even before I realized the files were all of people I'd transformed, a list of bodies that were never found— and haven't been found since. More missing memories.

"We've got to get going," I say. The classroom has emptied out, and a few students are starting to come in for the next class. "We're going to be late."

She reluctantly lets go of my arm and follows me out the door. It's funny how our positions are reversed. Now she's the one trying to corner me.

"We were working on that case together," Daneca says. Which is sort of true. *"What did you do?"* she whispers.

I look down at her face, searching for what she thinks the answer is. "I never hurt Philip. I never hurt my brother."

"What about Barron? What did you do to him?"

I frown, so confused that for a moment I can't think of what to say. I have no idea where she got that from. "Nothing!" I say, throwing my hands wide for emphasis. "Barron? Are you crazy?"

A faint flush colors her cheeks. "I don't know," she says. "You did something to *someone*. You needed immunity. Good people don't need immunity, Cassel."

She's right, of course. I'm not a good person. The funny thing about good people—people like Daneca—is that they really honestly don't *get* the impulse toward evil. They have an incredibly hard time reconciling with the idea that a person who makes them smile can still be capable of terrible things. Which is why, although she's accusing me of being a murderer, she seems more annoyed than actually worried about getting murdered. Daneca seems to persist in a belief that if I would just *listen* and understand how bad my bad choices are, I'd stop making them.

I pause near the stairs. "Look, how about I meet you after dinner and you can ask me whatever you want? And we can talk about Sam." I can't tell her everything, but she's my friend and I could tell her more than I have. She deserves as much truth as I can afford to give. And who knows, maybe if I just *listen* for once, I will make some better choices.

I couldn't make much worse ones.

Daneca brushes a brown curl behind her ear. Her purple glove is smeared with ink. "Will you tell me *what* you are? Will you tell me that?"

I suck in my breath in honest surprise. Then I laugh. I've never told her my biggest secret—that I'm a transformation worker. I guess it's time. She must have worked out something or she wouldn't have asked.

"You got me," I say. "You got me there. Yeah, I'll tell you that. I'll tell you everything I can."

She nods slowly. "Okay. I'll be in the library after dinner. I have a paper to start."

"Great." I jog down the stairs, running full tilt when I hit the quad so I can make it to ceramics before the final bell. I already have two demerits. I've been in enough trouble for a single day.

My pot comes out totally misshapen. It must have had an air bubble in it too, because when I put it into the kiln, it explodes, taking out three other people's cups and vases along with it.

On my way to track practice, my phone rings. I flip it open and cradle it against my cheek.

"Cassel," Agent Yulikova says. "I'd like you to stop by my office. Now. I understand your classes are over for the day, and I've arranged for you to be excused. The office understands that you have a doctor's appointment."

"I'm on my way to track," I say, hoping that she'll hear the hesitation in my voice. I have a gym bag slung over my shoulder, bouncing off my leg. Overhead the trees are blowing in the wind, covering the campus in a drifting carpet of leaves with the colors of a sunrise. "I've missed a lot of meets."

"Then they won't notice if you miss another one. Honestly, Cassel. You almost got yourself killed yesterday. I would like to discuss the incident."

I think of the gun, taped in the closet of my dorm room. "It wasn't any big thing," I say.

"Glad to hear it." With that, she hangs up.

I head toward my car, kicking leaves as I go.

CHAPTER THREE

A FEW MINUTES LATER

Agent Yulikova is gathering up piles of paper and shifting them out of the way so that she can get a better look at me. She's got straight gray hair, chopped to hang just beneath her jawline, and a face like a bird's—delicate and long nosed. Masses of chunky beaded necklaces hang around her throat. Despite holding a steaming cup of tea and wearing a sweater under her navy corduroy jacket, her lips have a bluish tint, like she's cold. Or maybe like she *has* a cold. Either way she more closely resembles a professor from Wallingford than the head of a federal program to train worker kids. I know she probably dresses the way she does on purpose, to lure trainees into feeling comfortable. She probably does everything on purpose.

It still works.

She's my handler, the one who's responsible for ushering me into the program as soon as I am eighteen, per the deal I made with the Feds. Until then, well, I don't know what she's supposed to do with me. I suspect she doesn't know either.

"How are you doing, Cassel?" she asks me, smiling. She acts like she really wants to know.

"Good, I guess." Which is a huge, ridiculous lie. I'm barely sleeping. I'm plagued with regrets. I'm obsessed with a girl who hates me. I stole a gun. But it's what you say to people like her, people who are evaluating your mental state.

She takes a sip from her mug. "What's it been like shadowing your brother?"

"Fine."

"Philip's death must make you feel more protective of Barron," she says. Her gaze is kind, nonthreatening. Her tone is neutral. "It's just the two of you now. And even though you're the younger brother, you've had a lot of responsibility placed on you. . . ." She lets her words trail off.

I shrug my shoulders.

"But if he put you in any danger yesterday, then we need to put a stop to things immediately."

"No, it wasn't like that," I say. "We were just following someone—a random person—and then Barron got a call. So I was on my own for a couple minutes, and I saw the murder. I chased after the kid—the killer—which was stupid, I guess. But he got away, so that's that."

"Did you talk to him?" she asks.

"No," I lie.

"But you cornered him in the alley, correct?"

I nod, then think better of it. "Well, for a second he was cornered. Then he went for the fence."

"We found a broken plank near the scene. Did he swing it at you?"

"No," I say. "No, nothing like that happened. Maybe he stepped on it as he was running. It all happened so fast."

"Could you describe him?" She leans forward in her seat, peering at me, like she can see my every fleeting thought in the involuntary flinches and flushes of my body. I really hope that's not true. I'm a good liar, but I'm not world class. My experience has been mostly with two different kinds of adults—criminals, who act in ways I can anticipate, and marks, who can be manipulated. But with Yulikova I'm out of my depth. I have no idea what she's capable of.

"Not really," I say with a shrug.

She nods a few times, like she's taking that in. "Is there anything else you want to tell me about what happened?"

I know I should admit to taking the gun. If I confess now, though, she'll ask me why I took it. Or maybe she'll just ask Barron what we were doing. Who we were tailing. If he's in the right mood, he might even tell her. Or worse, he'll make up a story so fanciful that it leads her straight to Lila faster even than the truth would.

It's not that I want to be this person, doing the wrong thing again, lying to Yulikova. I want to learn how to do the right thing, even if I hate it. Even if I hate her for it. I just *can't* this time.

But next time—next time I'll do better. I'll tell her everything. Next time.

"No," I say. "It really was no big thing. I was just stupid. I'll be more careful."

She picks up a clipped packet of papers from her desk and drops them in front of me with a significant look. I know what they say. Once I sign them, I'm no longer a regular citizen. I will be agreeing to a private set of regulations and laws. If I screw up, I will have agreed to be tried in a private court. No more jury of my peers. "Maybe it's time for you to leave Wallingford early and train with Barron and all the other students full-time."

"You've said that before."

"And you've said no before." She smiles. Then, opening up one of the drawers of the desk, she pulls out a tissue. She coughs into it. I see something dark stain the paper before she wads it up. "I'm guessing you're going to say no again now."

"I want to be a federal agent and work for the LMD. I want—" I stop. *I want to be better. I want you to make me better.* I can't say that, though, because it's crazy. Instead I say, "Becoming a high school dropout isn't exactly a dream of mine. And anyway, my immunity agreement—"

She cuts me off. "We might be able to scare up a diploma for you."

I imagine not having to see Lila, her white-gold hair long enough to curl at the nape of her neck, her smoky voice distracting enough that I can barely pay attention to whatever it is that I'm doing when she speaks. I imagine not having to grit my teeth to avoid calling her name every time I pass her in the hall. "Soon. I just want to finish out the year."

Yulikova nods, like she's disappointed but not surprised. I wonder about her coughing and the tissue—was that blood on it? I don't feel right asking. None of this feels right.

"How are you doing with the charms?" she asks.

I reach into my pocket and pull them out. Five perfect circles of stone with holes bored in the middle. Five transformation amulets to stop a curse from a worker like me, not that there are many workers like me. Making the charms was draining, but at least there was no blowback involved. They'd been sitting in my glove compartment for a week, waiting for me to deliver them.

"Very rare," she says. "Have you ever worn one of these amulets and cast a curse?"

I shake my head. "What would happen if I did?"

Yulikova smiles. "A lot of nothing. The stone would crack and you would be exhausted."

"Oh," I say, oddly disappointed. I don't know what I was expecting. Shaking my head at myself, I drop the amulets onto the desk in front of her. They roll and spin and clatter like coins. She looks at them for a long moment, then raises her eyes to me.

"It's personally important that you stay safe." She takes another sip of her tea and smiles again.

I know that she probably says that to dozens of potential recruits, but I still like it when she says it to me.

On the way out her gloved hand touches my arm briefly. "Have you heard from your mother?"

Yulikova's voice is soft, like she's really concerned about a seventeen-year-old boy on his own and scared for his mother. But I bet she's fishing for information. Information I wish I had.

"No," I say. "She could be dead for all I know." For once I'm not lying.

"I'd like to help her, Cassel," she says. "Both you and Barron are important to us here in the program. We'd like to keep your family together."

I nod noncommittally.

Criminals get caught eventually—it's a tenet of being in the life. But maybe things are different for government agents. Maybe their mothers stay out of prison forever. I guess I ought to hope so.

From the outside the building is nondescript, a dull medium-size concrete structure in the middle of a parking lot, its mirrored windows gleaming with reflected light from the setting sun. No one would guess that a federal agency occupies the upper floors, especially since the sign out front promises RICHARDSON & CO., ADHESIVES AND SEALANTS and almost everyone coming in and out is wearing a sharp-looking suit.

Above me the trees are mostly brown and bare, the reds and golds of early autumn faded by the cold October wind. My Benz is right where I left it, reminding me of the life I could have had if I'd accepted Lila's father's offer and become his secret weapon.

More and more I feel like the boy who cut off his nose to spite his face.

I drive back to Wallingford, arriving with just enough time to dump off my gym bag and grab a granola bar before I have to meet Daneca at the library. I jog up the stairs and am about to unlock the door to my room when I realize it's already open.

"Hello?" I say as I go in.

Sitting on my bed is a girl. I've seen her around campus, but I don't think we've ever spoken. She's a sophomore, Asian—Korean, I think, with long black hair that hangs to her waist like a waterfall, and thick white socks that come almost to her knees. Her eyes are lined with glittering blue pencil. She looks up at me from under long lashes and smiles shyly.

I'm a little flustered, I have to admit. This doesn't happen a lot. "Are you waiting for Sam?"

"I was hoping to talk to you." She stands, lifting her pink book bag and biting her bottom lip. Then, hesitating, she adds, "I'm Mina. Mina Lange."

"You're really not supposed to be in my room," I say, dropping my gym bag.

She grins. "I know."

"I was just about to head out," I say, glancing toward the door. I have no idea what kind of game she's playing, but the last time a girl turned up on my bed, everything went directly to hell sans handbasket. I'm not exactly optimistic. "I don't mean to be rude, Mina, but if there's something you want to tell me, you should probably do it now."

"Can't you stay?" she asks, taking a step toward where I'm standing. "I have a really big favor to ask, and there's no one else who can help."

"I find that hard to believe." My voice comes out a little strained-sounding. I think of Daneca and all of the explaining I have ahead of me. The last thing I need is to be late and have one more thing to explain. "But I guess I could wait a few minutes if it's important."

"Maybe we could go somewhere else," she says. Her lips are glossy pink, soft-looking. Her white-gloved finger wraps around a strand of her long black hair, twirling it nervously. "Please."

"Mina, just tell me," I say, but the tone of my voice isn't very commanding. I don't mind indulging in the illusion that there's something absolutely vital that I can do for a beautiful girl, even if I don't believe it myself. I don't mind lingering a little while longer, pretending.

"You're busy," she says. "I shouldn't keep you. I know that we're not—I know you don't know me that well or anything. And this is all my fault. But please, please can we talk sometime?"

"Yeah," I say. "Of course. But didn't you want—"

She cuts me off. "No, I'll come back. I'll find you. I knew you'd be nice, Cassel. I just knew it."

She brushes past me, close enough that I can feel the warmth of her body. Moments later I hear her light step in the hall. I stand alone in the middle of my room for a long moment, trying to figure out what just happened.

The air has turned from chilly to the kind of cold that seeps into your bones and lives in your marrow. The kind of cold that keeps you shivering after you've come into a warm room, as if you have to shudder ice from your veins. I am almost to the library.

"Hey," someone calls from behind me. I know the voice. I turn.

Lila's standing at the edge of the grass, looking up. She's wearing a long black coat, and when she speaks, her breath condenses in the air like the ghosts of unspoken words. She looks like a ghost herself, all black and white in the shadow of leafless trees. "My father wants to see you," she says.

"Okay," I say, and follow her. Just like that. I'd probably follow her off a cliff.

She leads me to a silver Jaguar XK in the parking lot. I don't know when she got the car—or her license—and I want to say something about that, offer her some kind of congratulations, but when I open my mouth, she gives me a look that makes me swallow the words.

I get in quietly on the passenger side and take out my phone. The inside smells like spearmint bubble gum and perfume and cigarette smoke. A half-empty bottle of diet soda is resting in the cup holder.

I take out my phone and text Daneca: *Can't make it 2nite.*

A few seconds later the phone starts ringing, but I set it to vibrate and then ignore it. I feel guilty for standing her up after making a promise to be more honest, but explaining where I am going—no less why—seems impossible.

Lila looks over at me, half her face lit by a streetlight, blond lashes and the arch of her brow turned to gold. She's so beautiful that my teeth hurt. In psychology class fresh-man year our teacher talked about the theory that we all have a "death instinct"—a part of us that urges us toward oblivion, toward the underworld, toward Thanatos. It feels exhilarating, like taking a step off the edge of a skyscraper. That's how I feel now.

"Where's your dad?" I ask her.

"With your mom," Lila says.

"She's alive?" I am so surprised that I don't have time to be relieved. My mother is with Zacharov? I don't know what to think.

Lila's gaze finds mine but her smile gives me no comfort. "For now."

The engine starts, and we pull out of the parking lot. I see my own face reflected back in the curve of the tinted window. I might be going to my own execution, but I don't look all that torn up about it.

CHAPTER FOUR

WE DRIVE INTO THE basement garage, and Lila parks in a numbered spot next to a Lincoln Town Car and two BMWs. It's a car thief's dream lot, except for the fact that anyone who steals from Zacharov will probably get dropped off a pier with cement boots on.

As Lila kills the engine, I realize that this will be the first time I've ever seen the apartment where she lives when she's with her father. She was quiet on the drive, leaving me with plenty of time to wonder if she knows that I followed her yesterday, if she knows that I'm being recruited for the Licensed Minority Division, if she knows that I saw her order a hit or that I have Gage's gun.

To wonder if I'm about to die.

"Lila," I say, turning in my seat and putting my gloved hand on the dashboard. "What happened with us—"

"Don't." She looks directly into my eyes. After a month of being forced to avoid her, I feel stripped bare by her gaze. "You can be as much of a charming bastard as you want, but you're never going to bullshit your way into my heart again."

"I don't want that," I say. "I never wanted that."

She gets out of the car. "Come on. We have to get back to Wallingford before curfew."

I follow her into the elevator, trying to behave myself, trying to puzzle through her words. She pushes the P3 button. I guess the *P* stands for "penthouse," because soon we are whirring up the floors so fast that my ears pop. She lets her messenger bag drop off her shoulder and hunches forward in her long black coat. For a moment she looks frail and tired, like a bird huddling against a storm.

"How did my mother wind up here?" I ask.

Lila sighs. "She did a bad thing."

I don't know if that means working Patton or something else. I think about the reddish stone my mother was wearing on her finger the last time I saw her. I think too of a picture I found in the old house, of a much younger Mom decked out in lingerie and looking like Bettie Page— a picture obviously taken by a man who wasn't my father and who might have been Zacharov. I have a lot of reasons to worry.

The elevator doors open into a massive room with white

walls, a black and white marble floor, and what looks like a Moroccan style wood ceiling at least eighteen feet above us. There's no carpet, so the tap of our shoes echoes as we walk toward the lit fireplace on the opposite wall, flanked with sofas, and with two people mostly hidden by shadows. Three huge windows show Central Park at night, a patch of near blackness in the shimmering city surrounding it.

My mother sits on one of the couches. She has an amber-colored drink in her hand and is wearing a filmy white dress I've never seen on her before. It looks expensive. I expect her to jump up, to be her usual exuberant self, but the smile she gives me is subdued, almost fearful.

Despite that I nearly collapse with relief. "You're okay."

"Welcome, Cassel," Zacharov says. He's standing by the fire, and when we get close, he crosses to where Lila is and gives her a kiss on the forehead. He looks like the lord of some baronial manor, rather than a seedy crime boss in a big Manhattan apartment.

I incline my head in what I hope is a respectful nod. "Nice place."

Zacharov smiles like a shark. His white hair looks gold in the firelight. Even his teeth look golden, which reminds me uncomfortably of Gage and the gun taped to the wall of my closet. "Lila, you can go do your homework."

She touches her throat lightly—gloved fingers tracing the marks she took, the marks that make her an official member of his crime family, not just his daughter—rage in every line of her face. He barely notices. I'm sure he doesn't realize that he just dismissed her like a child.

My mother clears her throat. "I'd like to talk to Cassel alone for a moment, if that's all right, Ivan?"

Zacharov nods.

She gets up and walks to me. Linking her arm with mine, she marches me down a hallway to a massive kitchen with ebony wood floors and a center island of a bright green stone that looks like it might be malachite. While I sit down on a stool, she puts a clear glass kettle on one of the burners. It's eerie, the way she seems to know Zacharov's apartment.

I want to grab her arm to reassure myself that she's real, but she's moving restlessly, not seeming to notice me.

"Mom," I say. "I'm so glad that you—but how come you didn't call us or—"

"I made a big mistake," Mom says. "Huge." She takes a cigarette from a silver case, but instead of lighting it she sets it down on the counter. I've never seen her so agitated before. "I need your help, sweetheart."

I am uncomfortably reminded of Mina Lange. "We were really worried," I say. "We didn't hear from you for weeks, and you're all over the news, you know? Patton wants your head."

"We?" she asks, smiling.

"Me. Barron. Grandad."

"It's nice to see you and your brother so close again," she says. "My boys."

"Mom, you are on every news channel. Seriously. The cops are looking everywhere for you."

She shakes her head, waving away my words. "When

I got out of prison, I wanted to make some quick money. It was hard, sweetheart, inside. I spent all the time when I wasn't planning that appeal planning what I would do when I got out. I had a few favors to call in and a few things put away for a rainy day."

"Like?" I say.

Her voice goes low. "The Resurrection Diamond."

I saw it on her finger. She wore it once, out to lunch, after Philip died. The stone's a pretty distinctive color, like a drop of blood spilled into a pool of water. But even when I saw it, I thought I must have been mistaken, must have misunderstood, because even though I knew Zacharov wore a fake diamond on his tie pin, that didn't mean he'd lost the original. And it certainly didn't mean *my mother* had taken it.

"You stole it?" I mouth, pointing to the other room. "From *him*?"

"A long time ago," she says.

I can't believe that she's treating this so lightly. I keep my voice low. "Back when you were screwing him?"

After all these years I think I've finally shocked her. "I—," she starts.

"I found a photo," I say. "When I was cleaning out the house. The guy who took it was wearing the same ring that I saw Zacharov wearing in a picture at Grandad's place. I wasn't sure, but now I am."

Her gaze goes toward the other room, then back to me. She bites her lower lip, smearing lipstick on her teeth. "Yes, fine, back then," she says. "One of those times. Anyway, I stole it and got a copy made of it—but I knew he would want the real one back, even after all this time. It doesn't make him look good not to have the real one."

The understatement of the year. If you're the head of a crime family, then, no, you don't want people to find out that your most valuable possession was stolen. You certainly don't want people to know that it was stolen years ago and you've been wearing a fake ever since. Especially if your most valuable possession is the Resurrection Diamond, which, according to legend, makes its wearer invulnerable; the loss of it is going to make you seem suddenly vulnerable. "Yeah," I say.

"So I thought I would sell it back to him," Mom says.

I forget to keep my voice down. "You *what*? Are you *crazy*?"

"It was all going to be fine." Now she puts the cigarette to her lips and leans into the burner on the stove to catch the edge of the flame. She inhales deeply, and embers flare. She blows smoke.

The tea water is starting to boil. Her hand is shaking.

"He doesn't care if you smoke in the house?"

She goes on without answering me. "I had a good plan. Worked through a middleman, everything. But it turned out that I didn't have the real thing. The stone's gone."

I just stare at her for a long moment. "So someone found yours and switched it out?"

She nods quickly. "That must have been it."

This is turning into one of those stories where each new piece of information is so much worse than the thing before that I don't want to ask for more details, but I am pretty sure there's no way around it. *"And?"*

"Well, Ivan might not have minded paying a little bit

to get his property back, especially since he'd probably given up on getting the real thing returned to him. I think he would have just made the exchange. But when he found out the stone was a *fake*, well, he killed the middleman and found out I was behind it."

"How'd he find that out?"

"Well, the *way* he killed the middleman was—"

I hold up my hand. "That's okay. Let's skip that part."

She takes a deep drag from her cigarette and blows three perfect rings of smoke. When I was a kid, I loved those. I would try to pass my hand through them without the breeze from the movement blowing them apart, but it never worked. "So, Ivan—he was angry. Well, but he knows me, so he didn't want to kill me right out. We have history. He told me I had to do a job for him."

"A job?"

"The Patton job," she says. "Ivan has always been interested in the government. He said that it was important to stop proposition two from passing in New Jersey, because if it passed in one state then it could pass elsewhere. All I had to do was make Patton renounce it, and Ivan thought the whole thing would just collapse. . . ."

I put a hand to my forehead. "Stop. Wait. It doesn't make any sense! When did all this happen? Before Philip died?"

The kettle starts to wail.

"Oh, yes," Mom says. "But you see, I blew it. The job. I didn't manage to discredit Patton at all. In fact, I think I made the chance of proposition two passing better than ever. But you know, sweetie, it's never really been my thing—politics. I know how to make men give me things, and I know how to get away before things get too hot. Patton's nosy aides were always asking questions and looking up things about me. That's just not the way I work."

I nod numbly.

"So now Ivan says I have to get the stone back. Only, I have no idea where it is! And he says he won't let me leave until I give it back—but how can I give it back when I can't even look for it?"

"So that's why I'm here."

She laughs, and for a moment she's almost like herself. "Exactly, sweetheart. You'll find the stone for Mommy, and then I'll be able to come home."

Sure. She'll be able to waltz right out of Zacharov's apartment and into the waiting arms of every cop in New Jersey. But I nod again, trying to work through everything she's said. "Wait. When I met you and Barron for sushi— the last time I *saw* you—you were *wearing* the ring. Had Zacharov already put you on the Patton job?"

"Yes. I already told you. But I figured that since the diamond was a fake, I might as well wear it."

"Mom!" I groan.

Zacharov appears in the doorway, a silver-haired shadow. He walks past both of us to the stove, where he clicks off the burner. Only when the kettle stops its screaming do I realize how loud it had became.

"Are you two finished?" he asks. "Lila says it's time for her to go back to Wallingford. If you'd like to go with her, I suggest you go now."

"One more minute," I say. My palms are sweating inside my gloves. I have no idea where to even start looking for the real Resurrection Diamond. And if I don't find it before Zacharov runs out of patience, my mother could wind up dead.

Zacharov takes a long look at my mother and then me. "Quickly," he tells us, heading back down the hallway.

"Okay," I say to my mother. "Where was the stone last? Where did you keep it?"

She nods. "I hid it wrapped up in a slip in the back of a drawer of my dresser."

"Was it still there when you got out of prison? In the same exact place?"

She nods again.

My mother has two dressers, both of them blocked by huge piles of shoes and coats and dresses, many rotted through, most moth-eaten. The idea that someone went through all that and then her drawers seems unlikely— especially if they didn't know to target the bedroom.

"And no one else knew it was there? You didn't tell anyone? Not in prison, not at any time? No one?"

She shakes her head. The ash on her cigarette is burning long. It's going to fall on her glove. "No one."

I think for a long moment. "You said you switched the stone with a fake. Who made the fake?"

"A forger your father knew up in Paterson. Still in business, with a reputation for discretion."

"Maybe the guy made two forgeries and kept the real one for himself," I say.

She doesn't look convinced.

"Can you just write down his address?" I say, looking toward the hall. "I'll go talk to him."

She opens a few drawers near the stove. Knives in a wooden block. Tea towels. Finally she finds a pen in a drawer full of duct tape and plastic garbage bags. She writes "Bob—Central Fine Jewelry" and the word "Paterson" on my arm.

"I'll see what I can find out," I say, giving her a quick hug.

Her arms wrap around me, bone-achingly tight. Then she lets me go, turns her back, and throws her cigarette into the sink.

"It's going to be all right," I say. Mom doesn't reply.

I head into the other room. Lila is waiting for me, bag slung over her shoulder and coat on. Zacharov stands beside her. Both their expressions are remote.

"You understand what you have to do?" he asks me.

I nod.

He walks us to the elevator. It's right where other people would have front doors to their apartments. The outside of it is golden, etched with a swirling pattern.

When the doors open, I look back at him. His blue eyes are as pale as ice.

"Touch my mother, and I'll kill you," I say.

Zacharov grins. "That's the spirit, kid."

The doors close, and Lila and I are alone. The light overhead flickers as the elevator begins its descent.

We pull out of the garage and start toward the tunnel out of the city. The bright lights of bars and restaurants and clubs streak by, patrons spilling out onto the sidewalk. Cabs honk. In Manhattan the night is just starting in all its smoky glory.

"Can we talk?" I ask Lila.

She shakes her head. "I don't think so, Cassel. I think I've been humiliated enough."

"Please," I say. "I just want to tell you how sorry—"

"Don't." She flips on the radio, adjusting it past the news, where the host is discussing Governor Patton's terminating the employment of all hyperbathygammic individuals in government positions, whether or not they've been convicted of a crime. She leaves it on a channel blasting pop music. A girl is singing about dancing inside someone else's mind, coloring their dreams. Lila cranks it up.

"I never meant to hurt you," I yell over the music.

"I'm going to hurt *you* if you don't shut up," she shouts back. "Look, I know. I know it was awful for you to have me crying and begging you to be my boyfriend and throwing myself at you. I remember the way you flinched. I remember all the lies. I'm sure it was embarrassing. It was embarrassing for both of us."

I press the radio button, and the car goes abruptly silent. When I speak, my voice sounds rough. "No. That's not how it was. You don't understand. I wanted you. *I love you*—more than I have ever loved anyone. More than I ever will love anyone. And even if you hate me, it's still a relief to be able to tell you. I wanted to protect you—from me and the way I felt—because I didn't trust myself to keep remembering that it wasn't really—that you didn't feel like I— Anyway, I'm sorry. I'm sorry you're embarrassed. I'm sorry I embarrassed you. I hope I didn't— I'm sorry I let things go as far as they did."

For a long moment we are both quiet. Then she jerks the wheel to the left, tires screeching as she veers off the road, making a turn that takes us back into the city.

"Okay, I'm done," I say. "I'll shut up now."

She slams her hand down on the radio, turning it on and up so that it drowns the car in sound. Her head is turned away from me, but her eyes are shining, as if wet.

We careen around another block, and she pulls up to the curb abruptly. We're in front of the bus station.

"Lila—," I say.

"Get out," she tells me. Her head is turned away from me and her voice shakes.

"Come on. I can't take the bus. Seriously. I'll miss curfew and I'll get expelled. I already have two demerits."

"That's not my problem." She fumbles around in her bag and lifts out a large pair of sunglasses. She pushes them on, hiding half her face. Her mouth is curved down at the corners, but it's not nearly as expressive as her eyes.

I can still tell that she's crying.

"Please, Lil," I say, using a name I haven't called her since we were kids. "I won't say a thing for the whole way back. I swear. And I'm sorry."

"God, I hate you," she says. "So much. Why do boys think that it will be better to lie and tell a girl how much they loved her and how they only dumped her for her own good? That they only tried to rearrange her brain for her own good? Does it make you feel better, Cassel?

Does it? Because from my perspective, it really sucks."

I open my mouth to deny it but then remember I promised not to talk. I just shake my head.

She pulls away from the curb suddenly, the force of acceleration enough to throw me back against the seat. I keep my eyes on the road. We're quiet all the way back to Wallingford.

I go to sleep tired and get up exhausted.

As I pull on my uniform, I can't stop thinking about Zacharov's cold vast apartment where my mother is now imprisoned. I wonder what it's like for Lila to wake up there on a Saturday morning and wander into that kitchen for coffee.

I wonder how long she's going to be able to look at my mother before she tells Zacharov what Mom did to her. I wonder if each time Lila sees her, she remembers what it was like to be forced to love me. I wonder if each time, she hates me just a little bit more.

I think of her in the car, her head turned away from me, her eyes filled with tears.

I don't know how to even start to make Lila forgive me. And I have no idea how to help Mom. The only thing I can think of—aside from finding the diamond—that might keep Zacharov pacified is if I agree to work for him. Which means betraying the Feds. Which means giving up on trying to be good. And once I start working for the Zacharovs— Well, everyone knows that paying off a debt to the mob is impossible. They just keep piling on interest.

"Come on," Sam says, scratching his head and making his hair stand straight up. "We're going to miss breakfast again."

I grunt and head to the bathroom to brush my teeth. I shave. When I sweep back my hair from my face, I grimace at the redness of my eyes.

In the cafeteria I make a mocha with coffee and a packet of hot chocolate. The sugar and caffeine wake me up enough to finish up a couple of problems due for Probability & Statistics. Kevin Brown glowers at me from across the room. There's a bruise darkening his cheekbone. I can't help it; I grin at him.

"You know, if you did your homework at night, you wouldn't have to do it in your other classes," Sam says.

"That would also be true if someone would let me copy their answers," I tell him.

"No way. You're on the straight and narrow now. No cheating allowed."

I groan and get up, shoving aside my chair. "See you at lunch."

I sit through morning announcements, resting my head on my arms. I turn in my hastily done homework and copy down new problems from the board. As I come out of third-period English and trudge through the hallway, a girl falls into step beside me.

"Hi," Mina says. "Can I walk with you?"

"Uh, sure." I frown. No one's asked me before. "Are you okay?"

She hesitates and then says the words all in a rush. "Someone's blackmailing me, Cassel."

I stop walking and stare at her for a long moment as students rush around us. "Who?"

She shakes her head. "I don't know. It doesn't matter, does it?"

"I guess not," I say. "But what can I do?"

"Something," she says. "You got Greg Harmsford kicked out of school."

"I didn't," I say.

She looks up at me through lowered lashes. "Please. I need your help. I know you can fix things."

"I really don't think that I can do as much as—"

"I know you made rumors go away. Even when they were true." She looks down when she says it, like she's afraid I'm going to be mad.

I sigh. There were some perks to being the school bookie. "I never said I wouldn't *try*. Just that you shouldn't expect too much."

She smiles at me and tosses that gleaming mane of hair over her shoulders. It falls down her back like a cloak.

"And," I say, holding up one hand, cautioning her against being so thrilled by my answer, "you're going to have to tell me what's going on. All of it."

She nods, her smile fading a little.

"Now would be good. Or you can keep putting it off and—"

"I took photos." She blurts it out, then presses her lips together nervously. "Photos of me—naked ones. I was going to send them to my boyfriend. I never did, but I kept them on my camera. Stupid, right?"

Some questions have no good answer. "Who's this boyfriend?"

She looks down and reaches across her body to adjust the shoulder strap of her bag, making her seem smaller and more vulnerable. "We broke up. He didn't even know. He couldn't have anything to do with this."

She's lying.

I'm not sure which part is the lie, but now that we're getting to the details, she's exhibiting tells. Avoiding eye contact. Fidgeting.

"So I guess someone got a hold of them," I say, prompting her to continue.

She nods. "My camera got taken two weeks ago. Then this past Sunday someone slipped a note under my door. It said that I have a week to get five thousand dollars. I have to bring that to the baseball pitch at six in the morning next Tuesday or the person's going to show the photos to everyone."

"The baseball pitch?" I frown. "Let me see the note."

She reaches into her book bag and gives me a folded piece of white printer paper, probably from one of the computer labs on campus. The note says exactly what she told me.

I frown. Something doesn't add up.

She swallows. "I don't have that kind of money—not like the note wants—but I could pay you. I could find *some* way to pay you."

The way she says it, with her lashes fluttering and her bruised voice, I know what she's implying. And while I don't think she'd actually follow through, she must be panicked to try that angle.

Plenty of people get conned because they don't know any better. They're just gullible. But lots of people *are* suspicious at the start of a con. Maybe the initial investment is small enough that they can afford to lose it. Maybe they're bored. Maybe they're hopeful. But you'd be surprised how many people start a con knowing there's a good chance they're being conned. All the signals are there. They just keep ignoring them. Because they want to believe in the possibility of something. And so, even though they know better, they just let it happen.

"So you'll find a way to help me?" she asks. "You'll try?"

Mina's lack of skill at lying touches my heart. I know I'm being conned—just like all those other suckers—but somehow, in the face of her enormously obvious attempt at manipulation, I can't turn her down.

"I'll try," I say.

I don't understand much about this situation, except there's a pretty girl and she's looking at me like I can solve all her problems. I want to. Of course, it would help if she told me the truth about what they were.

I could really use a win.

She throws her arms around my neck as she thanks me. I inhale the scent of her coconut body wash.

CHAPTER FIVE

I STALK INTO PHYSICS and slide into my new spot, next to Daneca. She's opening her notebook and smoothing down the pleats of her black skirt. She turns to give me a poisonous look. I glance away from her eyes and notice that the gold thread on the Wallingford patch over the pocket of her blazer is fraying.

"I'm really sorry I didn't make it to the library yesterday," I say, putting my gloved hand to my heart. "I really meant to be there."

She doesn't reply. She tugs back a mass of her purple-tipped hair and rolls it into a loose bun, then slips an elastic band off her wrist and around the whole thing. It doesn't seem like it should hold, but it does.

"I saw Lila," I say. "She had to tell me something about my family. It really couldn't wait."

Daneca snorts.

"Ask her, if you don't believe me."

She takes a chewed-on pencil out of her bag and points it in my direction. "If I asked *you* one question, would you answer it honestly?"

"I don't know," I say. There are some things I can't talk about and other things I'm not sure I want to. But at least I can be honest with her about my uncertainty. I'm not sure she sees that as the same step forward I do, though.

"What happened to that cat we saved from the animal shelter?"

I hesitate.

Here's the problem with telling the truth—smart people figure out the parts you don't say. A lie can be airtight, easy. The truth is a mess. When I told Daneca the story about my brothers changing my memory, about how they wanted me to kill Zacharov and how they'd held Lila captive, I left out one essential detail. I never told her that I was a transformation worker.

I was too scared. I was already trusting her so much that I couldn't bring myself to give up that last secret. And I was scared of the secret itself, scared to say the words out loud. But now Daneca's put the whole thing together and found the gap. The cat that she saw me hold—the one that she never saw again.

"I can explain," I start.

Daneca shakes her head. "I thought you'd say that." She turns away from me.

"Come on," I say. "I really can explain. Give me a chance."

"I already did," she whispers as Dr. Jonahdab starts taking attendance. "You blew it."

No matter how angry Daneca is with me, I know she always wants answers. But maybe she feels like she already has them.

Something prompted her to start thinking about stuff that happened seven months ago. Lila must have said something—maybe even told her that I was a transformation worker, that it was because of me she spent years trapped in a body that wasn't hers, that she was the cat we stole. She and Daneca have been hanging out a lot. Maybe Lila needed to talk to someone. It's as much Lila's secret as it is mine.

Now I guess it's Daneca's secret as well.

I skip track practice, flop down on the sofa in the common room of my dorm, and Google Central Fine Jewelry in Paterson. There's a crappy website that promises to pay cash for gold and claims to accept consignments. It's open only until six, so there's no way I can make it there before closing time.

I dial the number listed. I pretend to be a regular, checking when Bob works, claiming he's the only one I'll trust with some estate pieces. The grouchy woman on the other end of the line says he'll be in on Sunday. I thank her and hang up. I guess I have plans for the weekend.

Central Fine Jewelry doesn't seem like the kind of place where you keep working after you make a mint reselling the Resurrection Diamond, though, so I'm not feeling optimistic.

They do have a page on the site featuring amulets. It looks pretty legit. They don't claim to have any transformation amulets. Claiming to have one is a sure sign of a scam, since no one but a transformation worker can make them. Most of the stones in stock are for luck magic. They list a few more unusual amulets, ones to prevent memory work and death work—well, prevent it once, before the amulet snaps and you're left buying a new one—but nothing too good to be true. I figure that since he knew my dad, Bob used to have ties to curse workers. His inventory is proof that he still does.

It figures that a forger would be in with workers. The thing about curse magic being illegal is that it turns everyone who uses it into a criminal. And criminals stick together.

That thought makes my mind turn inevitably toward Lila.

As much as she hates me now, she will hate me that much more once I sign the papers and become a federal agent. Down in Carney, where we spent our summers growing up, if a curse worker joined the government, that person was considered a traitor, the lowest of the low, someone not worth spitting on if he was on fire.

There's some part of me that takes a perverse delight in doing the one thing that is going to make a bunch of murderers, con men, and liars all gasp and clutch their pearls.

I bet they didn't think I had it in me.

But I never wanted to hurt Lila—at least not hurt her worse than I already have. And no matter what any of them think of me, I will never let the government get its claws in her.

Another senior, Jace, comes into the common room and turns on the television. He flips the channel to some reality show about beauty queens stranded on a desert island. I'm not really watching. My mind is skipping to Mina Lange and blackmail.

I don't want to even consider how thinking about Lila brought me to Mina.

Still, I turn her story over and over in my head, trying to see if there is some clue I can glean from the little she told me. Why did it take the thief two weeks after stealing the camera to start blackmailing Mina? Don't people who steal cameras usually want the *camera* more than what's on it, anyway? Who bothers flipping through another person's pictures? But then, it's not like most kids at Wallingford can't afford to buy a camera, and it's weird how many rich kids steal for fun. They'll shoplift from the convenience store down on the corner, break into each other's rooms to grab boxes of cookies, and clumsily jimmy open doors so that they can grab iPods.

Which, unfortunately, only widens the suspect pool, instead of shrinking it. The blackmailer could be anyone. And, more than probably, the person is joking about the five grand and the baseball field, trying to scare Mina. The remote cruelty points to a girl or a bunch of girls. Whoever she is, she probably just wants to make Mina squirm.

If I'm right, it's a pretty good con. Even if Mina calls their bluff, she can't do much about it, because she won't want the pictures to get out. But the girls probably can't resist giggling when Mina comes into the cafeteria or teasing her in class, even if they don't say anything about the pictures.

I just wish I was sure Mina was telling me the truth.

Assignments like these are what FBI agents do, right? On a grander scale but still, using the same techniques. This might be like one of the exercises that Barron is given, except that this one is mine. A little investigation for me to practice on in secret. So that when I finally join up, I'll be better than him at something.

A little investigation to prove to myself that I am making the right decision.

I'm still running through ways to draw out the blackmailer when the beauty queen program is interrupted by news footage of Governor Patton. He's on the steps of the courthouse, surrounded by microphones, railing loudly.

"Did you know that government bodies exist staffed entirely by curse workers—curse workers with access to your confidential files? Did you know that no one requires testing of applicants to government jobs to determine who among us are potentially dangerous criminals?" he says. "We must root all workers out of our government! How can we expect our legislators to be safe when their staffers, their aides, even their constituents could be seeking to undermine policies directed at bringing these sinister predators to light, because those policies would inconvenience them."

Then we cut to the reporter's serious, perfectly made-up face and are told that a senator from New York, Senator James Raeburn, has made a statement denouncing Patton's position. When they show Senator Raeburn, he appears in front of a blue curtain, at a lectern with the state insignia on it.

"I am deeply disappointed by the recent words and actions of Governor Patton." He's young for a senator, with a smile like he's used to talking people into and out of things, but he doesn't look slick. I want to like him. He reminds me of my dad. "Are we not taught that those who have confronted temptation and triumphed over it are more virtuous than those who have yet to face their own demons? Are not those who are born hyperbathygammic and tempted into a life of crime—tempted to use their power for their own benefit—are not those people just like us, who resist temptation and choose instead to work to shield us from their less moral kind, are they not to be celebrated rather than treated to Governor Patton's witch hunt?"

The newscaster tells us that more details will be forthcoming and more statements are expected from other members of government.

I fumble for the remote and switch the channel to a game show. Jace has his laptop open and doesn't seem to notice, for which I am grateful. I guess anything that distracts Patton from talking about my mother is a good thing, but I still hate the sight of him.

Before dinner I head up to my room to drop off my schoolbooks. As I get to the top of the stairs, I see Sam storming down the hall. His hair is a mess and his neck and cheeks are flushed. His eyes look too bright, the way they do in people who are in love, people who are enraged, and people who are completely bonkers.

"What's wrong?" I ask.

"She wants all her stuff back." He slams his hand into the wall, cracking the plaster, a move so uncharacteristic that I just stare. He's a big guy, but this is the first time I've ever seen him use his size for violence.

"Daneca?" I ask, like an idiot, because *of course* he's talking about Daneca. It's just that the whole thing doesn't make sense. They've been fighting, sure, but the fight is over something stupid. They both care about each other—surely more than they care about an exaggerated misunderstanding. "What happened?"

"She called me and told me it was over. That it had been over for weeks." He sags now, arm bent against the wall, his forehead resting on his arm. "Didn't even want to see me to get her things. I told her that I was sorry—over and over I told her—and that I would do anything to get her back. What else am I supposed to do?"

"Maybe she just needs some time," I say.

He shakes his head pitifully. "She's seeing somebody else."

"No way," I say. "Come on. You're just being—"

"She is," he says. "She said she was."

"Who?" I try to think of anyone I saw Daneca talking to—anyone who she looked at lingeringly or walked down the halls with more than once. I try to think of any guy who

stayed behind after HEX meetings to talk with her. But I come up blank. I can't picture her with anyone.

He shakes his head. "She wouldn't tell me."

"Look," I say, "I'm really sorry, man. Let me dump my bag and we can go off campus—get some pizza or something. Ditch this place for a couple of hours." I was planning on meeting Mina tonight in the dining hall, but I push that thought aside.

Sam shakes his head. "Nah. I just want to be by myself for a little while."

"You sure?"

He nods and lurches away from the wall to thud down the stairs.

I go into our room and toss my bag of books onto my bed. I'm about to go out again, when I see Lila, on her knees, peering under Sam's dresser. Her short gold hair is hanging in her face, the sleeves of her dress shirt rolled up. I notice that she's not wearing tights, just ankle socks.

"Hey," I say, stunned.

She sits up. I can't read her expression, but her cheeks look a little pink. "I didn't think you were going to be here."

"I live here."

She turns so that she's sitting on the floor with her legs crossed, pleated skirt riding high over her thighs. I try not to look, not to recall what her skin felt like against mine, but it's impossible. "Do you know where Daneca's stuffed owl is? She swears she left it here, but Sam says he never saw it."

"I never saw it either."

She sighs. "How about her copy of Abbie Hoffman's *Steal This Book*?"

"My bad," I say, and take it out from one of my drawers. She gives me a look. "What? I thought it was Sam's when I borrowed it."

She gets up in a single fluid movement and snatches the book from my gloved hand. "It's not that. I don't know. I don't know how I got talked into this. Daneca was just so upset."

"She was upset? She's the one who just broke his heart."

I expect Lila to say something cruel about Sam or me or about love in general, but she just nods. "Yeah."

"Last night—," I start.

She crosses the room, shaking her head. "How about a T-shirt with the words 'NERD HERD' on it? Have you seen one of those?"

I shake my head as she starts picking up laundry off the floor. "So I guess you guys got really close? You and Daneca?" I ask.

Lila shrugs. "She's been trying to help me."

I frown. "With what?"

"School. I'm a little behind. I might not be here for that much longer." Lila straightens, a wadded-up shirt in her hand. When she looks at me, she looks more sad than angry.

"What? Why?" I take a step toward her. I remember something Daneca said about Lila having to do remedial work. She hasn't been taking classes since she was fourteen; that's a lot to catch up on. Still, I figured she could handle it. I figured she could handle anything.

"I only came here for you. I'm no good at this school stuff." She unsticks a postcard from the wall over Sam's bed, which involves her climbing onto the mattress in a way that ignites every bad thought I've ever had. "Okay. I think that's it," she says.

"Lila," I say as she walks toward the door. "You're one of the smartest people I know—"

"She doesn't want to see you, either," Lila says, cutting me off. "I have no idea what you did to Daneca, but I think she's madder at you than she is at Sam."

"Me?" I drop my voice to a whisper so that we won't be overheard. "I didn't do anything. You're the one who told her I turned you into a cat."

"What?" Lila's mouth parts slightly. "You're crazy. I never said that!"

"Oh," I say, honestly puzzled. "I thought you must have. Daneca was asking me all these questions—weird questions. Sorry. I didn't mean anything. It's your story to tell if you want to tell it. I've got no right—"

She shakes her head. "You better hope she doesn't figure it out. With her mother's crazy worker advocacy stuff, she'd probably go straight to the government. You'd wind up press-ganged into one of those federal brainwashing programs."

I smile guiltily. "Yeah, well, I'm glad you didn't say anything to her."

Lila rolls her eyes. "I know how to keep a secret."

As she leaves with Daneca's stuff, I am shamed into realizing how many secrets Lila *has* kept. She's had the means to ruin my life pretty much since she became human again. One word to her father, and I would be dead. Since my mother worked her, Lila has even more means and a better motive. The fact that she hasn't done it is a miracle. And I have not even the slightest idea why she hasn't, when she has every reason, now that the curse has worn off.

I lean back on my bed.

My whole life I've been trained as a con artist, trained to read what people mean underneath what they say. But right now I can't read her.

At dinner Mina denies knowing anyone who would blackmail her for spite. No one has ever teased her at Wallingford, no one has ever laughed behind her back. She gets along with absolutely everybody.

We sit together, slowly eating roast chicken and potatoes off our trays while she answers my questions. I wait for Sam to show up, but he never does. Lila doesn't come into the dining hall either.

When I press Mina, she tells me that her ex-boyfriend doesn't go to school at Wallingford. His name is Jay Smith, apparently, and he goes to public school, but she isn't sure which one. She met him at the mall, but she's a little fuzzy on where. His parents are very strict, so she was never allowed to go to his house. She deleted his number when they broke up.

Everything is a dead end.

Like she doesn't want me to suspect anyone. Like she doesn't want me to be investigating the very thing she asked me to fix.

Like she *already knows who's blackmailing her*. But that makes no sense. If she did, she'd have no reason to involve me.

When I get up from the table, Mina hugs me and tells me that I'm the sweetest boy in the world. Even though she doesn't mean it and she's probably saying it for all the wrong reasons, it's still nice.

I find Sam lying in bed when I get back to the room, headphones over his ears. He stays that way all through study hall, snuffling quietly into his covers. He sleeps in his clothes.

Wednesday he barely speaks and barely eats. In the cafeteria he picks at his food and responds to my most outrageous jokes with a grunt. When I see him in the halls, he looks haunted.

On Thursday he tries to talk to Daneca, abruptly chasing her out onto the school green after breakfast. I follow them, dread in the pit of my stomach. The skies are overcast and it's cold enough that I won't be surprised if we get sleet instead of rain. Wallingford looks bleached out, gray. For a moment Sam and Daneca are standing close together, and I think he's got a chance. Then she lurches back and starts off in the direction of the Academic Center, braids whipping behind her.

"Who?" he yells after her. "Just tell me who he is. Just tell me why he's better than me."

"I should have never told you anything," she shrieks back.

People want to lay bets on the identity of this mysterious guy, but no one's willing to go to Sam with their guesses. He looks wild-eyed, stalking around the campus like a madman. When they come to me, I am glad that I already gave up the business.

By Friday I'm worried enough that I make Sam come home with me. I leave my Benz at Wallingford and we drive over to my mom's old house in his grease-powered hearse. As we pull in, I notice there's already another car parked in the driveway. Grandad's come to visit.

CHAPTER SIX

I WALK IN THE FRONT door to the house, Sam right behind me. It's unlocked and I can hear the chug of the dishwasher. My grandfather is standing at the counter, chopping potatoes and onions. His gloves are off and the blackened stubs where his fingers used to be are clearly visible. Four fingers; four kills. He's a death worker.

One of those kills saved my life.

Grandad looks up. "Sam Yu, right?" he says. "The roommate."

Sam nods.

"You drove up from Carney," I say. "And you're making dinner. What's going on? How'd you even know I was going to come home this weekend?"

"Didn't. You heard from that mother of yours?" Grandad asks.

I hesitate.

He grunts. "That's what I thought. I don't want you to get caught up with her bullshit." He nods toward Sam. "Kid can keep a secret?"

"He's currently keeping almost all of mine," I say.

"Almost all?" Sam says, the corner of his mouth lifting. That's the closest he's been to smiling in days.

"Then both of you listen up. Cassel, I know that she's your mother, but there's nothing you can do for her. Shandra got herself in over her head. She's got to get her own self out. You understand?"

I nod.

"Don't be yessing me to death when you mean no," Grandad says.

"I'm not doing anything crazy. I'm just seeing if I can find something she lost," I say, glancing toward Sam.

"What she *stole*," says Grandad.

"She stole from Governor Patton?" Sam asks, clearly bewildered.

"I wish it was just that idiot she had to worry about," says Grandad, and he goes back to his chopping. "You two go sit down awhile. I'm making steaks. There's plenty for three."

I shake my head and walk into the living room, drop my backpack near the couch. Sam follows.

"What's going on?" he asks. "Who's your grandfather talking about?"

"My mother stole something and then tried to sell a fake back to the original owner." That seems like the simplest explanation. The details only make the whole thing more confusing. Sam knows that Lila's father is a crime boss, but I'm not sure he really thinks of anyone's parent as potentially lethal. "The guy wants the real version, but Mom doesn't remember where she put it."

Sam nods slowly. "At least she's okay. In hiding, I guess, but okay."

"Yeah," I say, not even convincing myself.

I smell the onions hit a hot pan of grease in the kitchen. My mouth waters.

"Your family is badass," Sam says. "They set a high bar of badassery."

That makes me laugh. "My family are *lunatics* who set a high bar for *lunacy*. Speaking of which, don't mind my grandfather. Tonight we can do whatever you want. Sneak into a strip club. Watch bad movies. Crank call girls from school. Drive down to Atlantic City and lose all our cash at gin rummy. Just say the word."

"Is there really gin rummy in Atlantic City?"

"Probably not," I admit. "But I bet there are some old folks who'd be willing to sit in on a game and take your money."

"I want to get drunk—so drunk," he says wistfully. "So drunk that I forget not just tonight but, like, the last six months of my life."

That makes me think uncomfortably of Barron and his memory curses. I wonder how much, right now, Sam would pay to be able to do just that. To forget Daneca. To forget he ever loved her.

Or to make her forget that she stopped loving him.

Like Philip got Barron to make Maura—Philip's wife—forget she was going to leave him. It didn't work. They just had the same fights over and over again as she fell out of love with him exactly the same way she had before. Over and over. Until she shot him in the chest.

"Cassel?" Sam says, shoving my shoulder with a gloved hand. "Anyone home in there?"

"Sorry," I say, shaking my head. "Drunk. Right. Let me survey the booze situation."

There's always been a liquor cabinet in the dining room. I don't think anyone's been in it since before Dad died and Mom went to prison. There was so much clutter in front of it that it wasn't exactly easy to get into. I find a couple of bottles of wine in the back, along with some bottles of brown liquor with labels I don't recognize, and a few newer-looking things in the front. The necks are coated in dust. I take everything out and pile it on the dining room table.

"What's Armagnac?" I call to Sam.

"It's fancy brandy," my grandfather says from the kitchen. A few moments later he sticks his head into the room. "What's all that?"

"Mom's liquor," I say.

He picks up one of the bottles of wine and looks at the label. Then he turns it upside down. "Lot of sediment. This is either going to be the best thing you ever drank or vinegar."

The inventory turns out to be three bottles of possibly sour wine; the Armagnac; a bottle of rye that's mostly full; pear brandy with a pale globe of fruit floating in it; and a container of Campari, which is bright red and smells like cough medicine.

Grandad opens all three bottles of wine when we sit down to dinner. He pours the first into a glass. It's a dark amber, almost the same color as the rye.

He shakes his head. "Dead. Toss it."

"Shouldn't we at least try it?" I ask.

Sam looks at my grandfather nervously, like he's expecting to get in trouble for our liquor cabinet raid. I don't point out that among most people I know, legal drinking age isn't going to exactly be a sticking point. Sam should cast his mind back to Philip's wake.

Grandad laughs. "Go ahead if you want, but you're going to be sorry. It'll probably do better in your gas tank than in your stomach."

I take his word for it.

The next one is nearly as black as ink. Grandad takes a sip and grins. "Here we go. You kids are in for a treat. Don't just glug this stuff."

In the kind of fancy magazines my mother reads when she's shopping for men, they rate wines, praising them for tasting like things that don't sound good to drink—butter and fresh cut grass and oak. The descriptions used to make me laugh, but this wine really does taste like plums and black pepper, with a delicious sourness that fills my whole mouth.

"Wow," says Sam.

We finish off the rest of the wine and start on the rye. Sam pours his into a water glass.

"So what's the matter?" Grandad asks him.

Sam bangs his head against the table lightly and then downs his drink in three long swallows. I'm pretty sure he's forgotten to be worried about getting in trouble with anyone. "My girlfriend dumped me."

"Huh," Grandad says, nodding. "The young lady with you at Philip's funeral? I remember her. Seemed nice enough. That's too bad. I'm sorry, kid."

"I really—I loved her," Sam says. Then he refills his glass.

Grandad goes into the other room for the Armagnac. "What happened?"

"She hid something big—and when I found out, I was really pissed. And she was sorry. But by the time I was ready to forgive her, she was the one who was pissed. And then I had to be sorry. But I wasn't. And by the time I was, she had a different boyfriend."

My grandfather shakes his head. "Sometimes a girl's got to walk away before she knows what she wants."

Sam pours some of the Armagnac into his glass, along with the dregs of the rye. He tops off the concoction with a shot of Campari.

"Don't drink that!" I say.

He toasts to us and then tosses the whole thing back.

Even Grandad winces. "No girl's worth the hangover you're going to have come morning."

"Daneca is," Sam says, words slurring.

"You got a lot of ladies to get through. You're still young. First love's the sweetest, but it doesn't last."

"Not ever?" I ask.

Grandad looks at me with a seriousness he reserves for moments when he wants me to really pay attention. "When we fall that first time, we're not really in love with the girl. We're in love with being in love. We've got no idea what she's really about—or what she's capable of. We're in love with our idea of her and of who we become around her. We're idiots."

I get up and start stacking dishes in the sink. I'm not too steady on my feet right now, but I manage it.

When I was a kid, I guess I loved Lila like that. Even when I thought I'd killed her, I still saw her as the ideal girl—the pinnacle of girlhood that nobody else was ever going to be able to get close to. But when she came back, I had to see her the way she was—complicated, angry, and a lot more like me than I'd ever guessed. I might not know what Lila is capable of, but I know her.

Love changes us, but we change how we love too.

"Come on," Sam says from the table, pouring bright red liquor into teacups he's found somewhere. "Let's do shots."

I wake up with the horrible taste of cough medicine in my mouth.

Someone is pounding on the front door. I turn over and cover my head with a pillow. I don't care who it is. I'm not going downstairs.

"Cassel!" My grandfather's voice booms through the house.

"What?" I shout back.

"There's somebody to see you. He says he's from the government."

I groan and roll out of bed. So much for my avoiding answering the door. I pull on jeans over my boxers, rub sleep out of my eyes, and grab for a shirt and a pair of clean gloves. Stubble itches along my cheeks.

As I brush my teeth, trying to scrub the taste of the night before out of my mouth, dread finally catches up with me. If my grandfather guesses that I'm thinking about working for Yulikova, I have no idea what he will do. There's no worse kind of traitor to guys like Grandad. And as much as I know he loves me, he's also somebody who believes in putting his duty before feelings.

I shuffle down the stairs.

It's Agent Jones. I'm surprised. I haven't seen him or Agent Hunt since they turned me and Barron over to the Licensed Minority Division. He looks unchanged—dark suit, mirrored sunglasses. The only difference I detect is that his pasty skin looks red across his cheeks, like sunburn or maybe windburn. He's standing in the doorway, shoulder against the frame like he's going to push his way in. Grandad obviously hasn't invited him over the threshold.

"Oh, hey," I say, coming to the door.

"Can I talk to you . . ." He gives my grandfather a dark look. "Outside?"

I nod, but Grandad puts a bare hand on my shoulder. "You don't have to go anywhere with him, kid."

Agent Jones is staring at my grandfather's hand like it's a snake.

"It's okay," I say. "He was working Philip's murder."

"Fat lot of good that did," says Grandad, but he lets go of me. He walks to the counter and pours coffee into two mugs. "You take anything in your coffee, government leech?"

"No, thanks," Jones says, and points at Grandad's hand. "You hurt yourself there?"

"Wasn't me that got hurt." Grandad hands me one of the cups.

I take a swig and follow Jones out through the sagging porch and into the front yard.

"What do you want?" I ask under my breath. We're standing near his shiny black car with the dark tinted windows. The cold breeze cuts through the thin fabric of my T-shirt. I cup the mug closer to me for warmth, but the coffee is cooling fast.

"Something the matter? Afraid the old man's going to find out what you've been up to?" His smile is gloating.

I suppose it's too much to expect that just because Jones and I are on the same side now, he's going to start acting like it.

"If you've got something to say to me, spit it out," I tell him.

He folds his arms over his chest. I can see the bulge of his gun. He reminds me of every mobster I've ever met, except less polite. "Yulikova needs to see you. She said to tell you that she's sorry for bothering you on a weekend, but something really big has come up. She says that you'll want to hear it."

"Too big for them to tell you what it is?" I don't know why I'm taunting him. I guess I'm scared, what with him flaunting my connection to the Feds right in front of Grandad. And I'm angry—the kind of anger that burns you up from the inside. The kind of anger that makes you stupid.

His lip curls. "Come on. Get in the car."

I shake my head. "No way. I can't. Tell her I'll come later today. I just have to come up with an excuse."

"You have exactly ten minutes to square this with your grandfather, or I'll tell him that you framed your own brother. That you ratted him out to us."

"Yulikova didn't tell you to do that," I say. A shiver runs through me that's only partially from the cold. "She'd be pissed off if she knew you were threatening me."

"Maybe. Maybe not. Either way, you're the one who's screwed. Now, are you coming with me?"

I swallow roughly. "Okay. Let me get my coat."

Agent Jones is still grinning when I go back into the house. I swallow the rest of the coffee, even though it's like ice.

"Grandad," I shout. "They want to ask me some questions about Mom. I'll be right back."

My grandfather comes halfway down the stairs. He's wearing gloves. "You don't have to go."

"It'll be fine." I tug on a long black coat and grab for my phone and wallet.

I feel like a terrible person.

Whatever else I'm shaky on, I'm pretty sure you're not supposed to con the people you love.

Grandad gives me a long look. "Do you want me to come along?"

"I think someone better stay with Sam," I say.

At the mention of his name, Sam looks up from where he's draped on the couch. A strange expression passes over his face, and a moment later, he lunges for the wastebasket.

Hard to believe it, but someone's about to have a worse morning than I'm having.

I don't say anything while Agent Jones drives. I play a game on my phone and look out the window from time to time, checking on our progress. At some point I realize we're not taking the right roads to get to Yulikova's office, but I still don't speak. What I do is start planning.

A couple more minutes and I am going to tell him I need a rest stop. Then I'm going to lose him. If I can scope out an old enough car nearby, I can hot-wire it, but it would be better if I could con a ride. I go over various stories in my head and settle on looking for a middle-aged couple—a husband who's big enough not to be intimidated by my height or my brown skin, and a wife to argue on my behalf, ideally a couple who might have kids about my age. I'm planning on giving them a story about a drunk friend who wouldn't give me his keys and stranded me without a way home.

I'll have to work fast.

As I am thinking it through, we pull into the parking lot of a hospital, three huge brick towers linked at the base, with an ambulance blinking its red lights in front of the emergency room entrance. I let out my breath. Escaping from a hospital is a piece of cake.

"We're meeting Yulikova here?" I ask incredulously. Then I think better of it. "Is she all right?"

"As all right as she ever is," he says.

I don't know what that means, but I don't want to admit it. Instead of responding, I try the handle, and when I can get it open, I jump out of the car. We walk together to one of the side doors. The hallway is antiseptic, typical. No one questions us.

Jones seems to know where we're going. We pass a nurse's station, and Jones nods to an elderly woman behind the desk. Then we walk down another long corridor. I glance inside an open doorway to see a man with a big grizzly beard and balloons around his wrists, so that he can't bring his own hands to his face. He turns to me with a haunted look.

We stop at the next door—this one closed—and Agent Jones knocks once before heading inside.

It's a regular hospital room but clearly both larger and better-furnished than some others we passed. There is a multicolored afghan thrown over the foot of the hospital bed and several jade plants along the window. There are also two comfortable- but generic-looking chairs sitting across from the bed.

Yulikova is in a batik-print robe and slippers. She's got a plastic cup and is watering the plants when we come in. She's not wearing makeup, and her hair looks not so much wild as uncombed, but she doesn't otherwise look unwell.

"Hello, Cassel. Agent Jones."

"Hi," I say, lingering in the doorway like I might with a sick relative that I haven't seen in a long while. "What's going on?"

She looks at her surroundings and laughs. "Oh, this. Yes, it must seem a little bit dramatic."

"Yeah—and Agent Jones hustled me over here like a house was on fire and I was the only bucket of water in town." I sound only half as annoyed as I am, which is plenty. "I didn't even get to shower. I'm hungover and probably stink like I've been using booze as aftershave—except that I also didn't get to shave. What's the deal?"

Jones glowers.

She laughs a little and shakes her head at him. "I'm sorry to hear that, Cassel. There's a bathroom through there that you are welcome to use, if you'd like. The hospital has little packets of toiletries."

"Yeah," I say. "I might."

"And Agent Jones can go down to the commissary and get us something to eat. The hospital doesn't have much, but it's not as terrible as hospital food used to be. They have decent burgers and snacks." She walks over to the other side of her bed and opens one of the drawers in the side table, taking out a brown leather pocketbook. "Ed, why don't you get a bunch of different sandwiches and cups of coffee. The egg salad isn't bad. And a couple of bags of chips, some fruit, and something for dessert. Get some extra packets of mustard for Cassel. I know he likes them. We'll sit down and have a nice lunch."

"Very civilized," I say.

Agent Jones ignores her looking for her wallet and goes to the door. "Fine. I'll be right back." He looks from me to her. "Don't believe everything that little weasel tells you. I know him from before."

When he walks out, she gives me an apologetic look. "I'm sorry if he was difficult. I needed to get an agent on this, and I wanted someone who'd worked with you before. The last thing we need is lots of people knowing you're a transformation worker. Even here, I can't count on total discretion."

"You worried about a leak?"

"We want to be sure that when and if people find out about you, they receive that information directly from us. You know there's a rumor that there's a transformation worker in China? Many people in our government feel that that information was carefully planted."

"If they have one at all, you mean?"

She nods, a smile pulling at one corner of her mouth. "Exactly. Now go freshen up."

In the bathroom I manage to slick my hair back with water and take a safety razor to my stubble. Then I gargle with mouthwash. When I emerge, I do so in a cloud of mint.

Yulikova's gotten a third chair from somewhere and is arranging them near the window. "Much better," she says.

It's something that a mother would say. Not *my* mother, but *a* mother.

"You need help with anything?" I ask her. It doesn't seem like she should be moving furniture.

"No, no. Sit down, Cassel. I'm fine."

I grab a chair. "I don't mean to pry," I say, "but we're in a hospital. You sure you're fine?"

She sighs heavily. "No getting anything past you, huh?"

"I also often notice when water is wet. I have a keen detective's mind like that."

She has the good grace to smile. "I'm a physical worker. Which means I can alter people's bodies—not to the extent that you can, but brutal basic things. I can break legs and heal them again. I can remove some tumors—or at least reduce them in size. I can draw out an infection in the blood. I can make children's lungs work." I try not to show how surprised I am. I didn't know physical workers could do that. I thought it was just pain—sliced skin, burns, and boils. Philip was a physical worker; I never saw him use it to help anyone.

"And sometimes I do all those things. But it makes me very sick. All of it, any of it, hurting and healing. And over time it has made me sicker. Permanently sicker."

I don't ask her about the legality of what she's doing. I don't care, and if she doesn't care either, well, then, maybe we have something in common after all. "Can't you heal yourself?"

"Ah, the old cry of 'Physician, heal thyself!'" she says. "A perfectly logical question, but I am afraid I can't. The blowback negates any and all positive effects. So occasionally I have to come here for a while."

I hesitate before I ask my next question, because it's so awful. Still, I need to know, if I'm about to sign my free will away on the strength of her promises. "Are you dying?"

"We're all dying, Cassel. It's just that some of us are dying faster than others."

I nod. That's going to have to do, because Agent Jones walks back into the room with an orange cafeteria tray, the whole thing piled with sandwiches, muffins, fruit, and coffee.

"Put it on my bed. We can buffet off of that," she tells him.

I retrieve a ham sandwich, a cup of coffee, and an orange and sit back down while Jones and Yulikova choose their food.

"Good," she says, pulling the wrapper off what looks like a lemon poppy seed muffin. "Now, Cassel, I'm sure you're familiar with Governor Patton."

I snort. "Patton? Oh, yeah. I love that guy!"

Jones looks like he wants to choke the sarcasm out of me, but Yulikova just laughs.

"I thought you'd say something like that," she says. "But you should understand—what your mother did to him and then what was done to fix him—he's become more and more unstable."

I open my mouth to object, but she holds up her hand.

"No. I understand your impulse to defend your mother, and it's very noble, but right now that's irrelevant. It doesn't matter who's to blame. I need to tell you something confidential, and I need your assurance that it won't leave this room."

"Okay," I say.

"If you've seen him on the news recently," Yulikova says, "you can almost see Patton losing control. He says and does things that are extreme, even for anti-worker radicals. But what you can't tell is how paranoid and secretive he's become. People very high up in the government are worried. Once proposition two passes, I'm afraid that he's going to try to lock down the state of New Jersey, then round up and jail workers. I believe—and I'm not the only one—that he wants to bring back the work camps."

"That's not possible," I say. It's not that I can't believe Patton might want that; it's that I can't believe he'd actually try to *do* it. Or that Yulikova would admit suspecting all of this, especially to me.

"He has a lot of allies in Washington," she continues. "And he's been putting more in place. The state police are behind him, and so are more than a few folks at Fort Dix. We know he's been having meetings."

I think of Lila pressing her hands to the bars as Sam, Daneca, and I sat in the jail cell after the protest rally in Newark. No phone calls, no charges, no nothing. And then I think of the other people, the ones that were reported as held there for days.

I look over at Agent Jones. He doesn't look like he much cares either way, but he should. Even if he doesn't want to admit it, the fact that he's working in this division of the federal government means that he's a worker too. If Patton is really that crazy, a badge isn't going to save Jones.

I nod, encouraging her to go on.

She does. "I've been in conference with my superiors, and we agree that we have to stop him before he does something even worse. There are rumors of murders— rumors of terrible things, but no hard evidence. If we arrest him now, he could use that to his political advantage. A very public trial, where we don't have enough evidence, would play right into his hands."

I nod again.

"I've gotten permission for a small operation to remove Patton from power. But I need your help, Cassel. I can promise that your safety will be our first priority. You can abort the mission at any time if you don't feel completely secure. We'll handle all the planning and manage the risks."

"What are we talking about here?" I ask.

"We want you to transform Patton." She looks at me with her kind eyes, as if any answer I give will be the right one. She takes a sip of her coffee.

"Oh," I say. For a moment I'm so shocked that her words just ring in my head.

But then I realize that of course this moment was going to come. Being a transformation worker is the most valuable thing about me—the reason they want me in the program, the reason that they let me get away with murder.

They let me get away with murder so that I can murder for them.

"Sorry," I say. "I'm just surprised."

"It's a lot to take in," Yulikova says. "I know that you're uncomfortable with what you can do."

Agent Jones snorts, and she gives him a dark look.

When she turns back to me, there is still some of that anger in her eyes. "And I know what I'm asking isn't easy. But we need for there to be no trace of him. This can't seem to be an assassination."

"Even though it is?" I say.

That seems to take her by surprise. "We'd like you to change him into a living creature. I understand that it would be possible for him to survive like that indefinitely. He won't be dead. He'll just be *contained*."

Being caged, trapped like Lila was in her cat body, forever, seems as awful as death. But maybe it will let Yulikova sleep better at night.

She leans toward me. "I have gotten approval to make you an offer, in light of the huge service you'll be doing for us. We'll make the charges against your mother go away."

Jones brings his hand down hard on the arm of his chair. "You're making *another* deal with him? That family of his is slipperier than black ice on a highway."

"Do I have to ask you to wait outside?" Her voice is steely. "This is a dangerous operation, and he isn't even a part of the program yet. He's seventeen years old, Ed. Let him have one less thing to worry about."

Agent Jones looks from me to her and then away from both of us. "Fine," he says.

"Here at the LMD we often say that heroes are the people who dirty their hands so other hands get to stay clean. We're terrible so you don't have to be. But in this case you do have to be—or at least we're asking you to be."

"What happens if I don't agree—I mean to my mother?"

Yulikova picks off a piece of her muffin. "I don't know. I'm authorized by my boss to offer you this, but he's the one who would be making it happen. I suppose your mother could continue to evade justice or she could be picked up and extradited—if she's out of the state. I'd be afraid for her safety if she were locked up in any place Patton could get to."

I am suddenly gripped with certainty that Yulikova knows exactly where my mother is.

They're manipulating me. Yulikova letting me see how sick she is, saying nice things, making us sit down to lunch. Jones being such an asshole. It's classic good cop–bad cop. Which isn't to say that it's not working.

Patton's a bad guy and he's out to get my mother. I want him stopped and I want her safe. I'm very tempted by any-thing that lets me have both. Plus there's the fact that I'm backed into a corner. Mom needs a pardon.

And if I don't trust my own instincts toward right and wrong, I have to trust someone's. That's why I wanted to join the government, right? So that if I was going to do bad things, it would at least be in the service of good people.

I am a weapon. And I have put myself in Yulikova's hands.

Now I have to let myself be used as she sees fit.

I take a deep breath. "Sure. I can do that. I can work him."

"Cassel," says Yulikova. "I want you to understand that you can decline this job. You can tell us no."

But I can't. She's seen to it that I really can't.

Jones doesn't say a single snarky thing.

"I understand." I nod to show that I really do. "I under-stand, and I'm telling you yes."

"This is going to be a very discreet mission," Yulikova says. "A very small team operating with the tacit support of my superiors—providing we can pull it off. Otherwise, they will disavow all knowledge. I will be running this—any questions should come directly to me. No one else needs to know. I trust I can count on both of your discretion."

"You mean if something goes wrong, it could be our careers," Jones says.

Yulikova takes another sip of her coffee. "Cassel isn't the only one with a choice. You don't need to be a part of this."

Agent Jones doesn't say anything. I wonder if it will hurt his career either way. I wonder if he even knows he's playing the bad cop. I kind of suspect he doesn't.

I eat my sandwich. A nurse pokes her head in and says that she'll be bringing medicine in about ten minutes. Yulikova stands and starts gathering empty cups and tossing them into the wastebasket.

"I can do that," I say, getting up and grabbing a sandwich wrapper.

She puts her gloved hands on my arms and looks into my eyes, like she's trying to see the answer to a question she hasn't asked. "It's okay to change your mind, Cassel. At any time."

"I'm not going to change my mind," I tell her.

Her fingers tighten. "I believe you. I do. I'll be in touch in a few days with more details."

"Let's not tire her out," Jones says, frowning. "We should go."

I feel bad leaving Yulikova with the mess, but now they're both looking at me with the expectation that our interview is over. Jones walks to the door, and I follow him.

"Just for the record, I don't like any of this," Agent Jones says, his gloved hand on the door frame.

She nods once, like she's acknowledging his words, but the ghost of a smile is on her mouth.

Their exchange makes me even more sure I made the right choice. If Agent Jones approved of what I was doing, that's when I'd be worried.

CHAPTER SEVEN

I FOLLOW AGENT JONES through the corridors of the hospital, but when I get to the parking lot, I'm done. The guy hates me. There's no way I'm letting him take me back to the old house. I don't want him talking to my grandfather again.

"I'm going to take off," I tell him. "See you around."

Agent Jones looks at me incredulously, then snorts. "You planning on walking?"

"I'll call a friend."

"Get in the car," he growls, switching from amused to impatient in a single breath. There is something in his face that makes me even more certain that going with him is a bad idea.

"Make me," I say. "I dare you."

When he doesn't actually lunge at me, I take out my cell phone and call Barron.

"Little brother," he drawls, picking up on the first ring. "You *need* to leave school and join up with the Feds. Last night we raided a worker strip club, and I was knee-deep in naughty gloves. Did you know no one uses Velcro on tear-away gloves anymore? The new kind are held together by magnets so they just *slide* right off the hand—"

"That's, uh, interesting," I say. "But what I really need right now is a ride."

"Where are you?" he asks.

I tell him the name of the hospital while Agent Jones watches me with a cold, furious look in his eyes. We don't like each other. He should be *relieved* that he isn't getting forced to spend any more time with me, but he's obviously brimming with rage instead. The more I study his expression, the more unnerved I am. He's not looking at me the way an adult looks at an obnoxious kid. He's studying me the way a man studies his opponent.

I sit on the cold stoop and wait, letting the chill seep into my skin. It takes a while for Barron to show—long enough that I start wondering if I should call someone else. But just as I decide that I'm going to have to go inside and get something warm to drink or con a blanket from one of the nurses, Barron pulls up in a red Ferrari. He rolls down a dark tinted window and flashes me a grin.

"You stole that," I say.

"Even better. This beautiful car was seized during a raid. Can you believe it? There's a whole warehouse of stuff that gets confiscated and then just sits around until the paperwork is sorted out. Best warehouse ever. Come on, get in."

I don't need to be told twice.

Barron is looking very pleased with himself. "Not only did I manage to get myself some new wheels, but I filled up the trunk with a bunch of tins of caviar and bottles of Krug that were just sitting around. Oh, and some cell phones I am pretty sure I can resell. Altogether a pretty good Saturday. How about yourself?"

I roll my eyes, but I'm already relaxing in the warmth of the heater, leaning back against the seat. "I've got to tell you some stuff. Can we go somewhere?"

"Anywhere you like, kid," Barron says.

Despite his extravagant offer, we wind up getting takeout Chinese and heading to his place in Trenton. He's fixed it up some, replacing the broken windows he'd previously just covered in cardboard. He even bought some furniture. We sit on his new black leather sofa and put our feet up on the trunk he's using for a coffee table. He passes me the tub of lo mein.

On the surface his place looks more normal than it used to, but when I go to the cabinet to get a glass, I see the familiar pattern of sticky notes on the fridge, reminding him of his phone number, his address, his name. Whenever he changes someone's memories, blowback strips out some of his—and he can't be sure which ones will go. He could lose something small, like his memory of eating dinner the night before, or something big, like the memory of our father's funeral.

It makes you a different person, to not have a past. It eats away at who you are, until what's left is all construct, all artifice.

I'd like to believe that Barron has stopped working people, the way he promised he would, that all these little reminders are here because of habit or in case of an emergency—but I'm not an idiot. That warehouse wasn't unguarded. I'm sure someone had to be made to "remember" paperwork that let Barron load up a car with whatever he wanted and drive it out of a government building. And then that same person had to be made to forget.

When I come back to the living room, Barron is mixing a concoction of duck sauce and hot mustard on his plate. "So what's up?" he asks.

I explain about Mom and her failed attempt to sell Zacharov back his own diamond, and the long-standing affair she appears to have had with him. Then I realize I have to explain how she stole it in the first place.

Barron looks at me like he's considering accusing me of lying. "Mom and Zacharov?"

I shrug. "I know. It's weird, right? I'm trying really hard not to think about it."

"You mean about the part that if Zacharov and Mom got married, that would make you and Lila brother and sister?" He starts laughing, falling back on the cushions.

I chuck a handful of white rice at him. A few of the grains stick to his shirt. More stick to my glove.

He keeps on laughing.

"I'm going to go talk to the forger tomorrow. Some guy up in Paterson."

"Sure, we could do that," he says, still giggling a little.

"You want to come?"

"Of course." He opens the chicken with black bean sauce and dumps it over his mustard and duck sauce concoction. "She's my mother too."

"There's something else I should tell you," I say.

He pauses with his hand on a packet of soy.

"Yulikova asked me if I would be willing to do something. A job."

He goes back to pouring out the sauce and taking a first bite. "I thought you couldn't get put to work, since you haven't officially joined up."

"She wants me to take out Patton."

Barron's brows draw together. "*Take out?* As in transform him?"

"No," I say. "As in *take out to dinner*. She thinks we'd make a good couple."

"So you're going to kill him?" He regards me carefully. Then he mimes a gun with his fingers. "Boom?"

"She didn't tell me much about the plan, but—," I start.

He throws back his head and laughs. "You should have joined the Brennans if you were just going to become an assassin anyway. We could have made a lot of money."

"This is different," I say.

Barron laughs and laughs. Now that he's off again, there's no stopping him.

I stab at the lo mein with my plastic fork. "Shut up. It is different."

"Please at least tell me that you're going to get paid," he says when he manages to catch a breath.

"They said they'd get the charges against Mom dropped."

"Good." He nods. "Any cold hard cash going along with that?"

I hesitate, then have to admit, "I didn't ask."

"You have a skill. You can do something *no one else* can," Barron says. "Seriously. You know what's good about that? It's *valuable*. As in you can trade it for goods or services. Or *money*. Remember when I said it was wasted on you? I was so right."

I groan and shove rice into my mouth so that I don't decide to dump the whole carton over his head.

After we finish eating Barron calls Grandad. He tells a long and complicated series of lies about the questions the federal agents asked and how we weaseled out of answering all of them through our inherent charm and wit. Grandad cackles down the line.

When I get on, Grandad asks me if any of what Barron said was true.

"Some," I tell him.

He stays quiet.

"Okay, very little," I finally admit. "But everything's okay."

"Remember what I said. This is your mother's trouble, not yours. Not Barron's, either. Both of you need to stay out of it."

"Yeah," I say. "Is Sam still there? Can I talk to him?"

Grandad gives the phone to Sam, who still sounds groggy but not all that upset to be abandoned for most of the day and the rest of tonight.

"It's okay," he informs me. "Your grandfather is teaching me how to play poker."

If I know Grandad, that means what he'll really be teaching Sam is how to cheat.

Barron offers to let me take his bed, saying that he can sleep anywhere. I'm not sure if he's suggesting that there are beds all over town for him to slip into or just that he's not picky about sleeping on furniture, but I take the sofa so I don't have to find out.

He digs up a couple of blankets that used to be at the old house. They smell like home, a somewhat dusty stale odor that's not entirely pleasant but that I inhale greedily. It reminds me of being a kid, of being safe, of sleeping late on Sundays and watching cartoons in my pajamas.

I forget where I am and try to straighten out my legs. My feet kick against the armrest, and I remember that I'm not a kid anymore.

I'm too tall to be comfortable, but I curl on the couch and manage to doze off eventually.

I wake up to the sounds of Barron making coffee. He pushes a box of cereal at me. He's terrible in the morning. It takes him three cups of coffee before he can reliably put together a whole sentence.

I take a shower. When I come out, he's wearing a dark

gray pin-striped suit with a white T-shirt under it. His wavy hair is gelled back, and he's got a new gold watch on his wrist. I wonder if that was in the FBI warehouse too. Either way, he looks like he made an impressive effort for a Sunday afternoon.

"What are you all dressed up for?"

Barron grins. "Clothes make the man. You want to borrow something clean?"

"I'll muck through," I tell him, pulling on my T-shirt from yesterday. "You look like a mobster, you know."

"That's another thing I'm good at that most trainees aren't," he says, getting out a comb and running it through his hair one last time. "No one would ever guess that I'm a federal agent."

By the time we're ready to leave, it's early afternoon. We get into Barron's ridiculous Ferrari and head upstate, toward Paterson.

"So how's Lila?" Barron asks once we're on the highway. "You still hung up on her?"

I give him a look. "Considering you locked her in a cage for several years, I guess she's okay. Comparatively speaking."

He shrugs, glancing in my direction with a sly look. "My choices were limited. Anton wanted her dead. And you surprised the hell out of us by transforming her into a living thing. After we got over the shock, it was a relief—although she made a terrible pet cat."

"She was *your girlfriend*," I say. "How could you have agreed to kill her?"

"Oh, come on," he says. "We were never that serious about each other."

I slam my hand down on the dashboard. "Are you crazy?"

He grins. "You're the one who changed her into a cat. And you were *in love* with her."

I look out the window. The highway is flanked by towering soundproofing walls, vines snaking through the gaps. "Maybe you made me forget almost everything, but I know I wanted to save her back then. And I almost did."

His gloved hand touches my shoulder unexpectedly. "I'm sorry," he says. "I really did start messing with your memories because Mom said it would be better for you not to know what you were. Then, when we got the idea to go into the killing business, I guess I thought that so long as you didn't remember, nothing we made you do counted."

I have no idea what to say in return. I settle for not saying anything at all. Instead I lean my cheek against the cool glass of the window. I look at the stretch of asphalt highway snaking in front of us, and I wonder what it would be like to leave all of this behind. No Feds. No brother. No Lila. No Mom. No mob. With just a little magic I could change my face. I could walk out of my life entirely.

Just a few fake documents and I'd be in Paris. Or Prague. Or Bangkok.

There I wouldn't have to try to be good. There I could lie and cheat and steal. I wouldn't really be me so it wouldn't really count.

Change my identity. Change my name. Let Barron take care of Mom.

Next year Sam and Daneca are going to be away at college. Lila will be doing whatever bootleg business her father tells her to do. And where will I be? Killing people for Yulikova. Everything's arranged, all for the best, and as bleak as a desert road.

Barron knocks on the side of my head. "Hey, anyone in there? You've been quiet for, like, fifteen minutes. You don't have to tell me that you forgive me or anything like that—but you could say *something*. 'Good talk.' 'Shut up.' Whatever."

I rub my face. "You want me to say something? Okay. Sometimes I think I am what you made me. And sometimes I don't know who I am at all. And either way I'm not happy."

He swallows. "Okay . . ."

I take a deep breath. "But if you want forgiveness, fine. You've got it. I'm not mad. Not anymore. Not at you."

"Yeah, *right*. You're pissed off at someone," he says. "Any idiot can see that."

"I'm just angry," I say. "Eventually it will burn off of me or something. It has to."

"You know, this might be your cue to say that you're sorry about forcing me to go into this whole federal agent training program—"

"You never had it so good," I say.

"But you didn't know that," he says. "I could be miserable right now, and it would be all your fault. And then you'd feel bad. Then you'd be sorry."

"Then I might. Now I'm not," I say. "Oh, and—good talk."

Really, it *was* a pretty good talk. About the best I could

expect from my sociopathic amnesiac jerk of an older brother.

We park on the street. Paterson is an odd collection of old buildings and bright awnings with neon signs advertising cheap cell phones, tarot card readings, and beauty salons.

I get out and feed a few quarters into the meter.

Barron's phone chirps. He takes it from his pocket and looks at the screen.

I raise my eyebrows, but he just shakes his head, like it's nothing important. His gloved fingers tap the keys. He looks up. "Lead on, Cassel."

I head toward the address of Central Fine Jewelry. It looks like all the other stores on the street—dirty and poorly lit. The front window is filled with a variety of hoop earrings and long chains. A sign in one corner reads WE'LL PAY CASH FOR YOUR GOLD TODAY. There's nothing special about it, nothing that makes the place stand out as the location of a master forger.

Barron pushes open the door. A bell rings as we walk in, and a man behind the counter looks up. He's short and balding, with huge horn-rimmed glasses and a jeweler's loupe on a long chain around his neck. He's dressed tidily in a black button-up shirt. Fat rings sparkle over his gloves on each of his fingers.

"Are you Bob?" I say, walking up to the counter.

"Who's asking?" he says.

"I'm Cassel Sharpe," I tell him. "This is my brother Barron. You knew our father. I don't know if you remember him, but—"

He breaks into a huge grin. "Look at you! All grown up. I saw pictures of the three of you Sharpe boys in your daddy's wallet, God rest his soul." He claps me on the shoulder. "Getting into the business? Whatever it is you need, Bob can make it."

I glance around the shop. A woman and her daughter are looking at a case of crosses. They don't seem to be paying attention to us, but we are probably the kind of people you try a little harder not to notice.

I lower my voice. "We want to talk to you about a custom piece you already made—for our mother. Can we go somewhere in the back?"

"Sure, sure. Come into my office."

We follow him past a curtain made from a blanket stapled to the top of a plastic door frame. The office is a mess, with a computer in the center of a sagging wooden rolltop desk, the surface covered completely in papers. One of the drawers is open, and inside are watch parts and tiny glassine bags with stones in them.

I pick up an envelope. The name on it is Robert Peck. Bob.

"We want to know about the Resurrection Diamond," Barron says.

"Whoa." Bob holds up his hands. "I don't know how you heard anything about that, but—"

"We saw the fake you made," I say. "Now we want to know about the real thing. We need to know what happened to it. Did you sell it?"

Barron walks intimidatingly close to Bob. "You know, I work memories. Maybe I could help you recall something."

"Look," Bob says, his voice quavering slightly, rising a little too high. "I don't know what's made the two of you take this unfriendly tone with me. I was a good friend to your father. And I never told nobody that I'd copied the Resurrection Diamond—that I knew who'd stolen it. How many people would do that, huh, when there was so much money on the line? If you think I know where your father kept it or if he sold it, I don't. We were close, but not close like that. All I did was make the fakes."

"Wait. I thought you made the stone for my *mother*," I say. "And what do you mean, *fakes*? How many?"

"Two. That's what your dad asked for. And there was no way I switched anything. He didn't let me keep the original diamond for longer than it took to take the measurements and some photographs. He was no fool, you know. You think he'd let something that valuable out of his sight?"

I exchange a look with Barron. Dad was a lot of things, but he wasn't lazy about a con.

"So what happened?" I ask.

Bob takes a few steps away from us and opens a drawer in his desk, pulls out a bottle of bourbon. He screws off the cap and takes a long pull.

Then he shakes his head, like he's trying to shake off the burn in his throat.

"Nothing," he says finally. "Your father came in here with that damn stone. Said he needed the two copies."

I frown. "Why two?"

"How the hell should I know? One fake I set on the gold tie pin where the original had been. The other I put in a ring. But the original, the real one? I kept that loose, just the way your father wanted it."

"Are they good fakes?" Barron asks.

Bob shakes his head again. "Not the one on the pin. Phil came in here, wanting it fast, you know? Within the day. But the second one, he gave me some more time. That was a fine piece of work. Now, are you two going to tell me what this is about?"

I glance at Barron. A muscle in his jaw is jumping, but I can't tell if he believes Bob or not. I'm trying to think, to play this thing through. So maybe Mom gives Dad the stone and says she needs a fake really fast, before Zacharov notices that the piece is gone. Dad goes straight to Bob, but he asks for *two* stones, because he already knows that he's going to steal the diamond for himself— maybe out of spite, since he discovered that Mom was screwing around with Zacharov? Anyway, Dad brings her one of the fakes, and she slips it back to Zacharov before he notices that it's gone. Then Dad tells her he has a present for her—a ring with the Resurrection Diamond set in it, which is actually the second fake. If that's what happened, the original could be anywhere. Dad could have sold it years ago.

But why put the diamond in a ring that Mom can't wear outside the house without drawing attention? That, I'm not sure about. Maybe he was so pissed off that he liked seeing it on her hand and knowing he'd gotten one over on her.

"What would something like that be worth on the black market?" I ask.

"The real thing?" Bob asks. "Depends if you really believe it'll keep you from getting killed. As a stone with historical value, sure, it's something, but the kind of people who buy rocks like that don't want something they can't show off. But if you believe— Well, what's the price on invulnerability?"

Barron gets a glint in his eye that tells me he's considering the question seriously rather than rhetorically, pricing the thing out in dollars and cents. "Millions," he says finally.

Bob pokes Barron's chest with his gloved finger. "Next time, before you come in here acting heavy, you get your story straight. I'm a businessman. I don't cheat the families, I don't cheat other workers, and I don't cheat my friends, no matter what your mother told you. Now, before you go, you better be buying something nice. Something expensive— you get me? Otherwise I'm going to tell a couple of my friends how rude you boys were to Bob."

We go out to the counter. Bob pulls out a couple of pieces that are in the right price range for our transgression. Barron picks out a diamond heart set in white gold for nearly a grand. I manage to seem convincingly broke— something that isn't hard, since it's true—and am allowed to buy a much cheaper ruby pendant.

"Girls like presents," Bob tells us as he lets us out of the store, adjusting his glasses. "You want to be a charming guy like me, you got to shower your girl with gifts. Give my best to your mother, boys. She looks good on the news. That woman always knew how to take care of herself!"

He winks, and I'm ready to slug him, but Barron grabs my arm. "Come on. I don't want to have to buy the matching earrings."

We march back to the car. Our first mission together, and it was pretty much a bust. I rest my head against the frame while Barron takes out the keys.

"Well, that was . . . interesting," he says, unlocking the doors with a click. "For a dead end."

I get in, sliding into the passenger seat with a groan. "How the hell are we going to find this thing? The stone's gone. There's just no way."

He nods. "Maybe we should try to think if there's something else we can give Zacharov?"

"There's me," I say. "I could—"

The car starts, and he pulls away from the curb, veering into traffic like he's daring the other cars to a game of chicken. "Nah. You're already mortgaged to the hilt. But hey, maybe we're looking at this the wrong way. Mom has a nice apartment to stay in and an older gentleman to keep her company. Three square meals. Patton can't get to her. What exactly are we trying to save her from? Given what we know about her history with Zacharov, she might even be getting—"

I hold up a hand to ward off whatever he's about to say next. "LALALA. I can't hear you."

He laughs. "I'm just figuring that *maybe* she *might* be better off unsaved—safer, happier—which is excellent, because, as you said, our chances of finding that stone are pretty much zero."

I tip my head back against the seat, looking up at the Ferrari's tinted sunroof. "Just drop me at Wallingford."

He pulls out his phone and texts while he drives, making him nearly pull into another lane by accident. A moment later his phone buzzes and he glances at the screen. "Yeah, okay. That's perfect, then."

"What do you mean?"

"Hot date," he says, grinning. "I need you gone."

"I knew it," I say. "I so knew you weren't dressed up like that to go to Paterson with me and meet Bob."

Barron takes his hands away from the wheel to straighten his lapels and to tuck his phone into the inside pocket of his jacket. "I think Bob appreciated my outfit. He made me buy the more expensive pendant. You might think that was to my disadvantage, but I accept that status comes with a price."

"Not usually so immediately." I shake my head. "You better not be hitting on federal agent ladies. They'll arrest you."

His grin widens. "I like handcuffs."

I groan. "There is something seriously wrong with you."

"Nothing that a night being worked over by a hot representative of justice couldn't fix."

I study the clouds through the sunroof. I think I see one in the shape of a bazooka. "Hey, so do you think Dad lied to Mom about the second fake diamond? Or do you think Mom lied to us?"

"To *you*," he says. "She didn't even try to tell me." The smile has curled off his mouth.

"Yeah." I sigh. "Either way it's a hell of a dead end."

Barron nods. His foot presses the accelerator harder, and he veers into the fast lane. I don't protest. At least he has something good to race back to.

Barron drops me in front of Strong House. I slide out of the car and stretch. Then I yawn slowly. It's just barely night-fall. The last of the sun is still blazing on the horizon, making all the buildings look like they're catching fire.

"Thanks for the ride," I say.

"Okay, well," he says, his voice full of impatience. "Sorry, but you've gotta scram. Call me when you talk to Mom—so long as it's not tonight."

I smirk and slam the car door. "Have fun on your date."

"Byeee," he says, and waves. As I head toward the dorm, I glance back at the parking lot. I keep expecting a sweep of headlights as he pulls out, but the Ferrari's still there. He's only rolled it forward a little. Is he seriously waiting until I get to the door of my dorm, like I'm a little kid who can't be trusted to make it home after dark? Am I in some danger I don't know about? I can't think of a good reason for him to keep idling near the curb when he so obviously wanted to get going.

I walk into the building, my scheming brain still rear-ranging the puzzle pieces. It takes me until I get to the hallway, fishing for my dorm key in the back pocket of my jeans, before I stop abruptly.

He wanted *me* to get going.

I run into the common room, ignoring Chaiyawat

Terweil's cry of protest when I jump over the cords connecting his PlayStation to the television. Then I drop to my knees in front of the window. Peering out, half-hidden behind a dusty curtain, I watch as a figure steps out of shadow, walks to where Barron is waiting, and opens the passenger side door.

She's not wearing her uniform, but I know her just the same.

Daneca.

Purple-tipped braids glowing under the streetlight. Heels a lot higher than anything I've ever seen her in—high enough for her to wobble as she bends down. There's no reason on earth why she should glance back at the Wallingford campus like she's afraid of someone seeing her, no reason for her to be getting into my brother's car, no reason for her to be dressed like that, no reason that makes sense. No reason but one.

The boy she's been dating is my brother.

CHAPTER EIGHT

THERE IS NO WAY
I can tell Sam.

He's in our dorm room, still looking pretty hung over, sipping on a can of coconut water. "Hey," he says, rolling toward me on his cot. "Your grandfather is a madman, you know that? After we finished with the poker, he showed me a bunch of old photos. I thought they were going to be pictures of you as a kid, but no. They were vintage snapshots of burlesque ladies with no gloves. From back in the day."

I force a grin. I'm still thinking about Daneca and my brother, wondering how many times she's been out with Barron, wondering *why* she ever went out with him even once. It's hard to concentrate. "You looked at porn with my grandfather?"

"It wasn't porn! Your *grandmother* was one of the ladies."

Of course she was.

"The costumes were amazing," he says dreamily. "Feathers and masks and sets like you wouldn't believe. Crescent moon thrones and a massive rose with petals that swung like doors."

"You were looking at the *sets*?" Now I'm laughing for real.

"I didn't want to stare at the women. I wasn't sure which ones were your relatives! And your grandfather was *right there*!"

I laugh some more. Mom told me about theaters back then, with curtained balcony seating where curse workers could conduct business while the show provided a legitimate front. Then came the raids. Now no one risks that kind of setup. "Imagine you in a place like that. You would be agitating them to do zombie burlesque in no time."

"Untried market," he says. Then he taps his gloved finger against the side of his head. "Always thinking. That's me."

He doesn't look happy, but he doesn't look crushed and miserable, the way he did all last week. If he's still thinking about Daneca, at least she isn't all he can think about. But if he knew about Barron—if he knew that my brother was the one she was seeing—that would change.

I know that if I'm going to be a better person, that includes being less of a liar. But sometimes a lie of omission is what you need until the world starts being fair on its own.

When Lila finds someone else, I hope they all lie to me.

I wake up with the alarm on my phone vibrating against my skull. Yawning, I glance over at Sam. He's still asleep, his comforter half-kicked to the floor. I get up quietly, grab some clothes, and pad into the bathroom.

I set my alarm to wake me up silently, so I could go find Daneca before Sam's up and noticing little things like me yelling at his ex-girlfriend. Before Daneca has a chance to see my good-for-nothing brother again. Before this situation gets even worse.

I shower and shave—so fast that I cut my neck right along my jawline. I wash the blood away, splash with stinging aftershave, and hurry to the cafeteria.

I'm early, which is rare. To celebrate I get myself two cups of black coffee and a piece of toast covered in crisp bacon. By the time Daneca comes in, I am considering a third cup.

Her hair is pulled back by a sandalwood hair band, and she's got on brown herringbone stockings with brown leather Mary Janes. She looks like she always does, which for some reason surprises me. My idea of who she is has changed completely. She's been seeing my brother secretly for days—maybe weeks. All that stuff she said, all the questions she suddenly had for me, now it makes sense. But the answer tilts my world on its axis.

I wait until she gets through the line, and then follow her back to her table.

"What do you want?" she asks me, setting her tray down.

"He's not who you think he is," I say. "Barron. Whatever he told you, it's not true."

Surprise makes her take a step back. Gotcha. Then she recovers herself, looking even more furious than she did before. Nothing makes people angrier than getting caught.

Trust me, I know.

"Yeah, I saw you last night," I say. "You suck at sneaking."

"Only you would think I should be ashamed of that," she snaps.

I take a deep breath, trying to control my anger. It's not her fault she got tricked. "Okay, look. Say whatever you want about me. *Think* whatever you want about me. But my brother is a *compulsive liar*. He can't even help it. Half the time I don't think he remembers the real story, so he just fills in whatever he dreams up."

"He's *trying*," Daneca says. "That's more than I can say about you. He told me what you did. To Lila. To Philip. To him."

"Are you kidding me?" I ask her. "Did he tell you what *he* did to Lila?"

"Stay away from me, Cassel."

Girls say that to me a lot lately. I'm starting to think I'm not as charming as I like to believe.

"Just please tell me he didn't take off his gloves," I say. "No, actually, I'd rather you said he did. Because there is no way the Daneca that I know would fall for my brother's crooked smile and his crooked patter."

"He told me you'd say that. He practically told me the

exact words you'd use. And he wasn't lying about that, was he?"

I sigh. My brother can be a smart guy when he wants to be.

"Daneca, look. There are two ways he could know what I'd say. One, he knows me really well. And two, he knows the truth. The actual truth. Which is what I'm telling you—"

"*You're* going to tell me the truth? That's a joke." She turns her back on me, picks up her toast, and starts toward the door.

"*Daneca,*" I call after her.

My voice is loud enough that people look up from their breakfasts. I see Sam in the entranceway to the cafeteria. Daneca brushes by him on her way out. He glances at her. Then he rounds on me. There is so much anger in his face that I stand, frozen, until he swivels on his heel and walks back out.

I call Barron before I walk into statistics, but I get his voice mail. The class is a blur. As soon as I walk out the door, I try him again.

This time he picks up. The connection is bad, staticky. "How's my favorite and only living brother?" he asks.

"Stay away from her." My hand shakes with the urge to deck him. I will bet anything that she was the girl he was talking to when I ran down that death worker. I will bet anything that he loved getting away with talking to Daneca right in front of me. Texting her from the car. Bragging about his date.

He laughs. "Don't be so dramatic."

I remember what he said long ago when I accused him of dating Lila just because she was Zacharov's daughter. *Maybe I'm dating her just to mess with you.*

"Whatever you're trying to pull . . . ," I say, keeping my voice level. "Whatever it is, it's not going to work."

"Me and her—it bothers you, doesn't it? I saw the way it got under your skin when I talked to her, first at Zacharov's little fund-raiser—where you got Anton killed—and then at Philip's funeral. It bothered you, but it made her blush. Guess you shouldn't have brought her around if you wanted her for yourself."

"Daneca is my friend. That's all. I don't want her to get hurt. I don't want you to hurt her. And I know it's impossible for you to date a girl and not hurt her, so I want you to leave her alone."

"You're only trying to convince me because you already failed to convince her. Nice try, Cassel, but are you really betting on my backing down?" His voice is smug.

The problem with cell phones is that you can't slam them down into a cradle when you hang up. Your only option is to throw them, and if you do, they just skitter across the floor and crack their case. It's not satisfying at all.

I close my eyes and bend down to pick up the pieces.

There is only one person I can think of with the power to convince Daneca to stay away from Barron. Lila.

I text Lila that I will meet her anywhere she wants, that I need to tell her something, that it's not about her or me, that it's important. She doesn't respond. I don't see her in the halls or the lunch room.

Sam grabs my arm the minute I walk into the cafeteria, though, so even if she was, there wouldn't be much I could say to her. He's got bed-head and is looking at me with the gaze of someone who's hanging on to their sanity by a very thin thread.

"Why didn't you wake me up?" he demands in a tone that suggests false calm. "You snuck out. You wanted me not to see you with her."

"Whoa." I hold up both of my hands in a sign of surrender. "You grunted and opened your eyes. I thought you were awake already." It's a lie, but hopefully a believable one. Lots of times I've said a few things, rolled over, and gone immediately back to sleep. It's just that Sam usually kicks my bed frame again before he heads out.

He blinks a couple times, rapidly, like he's restraining himself.

"What were you and Daneca arguing about this morning?" he asks finally.

"I said she was being a jerk," I tell him, frowning. "That you didn't deserve the way she was treating you."

"Yeah?" He slouches a little. I feel like the lout that I am. He wants to believe me, I can tell. "You sure? It seemed worse. She looked really mad."

"I guess maybe I didn't say it in a nice way," I say.

He sighs, but the fury has gone out of him. "You shouldn't talk to her like that. She's your friend too."

"Not anymore," I say, and shrug.

Then he looks grateful and I feel even worse, because I sound like a loyal friend who is declaring how firmly I'm on his side, when actually she's the one who's done with me.

"Cassel," a girl's voice says from just behind us. I turn to find Mina Lange looking up at me. She smiles, but she looks tired, which makes me feel suddenly protective. "Can we talk about tomorrow?"

Sam glances at her, then back at me. Then he looks up toward heaven, like that's the only possible explanation for luck like mine with women.

I can guarantee that's not where it comes from.

"Uh," I say. "Sure. I've been considering things, and—" I'm improvising, since I honestly haven't thought much about Mina's problem since our last conversation. The weekend came and swept everything away with it.

"Not here," she says, interrupting me.

I jerk my head toward the door. "Sure. We'll go to the library. There won't be that many people there, and we can find a quiet place in the back."

"What's going on?" Sam asks.

"Ah," I say. "Sam, Mina. Mina, Sam."

"We have a film studies class together," Sam says. "I know who she is."

"I'm just helping her out with something." It occurs to me that this is a perfect opportunity to distract Sam from all things Daneca-related. "But you should come to the library with us. Be the Watson to my Sherlock, the Hawk to my Spenser, the Mouse to my Easy, the Bunter to my Wimsey."

Sam snorts. "The fat Sancho Panza to your delusional

Quixote." Then he looks at Mina and his neck colors, as if he has realized that he just made both of us sound pretty bad.

"I really don't think—," Mina starts.

"Sam is completely trustworthy, if overly modest," I say. "Anything you can tell me, you can tell him."

She gives him a suspicious once-over. "Okay. But it's happening tomorrow. We need to get the camera back before then or find some way to pay them or—"

"The *library*," I say, reminding her.

"Okay." Mina nods, looking relieved.

I grab a few pieces of fruit from the bowl near the card swipe and we cross the quad together. A few students are sitting at library tables, studying through lunch. I navigate through and head for the far back, picking a spot near the stacks marked SOCIETIES, SECRET, BENEVOLENT, ETC. and sit down on the carpet.

I pass out the apples and take a bite of mine. "Let's start by going over the facts of the case one more time. This will get Sam up to speed and help us see the whole thing with fresh eyes."

Sam is looking a bit bewildered, possibly because I am talking like we really are playing detective here.

Mina looks at Sam. "Someone's blackmailing me. I'm supposed to pay that person five thousand dollars. Which I don't have. And I'm supposed to give it to them tomorrow morning." Then she looks back at me. "Please tell me that you know what I should do, Cassel."

"What do they have on you?" Sam asks. "Did you cheat on a test or something?"

Mina hesitates.

"Pictures," I say. "The naughty kind."

She flashes me a hurt look.

"Hey," Sam says. "Nothing to be ashamed of. We have all taken them. I mean, not me personally, but Cassel's *grandmother*, you should really see—"

"Okay," I say. "The point is, she had them on a camera. Then the camera got stolen. Mina, the more I think about it, the more I think that someone on your hall must have done it. One of the girls. Maybe she broke in to steal a packet of hot chocolate, saw the camera, and took it. Then a week later she started flipping through the images, found the naked pictures, and during one long night of giggling and eating too much junk food, she and her friends dreamed up a funny prank."

"You said you would help me." This time when she looks at me, her eyes are wet. She isn't crying exactly, but tears cling to her lashes, making her look lush and terribly vulnerable. Her misery makes me doubt myself.

"I am trying to help you," I say. "Honestly, it fits. But look, tomorrow morning Sam and I are going to get up early, go out to the baseball field, and watch. There's no way whoever is setting you up like this is going to be able to resist seeing if you bought it."

"You're upsetting her," Sam says.

Mina turns to him. "He doesn't believe me."

I sigh. I do think she's hiding something, but since I don't know what, it's no help. Telling her that I don't entirely believe her won't be any help either. "Look, if the blackmailer shows to get the money, we'll know who it is."

"But what about the money?" Mina says. "I won't have it."

"Just bring a big enough bag that it looks possible for you to have the cash."

Mina looks disconsolately out the window and takes a shaky breath.

"It's going to be fine," I tell her, curling my gloved hand around her arm in what I hope is a sympathetic way. She looks tired.

The bell rings, loud enough to startle us. Mina jumps up and brushes off her skirt. When she tosses her hair, it moves like a wave. It moves the way hair does only in movies.

No real hair moves like that.

I take another look at her as she pushes a lock of it behind her ear. "You seem really nice," she tells Sam. "Thanks for trying to help."

There are no split ends, I realize. And while her bangs make it hard to see, the part on top of her head shows a color that's subtly different from the rest of her skin.

Sam nods, expression grave. "Anything I can do."

"We'll figure this out," I say.

She gives me one of those almost-smiles that some girls seem to be able to summon up, the kind where her lip trembles and she looks so vulnerable that you find yourself desperate for a way to turn it into a real smile. Her lashes are still wet from tears that never fell. I wonder what it would feel like to wipe those tears with my thumb. I imagine the softness of her cheek against my bare skin. Then she picks up a messenger bag covered in pictures of singing anthropomorphic strawberries and marches out of the library.

Her wig swings behind her.

The rest of the day is a blur of hastily composed texts that don't get returned. Lila isn't in the common room of her building, and I had to promise Sharone Nagel a copy of my statistics homework to get her to look. Lila's car is not even in the lot. By the time I discover that she's not at dinner, I am practically crawling out of my skin with my desire to find her.

Daneca doesn't come to dinner either.

Sam at least is there, flipping through a catalog of masks, barely paying attention to the cooling mound of shepherd's pie piled on his plate. "So," he says, "are you going to tell me what this thing with Mina is really about?"

"Nothing to tell. We're going to save a maiden in distress like old-timey knights. I just wish I knew exactly what distress we were saving her from. The whole thing is fishy."

"You don't believe what she said about the pictures?" he asks, pausing on a page with a rubbery werewolf snout that is supposed to be attached with spirit gum.

"I don't know. All I'm sure of is that she's lying about *something*. But maybe it's nothing important. We all lie, right?"

That makes him snort. "So what's the plan, Sir Bonehead?"

"Pretty much what I said. We see who shows up to blackmail Mina or who shows up to laugh at how gullible she is."

I gaze across at where Mina is sitting with her friends, playing with a lock of her wig and drinking a diet soda. Even being nearly sure her hair isn't real, I wonder at it. It *looks* real, better than real, rippling down her back in a glossy sheet.

Was she sick? If so, it must have been long enough ago that no one at Wallingford remembers her absence from school, but not so long ago that her hair has grown back. Or I guess it could be something else. Maybe she just likes the convenience of not worrying about styling it in the morning.

I wonder what would make someone want to blackmail a girl like her. Anyone could tell that her family isn't flush if they just *looked*. Her watch is nice, but she always wears it. The leather band is worn. And her shoes are black ballet flats. Cute but cheap. It's not that she can't afford nice things. She has last year's cell phone and a two-year-old laptop covered in pink crystals. That's more than lots of people have. Plus she goes to Wallingford. It's just that she wouldn't be the person I'd target if I wanted to grift an easy five large. It has to be a prank.

Unless the blackmailer knows something I don't.

After dinner I go back out to the parking lot, but Lila's car still isn't there. I consider that maybe she and Daneca are together, since neither of them were at dinner. Maybe Daneca listened to what I said about Barron, no matter what she pretended. Maybe she even started to doubt him. If she ran into Lila, then maybe that's why Lila hasn't called me back. Daneca's house is close by; it would have been a small thing to go there for dinner. I imagine them in Daneca's kitchen, eating pizza and talking about what jerks those Sharpe boys are. I don't mind the thought. It is, in fact, a huge relief, compared to all the other possibilities. I have a couple of hours before in-room check and no better ideas, so I decide to drive by Daneca's house.

I know what you're thinking. You're thinking that it's ironic that Barron, who's wrong about so many things, is right about me being a stalker.

After parking on her leaf-lined street in Princeton, I walk down the block, past stately brick dwellings, each one with a manicured lawn, sculpted bushes, and a shining door knocker. Each yard is full of fall decorations—dried corn and gourds or planters with stacked pyramids of pumpkins, even the occasional leftover scarecrow.

As I walk up the path to her house, I realize that I figured wrong. Neither car is in the driveway, and I've just come this way for nothing.

I turn around and am about to walk away when the front door opens and the porch light flickers on.

"Hello?" Daneca's mother calls into the darkness. She's got a gloved hand up, shadowing her eyes. The porch light does the useless thing that porch lights often do, nearly blinding her and rendering me just a shadow.

I walk closer. "It's me, Mrs. Wasserman. Cassel. I didn't mean to scare you."

"Cassel?" she says, as though she's still nervous. Maybe more nervous. "Aren't you supposed to be at school?"

"I was looking for Daneca. We're seniors, so we can

go off campus as long as we're back on time. But, yeah, I should probably be at Wallingford. I'm going back there right now." I make a vague gesture in the direction of where I parked.

She's quiet for a long moment. Then she says, "I think you'd better come inside."

I walk over the worn marble threshold and step onto the gleaming wooden floors. I smell the remainder of whatever they had for dinner—something with tomato sauce—and hear the television from the living room. Daneca's father and her sort-of brother, Chris, are sitting on the couches, staring at the screen. Chris turns to glance in my direction as I pass, eyes bright with reflected light.

Mrs. Wasserman beckons me toward the kitchen, and I follow her.

"Do you want something to drink?" she asks, walking to the stove and filling the kettle. It reminds me uncomfortably of my mother in Zacharov's house.

"I'm okay."

She points to a chair. "Sit down at least."

"Thanks," I say, sitting awkwardly. "Look, I'm really sorry to bother you—"

"Why is it that you thought Daneca would be here instead of at Wallingford?"

I shake my head. "I don't know where she is. All I want to do is talk to her about her boyfriend. She's dating my brother. If you met him, you'd understand why I am—"

"I have met him," Mrs. Wasserman says. "He came to dinner."

"Oh," I say slowly, because I bet he told her something bad enough to explain her discomfort around me. "Barron came here? To dinner. Here?"

"I just want you to remember, Cassel, I know how hard things can be for worker kids. For every kid like Chris who finds a place to call home, there are lots of other kids who are kicked out onto the streets, taken in by crime families and then sold off to the rich—forced to endure continual blowback so that other people can line their pockets, or they're forced to become criminals themselves. And it must be even worse to be raised to believe you had to do those things. I don't know what you've done or what your brother's done, but—"

"What is it you think we did?"

She glances at my face, like she's searching for something. Finally she says, "I don't know. Daneca called here earlier today. She said that you didn't approve of her going out with your brother. I know you're worried about Daneca. You're Sam's roommate, and I can see that you want to protect her. Maybe you want to protect both of them. But if you expect to be forgiven for what you've done, then you have to see that your brother deserves a second chance too."

"What do you think I've done? What did he tell you that I did?"

"That's not important," she says. "It's in the past. I am sure you want it to stay there."

I open my mouth and close it again. Because I want to defend myself, but it's true that I've done bad things. Things that I want to stay in the past. But I also want to know what he told her, because I really doubt he told her the whole story.

The problem with people like Mrs. Wasserman is exactly this. She's *kind*. She's *good*. She wants to help people, even people that she shouldn't. Like Barron. Like me. It's easy to take advantage of her optimism, her faith in how the world should work.

I should know. I've already done it.

When I look into Mrs. Wasserman's face, I know that she's a born mark for this particular kind of con.

CHAPTER NINE

IF YOU ARE A CRAZY person who needs to have clandestine meetings, then, just like in real estate, what matters most is location, location, location.

You want to control the situation, so you better control the terrain. No surprises. No buildings, no trees, no shadowy corners where your enemies can hide. You want only those hidden spots that will be occupied by your people. But the place can't be *so* open that a passerby would have a clear sight line. Clandestine meetings have to stay clandestine.

The baseball field isn't a terrible choice. Far from other buildings. A nearby wooded area is the only place to hide, and it's not *that* close by. The time's good too. Six in the morning is too early for most students to be up, but there's no rule against it. Mina won't have to sneak out. And there's enough time for an exchange of goods before classes start. The blackmailer could get the money, take their sweet time stashing it, and still make it to breakfast.

On the other hand, six in the morning seems way too early for girls pulling a prank to be anywhere but in bed. I figure they'll be in their pajamas, leaning out of the windows of their dorm, jeering, when Mina returns from the baseball field after no one shows to the meeting. If I'm right, that's what's going to happen. Then the real negotiation starts, because I still have to somehow convince them to give up the camera and its contents. That's when we'll find out what's really going on.

Sam's alarm goes off like a siren at four thirty in the morning, an hour I hope I never see from this end again. I knock my phone onto the floor trying to turn it off, before I realize the sound is coming from a totally different part of the room.

"Get up," I say, and throw a pillow in his direction.

"Your plan sucks," Sam mumbles as he lurches out of bed and heads for the showers.

"Yeah," I say softly to myself. "Tell me one thing that doesn't suck right now."

It's too early for there to be any coffee. I stare dully at the empty pot in the common room, while Sam picks up a jar of instant grounds.

"Don't," I warn him.

He scoops up a heaping spoonful and, heedlessly, shoves it into his mouth. It crunches horribly. Then his eyes go wide.

"Dry," he croaks. "Tongue . . . shriveling."

I shake my head, picking up the jar. "It's dehydrated. You're supposed to add water. Good thing you're mostly made of water."

He tries to say something. Brown powder dusts his shirt.

"Also," I tell him, "that's decaf."

He runs to the sink to spit it out. I grin. There's nothing quite as funny as someone else's misery.

By the time we're outside, I feel a little more awake. It's so early that the hazy fog of morning is still settling over the grass. Dew has crystallized on the bare branches of trees and on piles of fallen leaves, turning them pale with frost.

We trek over to the baseball field, the dampness wetting our shoes. No one is there yet, which is the idea. You never want to be the last person to a clandestine meeting.

"Now what?" Sam asks me.

I point toward the woods. It's not ideal but will be close enough to see if anyone shows up, and after chasing down a death worker, I am confident that I can catch up to a student if I really have to.

The ground is frozen. The grass crunches as we sit. I get up to check from a few angles until I'm sure we're pretty well hidden.

Mina arrives about fifteen minutes later, just at the point when I think that Sam is about to fidget himself to death. She's clutching a paper bag nervously.

"Um, hello?" she calls from the edge of the trees.

"Here," I say. "Don't worry. Just go to the middle of the field—to the right, by first base—and make sure to turn so that we see you."

"Okay," Mina says, her voice shaking. "I'm sorry to have dragged you into this, but—"

"Not right now. Just go stand over there and wait."

Sam lets out a long-suffering sigh as she walks off. "She's *scared*."

"I know," I say. "I just didn't know how to— We don't have time for that."

"You must be the worst boyfriend in the whole world," Sam whispers.

"Probably," I say, and he laughs.

Waiting is hard. It's boring, and the more bored you get, the more you want to close your eyes and take a cat-nap. Or pull out your phone and play a game on it. Or talk. Your muscles get stiff. Your skin gets that pins-and-needles warning that your foot is falling asleep. Maybe no one's coming. Maybe you were spotted. Maybe you made one of a million other miscalculations. All you want is an excuse to leave your post and get a cup of coffee or take a nap in your own bed. Time slows to a jagged crawl, like the passage of an ant along your spine.

Getting through it once makes it easier to believe that it can be gotten through again. Sam shifts uncomfortably. Mina looks pale and anguished, pacing back and forth. I alternate between watching her face for some sign that the blackmailer has arrived, and planning what I will say to Lila.

Daneca won't believe me. Please just tell her what Barron did.

I get as far as that, and my mind stalls. I can't picture what she says back. I can't imagine the expression on her face. I keep thinking of how she wouldn't look at me after I told her that I loved her. The way she wouldn't believe me. And then I remember her mouth on mine and the way she looked up at me when we were lying on the same grass I am looking at now, except the grass was warm and she was warm and she said my name like nothing else in the world mattered.

I press the tips of my gloved fingers against my eyes, to force away the images.

Sam jerks next to me, and I take away my hands slowly. Mina's posture has stiffened, and she's looking across the grass at someone we can't quite see. Adrenaline floods my veins, making my heart pound. The risk at this point is that we'll be too eager. We need to wait until the blackmailer has his back to us, and then we need to move as quietly as we can.

Mina turns slightly as the figure approaches her. She does exactly what I told her, except for a glance in our direction. Our gazes lock, and I try to silently communicate that she needs to *never look over here again*.

Then the figure comes into view.

I don't know exactly what I was picturing, but it wasn't a freshman, tall and gangly and so twitchy that I relax at the sight of him. Maybe he found the camera and decided he'd make some fast cash. Maybe he thinks blackmail is the high school equivalent of shoving a girl you like into a mud puddle. I don't know. All I do know is that he is playing way out of his league.

It seems cruel to jump him, so instead I pull the lamest trick ever. Making sure his back is to me, I stuff my hand into the pocket of my jacket, point my first and middle fingers so that I'm making the little-kid gun shape.

I cross the lawn quickly, fast enough that by the time he hears me coming, I am pretty close.

"Freeze," I tell him.

It's comical, the sound that the kid makes when he sees me. A scream so high pitched, I can't hear half of it. Even Mina looks rattled.

Sam walks up until he's looming over the freshman. "That's Alex DeCarlo," he says, looking down. "We're in chess club together. What's he doing here?"

I raise my fake pocket gun. "Yeah. What exactly did you want with five grand?"

"No," Alex says, his face gone bright red with misery. "I didn't want to—" He looks over at Mina and takes a nervous breath. "I don't know about the five thousand dollars. I was just supposed to bring the envelope that, uh, *he* gave me. Mina's my friend, and I would never—"

Lying, lying. Everyone is *lying*. I can hear it in their voices. I can tell in the way their expressions don't quite match the words, in a dozen small tells.

Well, I can lie too. "If you don't tell me the truth, I am going to *blow your brains out*."

"I'm sorry," he squeaks. "I'm sorry. Mina, you didn't say

that he would have a gun." The kid looks like he's about to puke on his own shoes.

"*Alex,*" she says sharply, like a warning.

Sam takes a step closer to her. "Hey, it's going to be—"

Alex takes a trembling breath. "She said that all I had to do was come here and tell you this story, but I don't want to die. Please don't shoot. I won't tell anyone—"

"Mina?" I say incredulously. Dropping the pretense of the gun, I take my hand out of my pocket and snatch the envelope out of Alex's hand. "Let me see that."

"Hey!" says Alex. And then, as I start ripping open the package, he says, "Wait. That wasn't real? You don't have a gun?"

"Oh, he has a gun all right," Sam says.

"Don't!" Mina says. She reaches out to snatch the package from me. "Please."

I give her a dark look. There are printed-out pictures inside the envelope, not negatives or a SIM card or a missing camera.

But it's too late. I'm already looking.

There are three pictures, Mina standing in profile in all of the shots, her long black wig spilling over her shoulders. She's not naked. In fact, she's wearing her Wallingford uniform. The only thing naked about her is her right hand.

Her bare fingers touch the collarbone of the man beside her, Dean Wharton. His white dress shirt is open at the neck. His eyes are closed, perhaps with dread or with pleasure.

I let the photos fall. They scatter on the ground like dead leaves.

"You're ruining everything," Mina says, her voice almost feral. "I did this to make you believe me. I had to convince you."

Sam reaches down and picks up one of the photos. He stares at it, probably, like me, puzzling through what it could mean.

I roll my eyes. "Let me get this straight. You lied to us so that we'd believe you?"

"If you knew what was happening from the start, if you knew a dean was involved, you wouldn't have agreed to help me." Mina looks from me to Sam to Alex, like she's trying to figure out which one of us might still be vulnerable to her pleading. Her eyes are welling with tears.

"I guess we'll never know," I tell her.

"Please," she says. "You can see why I didn't want to— you can see why I was afraid."

"I have no idea," I say. "You've lied so much that I have no goddamn idea why you would be afraid."

"Please," she says tragically. Despite myself there is a part of me that really feels bad for her. I've been where she is, trying to manipulate people because I was too afraid to do anything else. Too convinced that they would never help me if I didn't con that help out of them.

"Liars don't get the benefit of being trusted twice," I tell her, trying to keep my voice firm.

She covers her face with one slender gloved hand. "You hate me now, I bet. You hate me."

"No," I say, relenting with a sigh. "Of course not. Just, this time, let's have the whole story okay?"

She nods quickly, wiping her eyes. "I promise. I'll tell you everything."

"You can start with your hair," I say.

She touches it self-consciously, gloved fingers threading through the black mass. "What?"

I lean forward and give a lock of it a hard tug. Her whole hairline slips to one side, and she gasps, her hands flying to try to correct it.

Alex gasps too.

"That's a wig?" Sam says, not really asking, but in that way when you haven't gotten your head around something yet.

She stumbles away from me, her face red. "I asked you to help me. All I wanted was your help!" Her voice is ragged and guttural. She sobs suddenly, and this time I am sure her reaction is entirely real. Her nose starts to run. "I just wanted—"

She turns and legs it back toward the dorms.

"Mina!" I call after her, but she doesn't turn.

Sam suggests that we should go off campus for breakfast, rather than standing in the middle of the baseball diamond, freezing our asses off discussing what information we got out of Alex after Mina ran. It's only a little after six in the morning, and we have until eight before classes start. I could do with pancakes.

I get into the passenger side of Sam's hearse. I lean back against the headrest and close my eyes. It's just for a moment, but the next thing I know Sam is shaking me awake. We're parked in back of the Bluebird Diner.

"Get up," Sam says. "No one gets to sleep in my car unless they're already dead."

I yawn and scramble out. "Sorry."

I wonder if this morning was any kind of useful training for being a federal agent. After I graduate from Wallingford in the spring and enroll in the official training program with Yulikova, I'll learn how to catch real blackmailers. Blackmailers who aren't like Alex DeCarlo and don't believe I'm holding a real gun when I push two fingers against my jacket pocket.

Blackmailers who are actually blackmailing someone.

We go inside. A waitress who has got to be at least seventy, her cheeks rouged like a doll's, seats us and passes out menus. Sam orders us a round of coffee.

"Refills are free," the waitress tells us with a frown, like she's hoping we're not the kind of people who ask for endless refills. I am already pretty sure we are exactly those people.

With a sigh Sam opens his menu and starts ordering food.

A few minutes later I am drinking my third cup of coffee and poking at a stack of silver dollar pancakes. Sam spreads cream cheese on half a bagel and tops it with salmon and capers.

"I should have spotted that wig," he says, pointing the dull knife toward his chest. "I'm the special effects guy. I should have noticed."

I shake my head. "Nah. I don't even know how I noticed. And besides, I have no idea what it means. Why do girls wear wigs, Sam?"

He shrugs and finishes off another cup of coffee. "My gran wears them to keep her head warm. Think it's that?"

I grin. "Maybe. Who knows, right? I mean, you'd think we could find out if she was being treated for a serious illness. She'd miss class."

"Doesn't hair fall out from stress? Maybe all this lying has really gotten to Mina. She's not the pro that you are."

I smirk. "Or sometimes people have a condition where they pull out all their hair. I saw it on some late-night reality TV show. They eat their follicles too. And they can get this giant deadly hair ball called a bezoar."

"Trichotillomania," he says, clearly smugly proud of himself for summoning that word from somewhere. Then he pauses. "Or it could be blowback."

I nod, conceding the point. I guess we were both thinking it. "You mean you think those are photos of Mina working Dean Wharton? I think so too. The first question is, who took them? And then the other question is, why give them to us? And the third question is, if she's working him, what's she *doing* to him?"

"'Why give them to us?' But she didn't. You grabbed them out of Alex's hands," Sam says, raising his cup, signaling to the waitress that we need another round of free refills. "There's no way she wanted us to see the photos."

"Nah. She must have," I say. "Or why even send Alex with them? And why take them in the first place? I think she got upset because we saw the pictures without hearing what she wanted us to hear."

"Wait. You think she *took* the pictures of herself? So

there's *no* blackmailer?" Sam is staring at me like he's waiting for me to tell him that Mina is a robot from the future come to doom our world.

"I think she's the blackmailer," I say.

After Mina left, we got Alex to explain the story he was supposed to give. Mina told him to say that the blackmailer was Dr. Stewart and that Stewart wanted five grand or he was going to ruin Wharton's career and Mina's reputation. Dr. Stewart was sending word through Alex for Mina to get the money and bring it to him. Or else.

I had Stewart last year. He's a hard-ass. The kind of teacher who seems delighted when you fail a quiz. I always figured him as a guy who loved rules—and who thought that if you didn't stick to the rules, then you deserved what you got.

Not exactly the criminal type.

There are several other problems with the story, besides the unlikely villain. One, involving Alex is just stupid. If Stewart was actually trying to cover his tracks by using Mina as a buffer between his identity and Wharton, then there's no way that he would be stupid enough to enlist a student with nothing to lose by telling everyone.

"I don't get it," Sam says.

"Neither do I," I say. "Not really. Is she a scholarship student?"

He shrugs. "Could be."

"We need to know if she's doing something to Wharton or for Wharton. Is he paying her, or is she making him—I don't know—do something that benefits her?"

"He's paying her," Sam says. "Because if he wasn't the one who was paying, then she wouldn't want there to be any documentation of what's going on, right? She wouldn't let us see the photos. Wouldn't have given them to Alex. Wouldn't rock the boat. If you're right about that part, then Wharton's hiring Mina."

I take out one of the photos and set it down in the center of the table. Sam moves mugs and plates so there's room.

We stare at Mina's bare fingers and the way that Wharton's head is turned away, like he's ashamed of what he's doing. We stare at the composition—the figures not centered, like maybe the photos were taken without anyone to aim. There's ways to do that, even with a cell phone. It can be programmed to take pictures every couple of minutes. The only hard part for Mina would be making sure that Wharton was standing in the right spot.

"Do you like her?" Sam asks.

I look up at him sharply. "What?"

"Nothing. Luck work, maybe. She could be a luck worker. He could have a gambling problem," Sam says.

"Or she could be a physical worker like Philip, although his hair didn't fall out." I try not to think about what Sam just asked me, but now I can't help wondering if he's interested in Mina. There's something about a lady in distress—we all want to save her. And there's nothing like getting dumped to make anybody eager for a rebound.

"Maybe she's a physical worker curing Wharton's *baldness*," Sam says, and we both laugh. "But seriously, what do you think? What was Mina trying to do?"

I shrug. "I guess she wanted the money, right? So she must have thought we could help her get it? Maybe she thought we'd find some way to squeeze Stewart for it or help her blackmail Wharton and blame Stewart."

The waitress sets the bill at the end of the table and clears our plates. We pause the conversation until she goes.

I wonder where Lila is now.

"But what does Mina need five grand for?" Sam asks, fumbling for his wallet with one hand and reaching for his refilled mug with the other. I drag my attention back to the present.

"It's money. Could be for anything—maybe just to have it. But if Wharton's been paying her to get himself worked, then I guess it's possible the payments are coming to an end. All grifters dream of the big score."

"The big score?" Sam grins, teasing.

"Sure," I say. "The one that you can live on forever. The legendary one. The one that your name becomes synonymous with. I admit that five large isn't *that* large, but it's pretty big for high school. And if she thinks that she's not going to be making money off him regularly anymore, maybe there's no reason not to go for it."

I throw ten bucks down onto the table. He does the same, and we slide out of the booth.

"No reason except getting caught," Sam says.

I nod. "That's why the big score is a myth. A fairy tale. Because no one ever quits after a successful job. They get stupid and cocky and think they're invulnerable. They convince themselves to do just one more, just this last time.

And then the time after that, because if a job goes sideways, then you want to do another to get the taste of failure out of your mouth. And if it goes well, you do another to chase that feeling."

"Even you?" Sam asks.

I look over at him, surprised. "Not me," I say. "I'm already on the hook with the Feds."

"My grandfather took me fishing a couple of times," Sam says as he unlocks the hearse. "I wasn't very good at it. I always had trouble reeling them in. Maybe it'll be like that."

I want to say something funny back, but the words stick in my throat.

Instead of going to class I head to Lila's dorm. I have some idea that I'm going to talk to her about Daneca, but it's become so jumbled up with a sheer, mad desire to see Lila that it doesn't make any real sense.

I thought I was getting better at this. I thought I was starting to make peace with being in love with a girl who despises me, but I don't think I'm so okay with it after all. Somewhere along the line I made a dark bargain with the universe without really being aware of it—a bargain that if I was allowed to see her, even if we never spoke, then I could live with that. And now a week without her has swallowed up all of my rational thinking.

I feel like a junkie, sick for my next fix and not sure if it will come.

Maybe she's eating breakfast in her room, I tell myself. That's a reasonable thought, a normal one. I can just catch her before she leaves. I won't let her see how much it matters.

I race up the stairs of Gilbert House, past a couple of freshmen girls, who giggle.

"You're not supposed to be here," one says, mock-scolding. "This is the girls' dorm."

I pause and give her my best smile, my coconspirator smile. The one that I practice in front of the mirror. The one that's supposed to promise all kinds of evil delights. "Good thing I have you to cover for me."

She smiles back, her cheeks going pink.

At the top of the steps I catch the door to Lila's hall as Jill Pearson-White comes out. She's got her backpack thrown over one shoulder and an energy bar in her mouth. She barely pays attention to me, taking the stairs two at a time.

I cross the corridor, fast, because if Lila's hall mistress sees me, I am totally screwed. I try Lila's door, but it's locked. I don't have time for anything fancy. I pull out a bank card from my wallet and slide it down the seam. That trick has worked on my own door before, and I'm lucky, because it works now.

I expect Lila to be sitting on her bed, maybe lacing her shoes. Or pulling on a pair of gloves. Or printing out a paper at the last possible minute. But she's not.

For a moment I think I'm in the wrong room.

There are no posters on the walls. There is no book-case, no trunk, or vanity or illicit electric kettle. The bed has been stripped down to the mattress, and there's nothing else there.

She's gone.

The door swings shut behind me as I cross the empty room. Everything feels like it has slowed down, the edges a little dim. The awfulness of it, the loss of her, hits me in the gut. Gone. Gone and there's nothing I can do about it.

My eyes are drawn to the window, where light's streaming in, casting an odd shadow. There on the sill, resting against one of the panes of glass, is a single envelope.

My name is written on it in her handwriting. I wonder how long it's been sitting there. I imagine her loading all her stuff into boxes and carrying it down the stairs, Zacharov himself helping her, like all the other dads did. With two goons, guns tucked into their waistbands, helping him.

The thought should make me smile, but it doesn't.

I sink to the floor, the paper clutched to my chest. I rest my head on the bare wood. Somewhere in the distance I hear a bell ring.

I've got no reason to get up, so I don't.

CHAPTER TEN

WHEN I FINALLY OPEN
the letter, it makes me smile, despite everything. And for
some reason, that makes it even more awful that she's gone.

4/ 8\6/5/3\ 9/6/8| 4/ 9\2\7// 6|6/ 4\6/6/3\ 2\8\
7//2/4|6/6/5/ - 9\3|5/5/ 4/6\ 6|6/8\ 4\6/6/3\
2\8\ 7//2\9/4/6|4\ 4\6/6/3\2|9/3| 3|4/8\4|3|7/
- 4/ 2\5/9\2\9/7// 5|6|3|9\ 9\4|2\8\ 4/ 9\2\7//
4\6/4/6|4\ 8\6/ 2|3| 9\4|3|6| 4/ 4\7/3|9\ 8|7\ -
4/ 2\5/9\2\9/7// 5|6|3|9\ 9\4|6/7//3| 7//4|6/3|7//
4/ 4|2\3\ 8\6/ 3/4/5/5/ - 2\6|3\ 4/ 6|3|8/3|7/
7//2\4/3\ 4/8\ 2|8|8\ 4/ 3|6|8/4/3|3\ 9/6/8| 3/6/7/
6|6/8\ 4|2\8/4/6|4\ 3|8/3|7/9/8\4|4/6|4\ 2\5/5/
7\5/2\6|6|3|3\ 6/8|8\ - 4/ 5|6|6/9\ 4/8\ 9\2\7//6|8\

2\5/9\2\9/7// 3|2\7//9/ - 7\3|6/7\5/3| 3\4/3\6|8\
8\7/3|2\8\ 9/6/8| 5/4/5|3| 9/6/8| 9\3|7/3|
4/6\7\6/7/8\2\6|8\ 2|8|8\ 9/6/8| 9\3|7/3| 3/7/3|3|

9/6/8| 7//8\4/5/5/ 2/2\6| 2|3| 2|8|8\ 9/6/8|7/3|
4\6/4/6|4\ 8\6/ 4|2\8/3| 8\6/ 8\7/9/ 4|2\7/3\3|7/
4/3/ 9/6/8| 9\2\6|8\ 8\6/ 7//8\2\9/ 8\4|2\8\ 9\2\9/

—5/4/5/2\

It's a code. One I recognize immediately, because Lila and I used it to leave notes for each other when we were kids. It's a simple one. Nobody with a real secret and any knowledge of cryptography would use this. You just take a phone and copy down the number that goes with each letter. Like *L* would become "5" and *A* would become "2." But since there's more than one letter for each number on a keypad, the code has a second symbol. A slash or straight line indicates the letter's position on the phone button, like this: \|/. So the final code for *L* is "5/" because *L* is to the far right on the key. And *A* is "2\" because *A* is to the far left. And if it's one of those numbers with four letters, then you add an extra slash, so that "9/" is *Y* and "9//" is *Z* and so on. It's time consuming to translate back, but easy, especially if there's a phone in front of you.

The existence of the letter—that she knew I would come here and find it, that she remembered our old code and believed I'd remember it too—makes my throat hurt. Nobody ever really sees me the way I am, underneath everything. But she did. She does.

I smooth the paper out on the floor, find the receipt from the diner and a spare pen, and start translating:

> *I told you I was no good at school. Well, I'm not good at saying good-bye either. I always knew what I was going to be when I grew up. I always knew whose shoes I had to fill. And I never said it, but I envied you for not having everything all planned out. I know it wasn't always easy. People didn't treat you like you were important, but you were free.*
>
> *You still can be, but you're going to have to try harder if you want to stay that way.*
>
> *—Lila*

I'm tracing my fingers over the coded paper, thinking about how long it must have taken her, picturing her lying on her bed, making mark after laborious mark, when my phone rings.

I fumble to answer, startled, suddenly reminded that I shouldn't be on the girls' hall—and that if someone hears a sound, they're going to investigate. The actual students who bunk here are all in class.

"Hello?" I say, keeping my voice low.

"Cassel?" It's Yulikova. "Is that you?"

I get up and cross the room, lean my arm against the closet door frame. "Yeah, I'm here. Sorry."

"The operation is moving forward. We're going to pick you up next Wednesday, okay? I need you not to tell anyone, but it looks like you're going to be gone for a few days. You'll need a story. Family member in the hospital, something like that. And pack a bag."

"A few days? When is the actual event—"

"I'm sorry. I'm not authorized to tell you that, although obviously I wish I could."

"Can you at least tell me what the plan is?"

Yulikova laughs. "We will, Cassel. Of course. We want you to be as involved as possible. But not over the phone."

Obviously. Of course.

The language of someone who's trying very hard to convince me. Too hard.

"Okay," I say. "So next week?"

"We want you to be safe, so please, just act normal. Spend time with your friends and plan out how you're going to get away for a while without anyone noticing. Start laying the groundwork for whatever excuse you think would work best. And if you need us to come up with something—"

"No," I say, "I've got it."

They don't trust me. She needs me, but she doesn't trust me. Not completely. Not enough. I wonder if Jones said something to her, but I guess it doesn't matter.

I've got it, but I don't have to like it.

I make it through my afternoon classes and try not to think about the morning ones I missed. About how close I am to getting chucked out of Wallingford. About how little I care. I try not to think about Lila.

At track practice I run in circles.

*   *   *

As soon as I can make an excuse, I change into normal clothes and head to my car, skipping dinner. I feel oddly distant, my gloved hands turning the wheel. There is a kind of dark hope in my heart—the kind that I don't want to examine too carefully. It's fragile. Just looking at it straight on could crush it dead.

I drive to Lila's apartment building. I don't even bother trying to get into the lot with its closed gates and coded lock. I find a space a couple blocks down, hope I won't get towed, and walk into the building.

At the desk a gray-haired man sitting in front of a bunch of monitors asks for my identification. Once I hand over my driver's license, he buzzes the Zacharov apartment. He picks up a battered gray headset, waits a few moments, and then mispronounces my name into it.

I hear static and a voice on the other end, so distorted that I don't recognize it. The front desk guy nods once, then pulls off the headset and hands me back my license.

"Go right up," he says with his slight Eastern European accent.

The elevator is just as shiny and cold as I remember.

When the doors open, Zacharov is there, pacing the floor in suit pants and a half-buttoned white shirt, staring at the television.

"I'm going to rip his head off," he yells. "With my bare hands."

"Mr. Zacharov," I say. My voice echoes. "Sorry—I—the doorman told me I could come up."

He turns around. "You know what that prick has done now?"

"What?" I ask, not sure who we're talking about.

"Look." He points at the flat screen.

Patton is shaking hands with a gray-haired man that I don't know. I look at the screen, and underneath the image are the words "Patton Proposes Joint Venture to Test Government Employees at Summit with Governor Grant."

"That's the governor of New York. Do you know how much money I've donated to his reelection campaign? And now he's acting like that lunatic has anything worthwhile to say."

Don't worry about Patton. He'll be gone soon. That's what I want to say, but I can't. "Maybe Grant's just humoring him."

Zacharov turns toward me, seeming to actually be aware of me for the first time. He blinks. "Are you looking for your mother? She's resting."

"I was hoping I could talk to Lila."

He frowns at me for a drawn-out moment, then points toward the sweeping staircase that leads to a rounded archway on the second floor. I don't know if he remembers that I don't know my way around or if he just doesn't care.

I jog up the steps.

When I'm halfway there, Zacharov calls, "I heard that useless brother of yours is working for the Feds. That's not true, is it?"

I turn back, keeping my face carefully blank, a little puzzled. My heart is beating so fast that my chest hurts. "No," I say, and force a laugh. "Barron's no good with authority."

"Who is, right?" asks Zacharov, and laughs too. "Tell him to keep his nose clean. I'd hate having to break his neck."

I lean against the railing. "You promised me—"

"Some betrayals even I can't afford, Cassel. He wouldn't just be turning his back on me. He'd be turning his back on you and your mother. He'd be putting you in danger. And Lila."

I nod numbly, but my heart is skipping along, like a stone on the surface of a lake right before it drops under. If he knew what I'd done, if he knew about Yulikova and the Licensed Minority Division, he would shoot me as soon as look at me. He would kill me six times over. But he *doesn't know*. At least I don't think he knows. His expression, the slight lift of one side of his mouth, tells me nothing.

I resume my walk up the steps, each footfall heavier than it was.

There's a hallway.

"Lila?" I call softly as I pass several glossy wooden doors with heavy metal trim on the hinges and knobs.

I open a door at random and see a bedroom, an empty one. It's too tidy to be anything but a guest room, which means that they have enough bedrooms to have my mother in one and at least another spare. The place is even bigger than I realized.

I knock on the next. No one answers, but down near the end another door opens. Lila steps into the hall.

"That's a linen closet," she says. "There's a washing machine and dryer in there."

"I bet you don't even need exact change to use them," I say, thinking of the dorms.

She grins, leaning against the door frame, looking like she just got out of the shower. She's got on a white tank and black skinny jeans. Her feet are bare, her toenails painted silver. A few locks of pale wet hair stick to her cheek; a few more stick to her neck where her scar is.

"You got my letter," she says, walking closer. Her voice is soft. "Or maybe—"

I touch the pocket of my jacket self-consciously and give her a lopsided grin. "Took me a while to translate."

She pushes the hair out of her face. "You shouldn't have come. I put everything in the letter, so that we wouldn't have to—" She stops speaking, as if the rest of the sentence has deserted her. Despite the words, she doesn't sound angry. She takes another half step toward me. We're close enough that if she whispered I'd hear it.

I look at her, and I think of how it felt when I saw her in my bedroom in the old house, before I knew that she'd been cursed, when everything still seemed possible. I see the soft line of her mouth, and the clear brightness of her eyes, and I remember dreaming about those features when it still seemed like she could be mine.

She was the epic crush of my childhood. She was the tragedy that made me look inside myself and see my corrupt heart. She was my sin and my salvation, come back from the grave to change me forever. Again. Back then, when she sat on my bed and told me she loved me, I wanted her as much as I have ever wanted anything.

But that was before we'd scammed our way into a high-rise and laughed ourselves sick and talked in the funeral parlor the way I've never talked to anyone and might never talk to anyone again. That was before she stopped being a memory and started being the only person who made me feel like myself. That was before she hated me.

I wanted her then. Now I barely want anything else.

I sway toward Lila, waiting for her to pull back, but she doesn't. My hands come up, gloved fingers closing around her upper arms, crushing her to me as my mouth catches hers. I'm braced for her to stop me, but her body folds against mine instead. Her lips are warm and soft, parting in a single sigh.

That's all it takes.

I push her back against the wall, kissing her the way I've never let myself. I want to swallow her up. I want her to feel my regret in the slide of my mouth and taste devotion on my tongue. She makes a sound that's half gasp and half a moan and pulls me closer against her. Her eyes close, and everything is teeth and breath and skin.

"We've got to—," she says against my mouth, her voice seeming to come from a great distance. "We've got to stop. We've got to—"

I stagger back.

The hallway seems very bright. Lila is still leaning against the wall, one hand against the plaster, like it's holding her. Her lips are red, her face flushed. She's looking at me with wide eyes.

I feel drunk. I am breathing so hard that I feel like I've been running.

"You should probably go," she says unsteadily.

I nod, agreeing, even though leaving is the last thing I want. "But I have to talk to you. It's about Daneca. That's why I came. I didn't mean—"

She gives me a nervous look. "Okay. Talk."

"She went out with my brother. She's *been* going out with him, I think."

"Barron?" She pushes off from the wall, paces the carpet.

"Remember when I thought that *you'd* told her about my being a transformation worker? Well, that was him. I don't know exactly what he told her, but he mixed up enough truth with the lies that I can't convince her to stay away from him. I can't convince her of anything."

"That's not possible. He's not the kind of boy she would like. Daneca's too smart for that."

"You went out with him," I say before I think better of it.

She gives me a scorching look. "I never said I was too smart." Her tone makes it clear that if she *were* smart, she wouldn't have just been up against the wall with my tongue in her mouth. "And I was a kid."

"Please," I say, "just talk to her."

Lila sighs. "I will. Of course I will. Not for your sake either. Daneca deserves better."

"She should have stayed with Sam."

"We all want things that aren't good for us." She shakes her head. "Or things that aren't what they seem."

"I don't," I say.

She laughs. "If you say so."

Down the hall a door opens, and we both jump. A man in jeans and a sweatshirt emerges, a stethoscope around his neck. He starts stripping off plastic gloves as he comes toward us.

"She's doing well," he says. "Rest is really the best thing for her now, but in another week I'd like to test her mobility with that arm. She's going to have to move it as soon as she's able to do so without pain."

Lila looks at me, her eyes slightly too wide. Like she's trying to gauge my reaction. Like there's something for me to be reacting about.

I take a chance. "Your patient is my mother," I say.

"Oh—I didn't realize. You can go see her now, of course." He reaches into his pocket and comes out with a card. He smiles, revealing a mouth full of crooked teeth. "Call me if you have any questions. Or if Shandra does. Gunshot wounds can be tricky, but this was a clean one. Through and through."

I take the card and shove it into my pocket as I start down the hallway. I'm walking fast enough that Lila would have to run to catch up.

"Cassel," she calls, but I don't even slow.

I push open the door. It's a regular guest room, like the other one. Big four-poster bed, but this one has my mother in it, propped up and watching a television that's on one of the dressers. She's got a bandage around her arm. Her face looks pale without her usual makeup. Her hair is a mess of curls. I have never seen her like this. She looks old and frail and nothing like my indomitable mother.

"I'll kill him," I say. "I'll murder Zacharov."

Shock distorts her features. "Cassel?" she says, fear in her voice.

"We're getting out of here." I come around to the side of the bed, ready to help her up. My eyes search the room for a weapon, any weapon. There's a heavy-looking brass cross over the bed. It's primitive-looking, with jagged sides.

"No," she says. "You don't understand. Calm down, sweetheart."

"You're kidding, right?"

The door opens and Lila's standing there, looking almost afraid. She pushes past me and gives my mother a quick glare.

"I'm sorry," she says, turning back to me. "I would have told you, but your mother made us promise not to. And she's okay. If she wasn't okay, I would have told you. No matter what. Honest, Cassel."

I look between them. It's hard to even imagine them being in the same room together. Maybe Lila's the one who shot her.

"Come here, baby," my mother says. "Sit on the bed."

I do. Lila stands by the wall.

"Ivan has been very good to me. This past Sunday he said I could go to church, so long as I went with some of his people. Isn't that nice?"

"You got shot in *church*?" I wonder which particular religion she's claiming to belong to, but I keep that question to myself.

"On the way back. If it wasn't for dear Lars, that would have been it. The car pulled up and I didn't even see it, but he did. I guess that's what he does, as a bodyguard and all. He pushed me and I fell, which made me mad when it was happening, but he saved my life. The first bullet hit me in the shoulder, but the rest missed and the car went screeching off." She sounds like she's reciting the plot of a particularly exciting episode of a soap opera, not telling me about something that actually happened to her.

"You think they were gunning for you? As in, you specifically? It wasn't some enemy of—" I glance at Lila. "You don't think it was a misunderstanding?"

"They had government plates," my mother says. "I didn't notice, but you can bet that Lars did. Amazing instincts."

Government plates. Patton. No wonder Zacharov was livid.

"Why didn't you call me right away? Or Barron? Either one of us. Or Grandad, for hell's sake. Mom, you're hurt."

She tilts her head and smiles at Lila. "Could you give the two of us a couple minutes alone?"

"Yeah," Lila says. "Of course." She heads out the door, closing it behind her.

Mom reaches out and pulls my face close to hers. She's not wearing gloves, and her bare nails sink into the skin of my throat. "What the hell have you boys been up to? Messing around with federal agents?" she hisses, low and vicious.

I push away, my neck stinging.

"I raised you better than this," she says. "Smarter. You know what they'll do to you if they find out what you are? They'll use you to hurt other workers. They'll use you. Against your grandfather. Against everyone you love. And Barron—that boy thinks he can wriggle out of anything, but if you got him into this, he's in over his head. The government put us in camps. And they'll do it again if they figure out a legal way to manage it."

I am left with the uncomfortable echo of Lila's words about Daneca being too smart to get involved with Barron. I guess we're all smart about some things and dumb about others. But the federal government isn't just some bad boyfriend. If Mom knew what they wanted me to do, I think she'd have a different opinion of them. If anything, looking at her, pale and furious in her pile of blankets, I am more committed than ever to getting rid of Patton.

"Barron can take care of himself."

"You're not denying it," she says.

"What's wrong with wanting to do something good with my life?"

She laughs. "You wouldn't know good if it bit you on the ass."

I look at the door. "Does Lila—does she know?"

"No one *knows*," Mom says. "They suspect. That's why I didn't want you to hear about my little accident. I didn't want you coming here—you or your brother. It's not safe. There was a boy who described you in connection with some agents."

"Fine," I say. "I'm going now. I'm glad you're okay. Oh, and I went to the jewelry store. It was a dead end, but I did learn one thing. Dad had two forgeries made. And by the way, it would have really helped if you'd mentioned that he was the one who met with Bob."

"*Two?* But why would he do—" She stops speaking as the obvious answer sinks in. She got conned by her own husband. "Phil would never do that. Never. Your father wasn't greedy. He didn't even want to sell the stone. He just wanted to keep it as insurance, in case we needed money. Our retirement fund, that's what he called it."

I shrug. "Maybe he was pissed off about your affair. Maybe he didn't think you deserved nice things."

She laughs again, this time without any malice. For a moment she seems like herself. "You ever hear of a sweetheart scheme, Cassel? You think your father didn't know?"

Sweetheart schemes have been Mom's bread and butter since Dad died. Find a rich guy. Curse him so he falls in love with her. Get his cash. She even went to jail for one of her less successful cons, although the conviction was overturned on appeal. But I never thought she'd done anything like that when Dad was alive.

I stare at her, my mouth parted. "So Dad knew about you and Zacharov?"

She snorts. "You really are such a prude, Cassel. Of course he did. And we got the stone, didn't we?"

"Okay," I say, trying to push away all thoughts of what she's done. "So, then, what *would* he do with it?"

"I don't know." Her gaze slides away from me as she contemplates the grooves of the plaster wall. "I guess a man is entitled to a few secrets."

I give her a long look.

"Just not very many," she says, and smiles. "Now come and give your mother a kiss."

Lila's in the hallway when I leave. She's leaning against the wall, near a modernist painting that's probably worth more than the entire contents of my mother's house. Lila's arms are folded against her chest.

I take out my phone and make a show of typing in the doctor's information from the card he gave me. It was just a number with no name attached, so I call him Dr. Doctor.

"I should have told you," she says finally.

"Yes, you should have told me," I say. "But my mother can be very convincing. And she made you promise."

"Some promises aren't worth keeping." Her voice drops low. "I guess it was stupid to think that I could just drop out and be gone from your life. We're all tangled up together, aren't we?"

"You're not *sentenced* to me," I say stiffly. "This thing with my mother will be resolved, you'll talk to Daneca, and then . . ." I make a vague gesture with my hand.

Then I'll be out of her life, more or less.

She laughs abruptly. "That's how it must have felt—me following you everywhere, begging for attention, obsessing over you—like you were sentenced to me. I even screwed up that on-again, off-again thing you had with Audrey, didn't I?"

"I think I screwed that one up all on my own."

Lila frowns. I can tell she doesn't believe me. "So *why*, Cassel? Why tell me that you loved me, then have Daneca work me so I couldn't feel anything for you, then tell me you love me all over again? Why come here and kiss me up against a wall? Do you just like messing with my head?"

"I— No!" I start to say more, to give her some explanation, but she keeps on going.

"You used to be my best friend in the world, and then, suddenly, you're the reason I'm a caged animal and you're acting like you don't even care. I know they took your memories, but I didn't know it then. I hated you. I wanted you dead. Then you were the one who freed me from my prison, and before I could come to terms with any of that, I was forced to be desperately in love with you. And now, when I see you, I feel everything, all those things, all at once. I can't afford to feel like that. Maybe you were right. Maybe I would be better off if I couldn't feel anything at all."

I don't know what to say. "I'm sorry," is all I manage.

"No, don't be. I don't mean it," Lila whispers. "I wish I wished that, but I don't. I'm just kind of a mess right now."

"You're not," I say.

She laughs. "Don't con me."

I want to reach for her, but her crossed arms keep me from it. I walk toward the stairs instead. At the top I look back at her. "No matter what happens, no matter what else I feel, no matter what else you believe, I hope you believe that I'll always be your friend."

One side of her mouth lifts. "I want to."

As I descend, I see Zacharov standing near the mantel talking to a boy. I recognize his braids, pulled back from his head like horns, and the flash of gold teeth. He looks up at me with dark unfathomable eyes and raises a perfectly manicured eyebrow.

I freeze.

Today he's dressed differently from the hoodie and jeans I saw him in when I chased him through the streets of

Queens. He's got on a purple motorcycle jacket over jeans, and has tapered gold plugs in his ears. He's wearing eyeliner.

Gage. That's the name he gave me.

Zacharov must see the look that passes between us. "Do you two know each other?"

"No," I say quickly.

I expect Gage to contradict me, but he doesn't. "No, I don't think it was him." He circles me, lifting a gloved hand to my chin, tilting my face toward him. He's a little shorter than I am. I pull back, jerking free of his grip.

He laughs. "Hard to believe I'd forget a face like that."

"Tell Cassel that story you told me," Zacharov says. "Cassel, take a seat."

I hesitate, glancing toward the elevator. If I ran, I think I could make it, but who knows how long it would take for the doors to open. And even if I got to the ground floor, I'd probably never get out of the building.

"*Sit down,*" Zacharov says. "I asked Gage to come over because the more I thought about your brother working for the Feds, the more I was sure that if it was true, you'd try to cover it up. Especially since I threatened his life. I take that back. But after Philip turned out to be a rat, I think we both understand that we have a lot to lose if your other brother started squealing."

I suck in a breath and sink onto one of the sofas. Flames flicker in the fireplace, filling the massive room with eerie shifting shadows. I can feel my palms start to sweat.

Lila looks over the edge of the railing. "Dad? What's

going on?" Her words echo through the big room, bouncing off the wooden ceiling and stone floors.

"Gage stopped by," Zacharov says. "I understand he ran into some complications the other day."

Gage looks up at her and grins. I wonder how long they've known each other. "I did that job like you wanted. It was quick. He was in the first place I looked."

Lila's face is shadowed. I can't read her expression.

"Charlie West didn't give you any trouble?" Zacharov asks.

Lila starts down the stairs.

Gage sucks his teeth, making a dismissive sound. "I didn't give him a chance for trouble."

Lila walks onto the black and white marble. Her bare feet make almost no sound as she pads across the floor. "Should Cassel be hearing this?"

It strikes me that once upon a time I thought of her as part of the class of people with magic. I knew that there were regular people and there were workers, and workers were better than regular people. That's what everyone in Carney believed, or it's at least what they told me. When I was a kid, Lila's cousin, my own brother's best friend, didn't even want me to be around her, because he thought I wasn't a worker.

But even among workers there are different roles. Lila is inheriting Zacharov's position, where you order murders but don't actually have to carry them out. She doesn't hold the gun, she just calls the shots.

"Let Gage tell his story," Zacharov says. "We trust Cassel, don't we?"

She turns her head toward me. The fire highlights the curve of her jawline, the point of her chin. "Of course we do."

Zacharov once asked me whether I would mind taking orders from his daughter. At the time, I said I wouldn't. Now I wonder what it would really be like. I wonder if I would resent it.

Gage clears his throat. "After I tap him, some psycho do-gooder decides to chase me through the streets and nearly breaks my arm." He laughs. "Guy picks up a plank and knocks my gun right out of my hand. If I was a couple of seconds faster, he would have got himself shot."

I concentrate on not reacting. I try to keep a vaguely interested expression on my face.

"You described him looking a lot like Cassel, didn't you?" Zacharov asks.

Gage nods, his gaze on me. He's laughing with his eyes. "Sure. Black hair, tan skin, tall. Cute. Stole my gun."

Zacharov crosses to where Lila is standing and puts his gloved hands on her shoulders. "Could it have been his brother? They look pretty alike."

"Barron is no do-gooder," I say.

Gage shakes his head. "Without a picture I'm not sure, but I don't think so."

Zacharov nods. "Tell him the rest."

"I have to climb a fence to get away," Gage says. "Three blocks later I get grabbed by guys in black suits. They hustle me into a car, and I think I'm done for, but they tell me that if I tell them what happened, they aren't going to investigate the hit."

"And did you tell them?" Zacharov asks, although I can tell he's already heard the story and knows the answer.

Lila pulls away from her father to perch on the edge of the couch.

"Well, at first I tell them no, I'm no snitch, but it turns out that they don't really care about who ordered me to do the job or even what I did. All they want to know about is the psycho do-gooder. They let me go, just for telling them about some guy I talked to for a couple of seconds. I said he took my gun."

I feel an odd sense of dizziness. It's almost like falling.

"They wanted to know if we knew each other. They wanted to know if he identified himself as a federal agent. I said no to both. Then, when they turned me loose, I came to Mr. Z, because I thought maybe he'd know what was going on."

"That sounds nothing like my brother," I say, giving them the steadiest look I can manage.

"A man can't be too careful," says Zacharov.

"Sorry I couldn't be more help," Gage says. "If you need anything else, let me know."

"I've got to get going," I say, standing up. "That is, if we're done here?"

Zacharov nods.

I start toward the elevator. My shoes tap a sharp rhythm on the stone tiles. I hear sudden footsteps following mine.

"Wait up," Gage says. "I'll ride down with you."

I look back to see Zacharov and Lila, across the room, watching us. Lila raises a hand in a half wave.

I get into the elevator and close my eyes as the doors shut.

"You going to kill me?" I ask in the silence that follows. "I hate waiting."

"What?" When I look at him, Gage is frowning. "You're the psycho who attacked me."

"You're a *death worker*. I figured you lied back there because you wanted some kind of personal revenge." I sigh. "Why did you do it? Why not tell Zacharov it was me?"

"No big thing. You let me go; I pay my debts." He's got sharp, almost delicate features, but he's muscled under his coat. I can tell from his shoulders. "All I want is my gun. It's a 1943 Beretta. A family heirloom. It belonged to my grandmother. She got it from some Italian boyfriend after the war—and she gave it to me when my parents kicked me out. I slept the whole bus ride to New York with that thing under what I was using for a pillow. It kept me safe."

I nod. "I'll get it to you."

"Just give the gun to Lila and she'll pass it along," he says. "Look, whatever those agents wanted you for, I figure it's none of my business. It didn't sound to me like you were one of them, and Lila wouldn't thank me for getting you in trouble with her father."

I frown. "What do you mean?"

"You're the youngest Sharpe brother, right? Cassel. Lila's been talking about you for *forever*." He grins appraisingly, raising both his eyebrows. "I didn't think you could possibly measure up, but it's the rare boy who can catch me."

I laugh. "How long have you known her?"

"I did a job for her father when I was thirteen. I guess

she was about twelve at the time. We got along like a house on fire. Used to go into her mother's room and try on her clothes and sing in front of her big double mirror. We were going to start a band called the Skies over Tokyo, but neither of us could play an instrument and neither of us could sing."

It takes me a moment to put it together that he means he killed someone for Zacharov when he was just a kid. I'm shocked before I remember that I was doing the same thing for Anton.

Then I realize that I'm going to do it again, for Yulikova this time. Yulikova, who knows I've already lied to her once.

My stomach sinks as the elevator doors open. I feel like the bottom is dropping out of the world.

CHAPTER ELEVEN

THE NEXT MORNING I am called into Dean Wharton's office right after morning announcements.

I stand in front of his burnished wooden desk and try not to think of the pictures I saw of him, with Mina's bare hand parting the collar of his starched white shirt. I guess everyone has a dark side, but I don't think I was prepared for that to extend to elderly Wallingford faculty.

Wharton's not a guy that I've thought a lot about. He's the dean of students, probably close to retirement age, with tufts of carefully combed-over silver hair on his head. He's never much liked me, but I've always given him plenty of reasons to feel that way, what with my bookmaking operation, the sleepwalking, and my mother being a convicted criminal.

I feel like I'm looking at him with fresh eyes now, though. I see today's newspaper, half-hidden in a stack of files, open to the crossword, a few shaky blue pen marks in the margins. I see the cap of a pill case under the desk and a single yellow pill. And perhaps most telling of all, I see the tremble in his left hand, which might be a nervous tic but shows how close he's playing to the edge. But then maybe I am reading him backward—seeing what I want to see. I know he's doing something bad, so I expect him to be nervous.

I just wish I knew exactly what he was doing.

"Mr. Sharpe, being in my office twice in as many weeks does not bode well for any student." His tone is as sternly exasperated as ever.

"I know that, sir," I say, as contritely as possible.

"You cut your morning classes yesterday, young man. Did you think there wouldn't be any consequences?"

"I'm sorry, sir. I wasn't feeling well, sir."

"Oh, is that right? And do you have a note from the nurse's office?"

"I just went back to sleep. Then, when I was feeling better, I went to class."

"So, no note?" he asks, raising both silver brows.

Okay, so say Mina's a luck worker. Say he has a gambling problem. Maybe he's coming up on retirement and realizes—for whatever reason—that he doesn't have enough socked away. I figure he's a guy who, at least mostly, stuck to the straight and narrow. But honest people get screwed too. The bottom falls out of the market. A family member gets sick and insurance doesn't even begin to cover it. For whatever reason, maybe he veers off the path.

My eye is drawn to the single yellow pill on the carpet.

Hiring a luck worker is pretty easy. He wouldn't need to target a student, although I guess maybe, being so straightlaced, he didn't know where else to go. But using luck work to win at gambling is a pretty uncertain proposition. Although sometimes people can get around it, most racetracks and casinos have ways to control for luck work.

Of course, he might need luck for some other reason. Maybe Northcutt is leaving and he wants to be the new headmaster.

"No note," I say.

"You're going to serve a Saturday detention with me, right here in this office, Cassel. I want you here at ten in the morning. No excuses. Or you're going to get that third demerit you're flirting with."

I nod. "Yes, sir."

The pill under his desk might be nothing. It could be aspirin or allergy medicine. But I don't have many clues, and I want this one. I should drop something, but all the little stuff that it would make sense to be holding is in my bag. I don't have keys or a pen or anything.

"You can go," he tells me, handing over a hall pass without really looking. I think about dropping that, but I imagine it fluttering to the floor far from where I need it to be. It's impossible to aim paper.

I stand and take a few steps toward the door before I have an idea. It's not a very good one. "Uh, excuse me, Dean Wharton?"

He glances up, brows knitted.

"Sorry. I dropped my pen." I walk over to his desk and bend down, grabbing for the pill. He pushes back his chair so he can look, but I'm up again fast.

"Thanks," I say, walking to the door before he can think too much about it.

As I start down the stairs, I look at the pill in my hand. There are ways to search online to find out about medication. You can put in details—like the color and shape and markings—and get a whole gallery of pills to compare against. I don't have to do any of that, because this pill has ARICEPT stamped into the top and 10 on the other side.

I know what it is; I've seen the commercials on late-night television.

It's medication to control Alzheimer's.

Daneca is waiting for me outside the cafeteria at lunch. She's sitting on one of the benches, her mass of brown and purple hair hanging in her face. She waves me over and shifts aside her hemp book bag so that I can sit down.

I lean back and stretch my legs. It's cold and a storm is rolling in, but there's still enough sun that it's nice to sit in a patch of it. "Hey," I say.

She shifts, and I can see what her hair hid before—red eyes and puffy skin around them. Streaks of salt on her cheeks marking the map of tears.

"Lila called you, huh?" I don't mean to sound callous, but the words come out that way.

She wipes her eyes and nods.

"I'm sorry." I reach into my pocket, hoping I have a tissue. "Honest."

She snorts and touches her cell phone where it's resting in the lap of her pleated Wallingford skirt. "I broke things off with Barron about ten minutes ago. I hope you're happy."

"I am," I say. "Barron is a sleaze bag. He's my brother—I should know. Sam is a much better guy."

"I know that. I always knew *that*." She sighs. "I'm sorry. I'm mad at you for being right, and I shouldn't be. It's not fair."

"Barron's a sociopath. They're very convincing. Especially if you're one of those girls who thinks she can fix a boy."

"Yeah," she says. "I guess I was. I *wanted* to believe him."

"You've got a real taste for darkness," I say.

She looks away from me, out at the overcast sky, the formless shifting mass of clouds. "I wanted to think there was a part of him that only I could see. A secret part that wanted kindness and love but didn't know how to ask for it. I'm stupid, right?"

"Oh, yeah. The taste for darkness, but not the stomach for it."

She flinches. "I guess I deserve that. I'm sorry I believed what he said about you, Cassel. I know you haven't told me everything, but—"

"No." I sigh. "I'm being a jerk. I'm mad because I wanted you to be the person that I could count on to always know right from wrong. That's not fair to expect from anyone. And I guess . . . I thought that we were better friends, despite all our sniping at each other."

"Friends screw up sometimes," she says.

"Maybe it'd help if I put my cards on the table. Tell me what Barron said, and I'll tell you the honest truth. This is a onetime offer."

"Because tomorrow you'll go back to lying?" she asks.

"I don't know what I'll do tomorrow. That's the problem." Which is one of the truest things I have ever said.

"You never told me what kind of worker you are, but Lila and Barron both did. I don't blame you for not telling me. That's a pretty big secret. And you really just found out last spring?"

"Yeah," I say. "I didn't think that I was a worker at all. When I was a kid, I used to pretend I was a transformation worker. I imagined that I could do anything, if I was one. That turns out to be almost true."

She nods, considering. "Barron said you told the federal agents . . . what you are, in exchange for immunity for all past crimes."

"I did," I say.

"Immunity for murdering Philip, for instance."

"*That's* what Barron thinks?" I shake my head and laugh without actually being amused. "That I killed Philip?"

She nods, braced. I'm not sure whether she's braced for me to tell her what an idiot she is or because she thinks

I'm about to confess to the whole thing. "He says the guy they're blaming for Philip's murder was dead way before Philip was."

"That part's true," I say.

She swallows.

"Oh, come on. I didn't kill Philip! I know who did, that's all. And, no, I'm not going to tell you, even if you ask, because it's got nothing to do with either one of us. Let's just say that the dead guy could afford to carry a murder charge in addition to his many other crimes. He was no angel."

"Barron said that you killed him—and that you kept him in the freezer of your house. That you were some kind of assassin. That you're the one who killed the people in those files you showed me after Philip's funeral."

"I'm no angel either," I say.

She hesitates. There's fear in her eyes, but at least she's not leaving. "Lila explained. She said that they—that Barron—messed with your memories. You didn't know what you'd done. You didn't know what you were or what happened to her."

Selfishly I wonder if Lila said anything else. I have no idea how I could persuade Daneca to tell me.

"He really kept her in a cage?" Daneca asks in a small voice.

"Yeah," I say. "Memory work—it erases part of who you are. If we're who we remember ourselves to be, then what's it like to have huge chunks of your identity missing? How you met the girl sitting next to you. What you had for dinner the night before. A family vacation. The law book you studied all last week. Barron's replaced all that with whatever he makes up in the moment. I have no idea if he really remembered who Lila was or even that he had a cat in the first place."

She nods slowly and pushes back a mass of curls. "I told him that it was contemptible, what he did. I told him that I would never forgive him for lying to me. And I told him he was an ass."

"That sounds like quite a lecture," I say, laughing. "I hope he was properly chastened."

"Don't make fun of me." She stands up, grabbing her bag. "He really sounded sad, Cassel."

I bite back everything I want to say to her. How he's an excellent liar. How he's the prince of liars. How Lucifer Morningstar himself could learn a thing or two from the conviction with which Barron lies.

"Lunch is almost over," I say instead. "Let's grab a sandwich while we can."

Afternoon classes slide by in a flurry of diligent note-taking and quizzes. A cup I made in ceramics comes out of the kiln in one piece, and I spend the better part of forty minutes painting it a muddy red, with the words RISE AND WHINE across it in big black letters.

Dr. Stewart is in his office when I swing by before track. He frowns at the sight of me.

"You're not in any of my classes this semester, Mr. Sharpe." His tone makes it clear that he considers that to be better for both of us. He adjusts his thick black-framed glasses. "Surely you aren't here trying to beg me to change a past grade? I maintain that anyone who misses as much school as you have shouldn't even be—"

"Mina Lange asked me to come by and drop something off for her," I say, pulling a paper bag out of my backpack.

It's not that I believe that Dr. Stewart has anything to do with blackmail or Wharton or Mina. It's that I want to be as sure as possible.

He crosses his arms. I can tell he's annoyed that I interrupted him before he could tell me once again how students suspended for almost falling off a roof should have to go to summer school, at the very least. "Mina Lange is not in any of my classes either, Mr. Sharpe."

"So this isn't for you?"

"Well, what is it?" he asks. "I can't imagine what she would be handing in to me."

"You want me to look?" I try to seem as unaware as possible. Just the stupid messenger.

He throws up both gloved hands in obvious disgust. "Yes, please do, and stop wasting my time."

I make a show of opening up the bag. "Looks like a research paper and a book. Oh, and it's for Mr. *Knight*. Sorry, Dr. Stewart. I really thought she said your name."

"Yes, well, I'm sure she's glad she trusted you to courier it over."

"She's not feeling well. That's why she couldn't bring it herself."

He sighs as though wondering why he is constantly

being punished by the presence of inferior intellects. "Good-bye, Mr. Sharpe."

He might not be a nice guy, but Stewart's never black-mailed anyone in his life.

I love running. I love the way that, even in a marathon, I only have to worry about my feet hitting the pavement and my muscles burning. No guilt and no fear. It's just me hurtling forward, as fast as I can, with no one to stop me. I love the cold wind against my back and the sweat heating my face.

Some days my mind is blank when I run. Other days I can't stop thinking, turning everything over and over again in my head.

Today I come to a couple of different conclusions.

One: No one is blackmailing Mina Lange.

Two: Mina Lange is a physical worker, fixing Wharton's Alzheimer's.

Three: Since Alzheimer's can never be cured, she can never stop working him, which means she just gets sicker and sicker, while he stays the same.

Four: Despite all her lies, Mina is probably actually in trouble.

Sam looks up from his bed when I walk into our dorm room. I've got a wrapped towel around my waist and am fresh from the shower.

He's got a bunch of brochures scattered beside him, colleges his parents want him to consider. None of them have a department that teaches visual effects. None of them will let him make his own rubber masks. All of them are Ivy League. Brown. Yale. Dartmouth. Harvard.

"Hey," he says. "Look, I was talking to Mina over lunch yesterday. She said she was sorry. She basically admitted what you said. That she wanted us to blackmail Wharton for her."

"Yeah?" I start rooting around for sweatpants, and put them on when I finally locate them under a pile of other clothes at the bottom of my closet. "Did she say why she needed the money?"

"Said she wanted to leave town. I didn't really understand it, but it seems like someone's brokering the deal between Wharton and her. That person won't let her leave, so she's got to run. Do you think it's her parents?"

"No," I say, thinking of Gage and myself and Lila and of what Mrs. Wasserman said when I was sitting in her kitchen. *Lots of kids are kicked out onto the streets, taken in by crime families and then sold off to the rich.* "Probably not her parents."

"Don't you think we can help her?" he asks.

"There's too much that's fishy about this situation, Sam. If she needs the money, then she should blackmail Wharton for it herself."

"But she can't. She's afraid of him."

I sigh. "Sam—"

"You nearly yanked her wig off in public. Don't you think you should make it up to her? Besides, I told her that the investigative firm of Sharpe & Yu was still on the case."

He grins, and I'm glad to see him distracted. I wonder again if he likes Mina. I really, really hope not.

"I think she's sick, Sam," I say. "I think that she's curing Wharton and it's making her sick."

"Even more reason to do something. Tell him he's got to give her the money. Explain the situation. You know, make it clear she's not alone. Wharton's the one who got her into this. We've got pictures."

"She's a player," I say. "She could still be playing us."

"Come on, Cassel. She's a lady in trouble."

"She *is* trouble." I scratch my neck, where I cut myself shaving. "Look, I have a Saturday detention with Wharton. He'll be alone in his office. Maybe we can talk to him then."

"What if she can't wait until the weekend?"

"We'll burn that bridge when we come to it." I open my laptop. "What's with the brochures?"

"Oh," he says. "I've got college applications to write. How about you?"

"I've got to plan an assassination," I say, logging into the school's wireless and bringing up the search engine. "I know. Weird, right?"

"Cassel Sharpe: boy assassin." He shakes his head. "You should have your own comic book."

I grin. "Only if you'll be my runty spandex-wearing sidekick."

"Runty? I'm taller than you are!" He sits up, and the springs of the bed groan, echoing his point.

I grin at him. "Not in my comic, you're not."

* * *

Killing someone is a lot like conning someone. You need to know a lot of the same things.

Maybe the Feds have to keep me in the dark, but I have to follow my own instincts. If something goes wrong with their plan, I'll need to improvise. And to do that I need to study my victim.

Patton's a public figure. Learning about him isn't hard— every detail of his life has been analyzed by the press, all his faults enumerated by his opponents. I look at photos until I know every detail of his face, until I can spot the lines of pancake makeup at the edges of his neck when he's camera-ready, until I see how he combs the few white hairs he's got and how he dresses to match the tone of his speeches. I look at pictures of him in his home, at rallies, kissing babies. I pore over news reports and gossip columns and restaurant guides to see who he meets with (many, many people), his favorite food (spaghetti Bolognese), what he orders at the diner he frequents (eggs over easy, buttered white toast, turkey sausage), and even how he takes his coffee (cream and sugar).

I study his security, too. He always has two bodyguards who follow him everywhere. They aren't always the same two guys, but they all have broken noses and smirking smiles. There are a few articles about Patton using funds to hire ex-cons to round out his security staff, men he personally pardoned. He never goes anywhere without them.

I watch several YouTube videos of him ranting about conspiracy theories, workers, and big government. I listen to the faint traces of his accent, the way he enunciates, and the way he pauses just before he says something he thinks is really important. I watch the way he gestures, reaching out to the audience like he's hoping to wrap them in his arms.

I call my mother and get a few more particulars while pretending to be interested in how she edged herself into his life. I find out where he buys his suits (Bergdorf; they have his measurements so he can just call and have a suit tailored and overnighted to a speaking engagement). What languages he speaks (French and Spanish). The medicine he takes for his heart (Capoten and a single baby aspirin). The way he walks, heel to toe, so that the backs of his shoes always wear down first.

I watch and look and listen and read until I feel like Governor Patton is standing over my shoulder and whispering into my ear. It's not a good feeling.

CHAPTER TWELVE

FRIDAY AFTERNOON, AS I'm coming back from classes, my phone buzzes in the pocket of my uniform pants. I take it out, but the number is blocked.

"Hello?" I say into the mouthpiece.

"We're coming to get you tomorrow night," says Yulikova. "Clear your schedule. We want to be moving by six p.m."

Something's wrong. Really, really wrong. "You said everything was happening *next* Wednesday, not this Saturday."

"I'm sorry, Cassel," she says. "Plans change. We have to be flexible right now."

I lower my voice. "Look, that thing with the death worker and me tailing him—I'm sorry I didn't tell you about the gun. I know you know. I just panicked. I still have it. I didn't do anything with it. I could bring it to you."

I shouldn't bring it to her. I promised it to Gage.

I should bring it to her. I should have given it to her in the first place.

She doesn't speak for a long moment. "That wasn't your smartest move."

"I know," I say.

"Why don't you turn the gun in tomorrow night and we'll just call the whole thing a misunderstanding."

"Right." My feeling of disquiet grows, although I can't say why. There's just something not right about her tone. Something that makes me feel like she's already distanced herself from this situation.

I'm surprised she's letting me off so easy about the gun. Nothing about this sits right.

"I was reading about Patton," I say, to keep her talking.

"We can talk about this when we pick you up." She says it kindly, but I can hear the dismissal in her voice.

"He has private security with him at all times. Tough guys. I was just wondering how we were getting around that."

"I promise you, Cassel, we've got good people handling this. Your part is significant but small. We're going to take care of you."

"Humor me," I say, putting some of the anger I feel into my voice.

She sighs. "I'm sorry. Of course you're concerned. We understand the risk you're taking, and we appreciate it."

I wait.

"We have one of them on the payroll. He's going to stall the other guard for long enough that you can take care of things. And he's going to watch your back."

"Okay," I say. "I'll meet you at Wallingford. Call me when you get here."

"Try not to worry," Yulikova says. "Good-bye, Cassel."

My heart's racing and my stomach is in knots as I close my phone. There is nothing worse than the creeping formless sense of dread—until that moment when it becomes clear what you should have been dreading all along. When you know it's not just all in your head. When you see the danger.

The Feds don't need me to bring in Patton. They don't need me at all. If they've really got one of his bodyguards on their payroll, they could disappear him anytime they wanted.

I sit down on the library steps and call Barron.

I can hear traffic in the background when he picks up. "You want something?" He sounds annoyed.

"Oh, come on," I say. I'm not exactly pleased with him, either. "You can't really be pissed off—just because you thought that I couldn't convince her you were lying when you were *actually lying*."

"So you called to gloat?" he asks.

"Yulikova moved up the date for the thing, and she has

an inside man already. Someone positioned to do this job a lot better than me. Does that sound fishy to you?"

"Maybe," he says.

"And that death worker I chased down. Her people picked him up after to see if I lied about anything."

"Did you?"

"Yeah. I took something from him and I . . . I kind of let him go. She knew that and never said anything."

"That does seem weird. I guess you're screwed. Sucks to be you, Cassel. Looks like the Feds aren't your friends after all."

He hangs up, leaving me with silence.

I don't know why I expected anything else.

I sit on the steps for a long time. I don't go to track practice. I don't go to dinner. I just turn the phone over and over in my hands until I realize I have to get up and go somewhere eventually.

I dial Lila's number. I don't expect her to answer, but she does.

"I need your help," I say.

Her voice is low. "We've helped each other enough, don't you think?"

"I just need to talk through some things with someone."

"It shouldn't be me."

I take a deep breath. "I'm working with the Feds, Lila. And I'm in trouble. A lot of trouble."

"I'm getting my coat," she says. "Tell me where you are."

We arrange to meet at the old house. I get my keys and head to my car.

*　*　*

I'm sitting in the kitchen in the dark when she opens the door. I'm thinking about the smell of my father's cigarillos and what it was like when we were very young and nothing really mattered.

She flips on the lights, and I blink up at her.

"Are you okay?" She comes over to the table and puts one gloved hand on my shoulder. She's wearing tight black jeans and a scarred leather jacket. Her blond hair is as bright as a gold coin.

I shake my head.

Then I tell her everything—about Patton, about Maura, about wanting to be good and falling short, about following her that day when I chased down Gage without knowing why, about Yulikova and the gun. Everything.

By the time I'm done, she's sitting backward in one of the chairs, resting her chin on her arms. She has shouldered off the jacket.

"How mad at me are you?" I ask. "I mean, exactly how mad—like on a scale of one to ten, where one is kicking my ass and ten is a shark tank?"

She shakes her head at my scale. "You mean because you watched me put out a contract on someone and then watched Gage kill him? That you're cooperating with the law, maybe even working for them? That you never told me any of this? I'm not *happy*. Does it bother you—what you saw me do?"

"I don't know," I say.

"You think I have ice in my blood?" She asks it lightly, but I know the answer matters.

I wonder what it would be like, being raised to be a crime lord. "You are what you always were going to be."

"Remember when we were kids?" she says. There's a slight smile on her mouth, but the way she's looking at me doesn't quite match up. "You thought I would be the one making deals and enemies, backstabbing and lying. You said you were going to get out, travel the world. Not get swept up in the life."

"Shows what I know."

"That's one long game you've been playing, Cassel. One long, dangerous game."

"I didn't mean for everything to get so crazy. It was one thing after another. I had to fix things. *Someone* had to fix things for Maura, and I was the only one who knew, so there just wasn't anyone else. And I had to keep Barron from going to the Brennans. And I had to stop myself—" I do stop myself there, because I can't say the rest. I can't explain how I needed to stop myself from being with her. I can't explain how I nearly didn't manage it.

"Okay, well, quit." She makes a wild gesture with her hands, as though stating something so obvious that it shouldn't have to be said. "You did what you thought you had to do, but you still have a way out, so take it. Get away from the Feds. And if they don't want to let you off easy, then go into hiding. I'll help. I'll talk to my dad. I'll try to see if he can take some of the pressure off the thing with your mother, at least until you can solve this. Don't let them play you."

"I can't quit." I look away, at the peeling wallpaper above the sink. "I can't. It's too important."

"What makes you so eager to throw away your life on whatever cause comes along?"

"That's not true. That's not what I was doing—"

"*None of it is your fault.* What is it that you feel so damn guilty about that makes you act like *you* don't matter?" Her voice rises, and she rises with it, coming around the table to push against my shoulder. "What makes you think that you've got to solve everyone's problems, even mine?"

"Nothing." I shake my head, turning away from her.

"Is it Jimmy Greco and Antanas Kalvis and the rest? Because I knew them, and they were really bad men. The world's a better place without them in it."

"Stop trying to make me feel better," I say. "You know I don't deserve it."

"*Why don't you deserve it?*" she yells, her voice sounding like the words are being ripped out of her gut. Her hand is on my upper arm; she's trying to get me to look at her.

I won't.

"You," I say, standing. "Because of *you.*"

For a moment neither of us speaks.

"What I did—," I start, but I can't make that sentence go anywhere good. I start over. "I can't forgive myself—I don't *want* to forgive myself."

I sink down to the linoleum tiles and say what I have never said before. "I killed you. I remember killing you. I killed you." The words, over and over and over, rolling out of me. My voice is catching. My voice is breaking.

"I'm alive," Lila says, sliding to her knees so that I have to look at her, have to see her. "I'm right here."

I take a deep, shuddering breath.

"We're alive," she says. "We made it."

I feel like I'm about to shake apart. "I've screwed up everything, haven't I?"

Now it's her turn not to meet my gaze. "I wouldn't let Daneca work me," she says, slowly and carefully, putting every word together as if having one out of place will make everything fall apart. "But I didn't stop loving you. Because I always have, Cassel. Since we were kids. You have to remember: I paraded around in my underwear at my own birthday party."

That startles a laugh out of me. I touch the ear she pierced that night, the hole closed now, and try to imagine a world where I wasn't the only one who felt something. "I didn't think that meant—"

"Because you're an idiot," she says. "An *idiot*. When the curse wore off, I couldn't let you see that I still had feelings. I thought I was the only one who'd ever had them."

She has woven her fingers together and is clenching them tight, the leather taut over her knuckles. "You were kind. You're always kind. I figured you pretended to love me until you couldn't pretend anymore. And I couldn't let you think you still had to. So I'd jab myself in the hand with scissors, or pens—with anything sharp in reach—whenever I thought of you. Until when I saw you I could concentrate on that moment of pain. . . . And despite that, I still wanted to see you."

"I haven't been pretending, Lila," I say. "I never was. I know how it looked, me asking Daneca to make you not feel anything. But I kissed you before I knew what my mother had done, remember? I kissed you because I had wanted to for a very long time."

She shakes her head. "I don't know."

"That night, in your dorm room— Lila, *you were cursed*," I say. "And I almost didn't care. It was awful, because you acted like you really felt all these things, and I had to constantly remind myself that it wasn't real—and sometimes I was overwhelmed by the awfulness. I wanted to blot out how bad I felt. I knew it wasn't right and I still didn't stop myself."

"Okay," she says. "It's okay."

"But I would never want—"

"I know that, Cassel," she says. "You could have explained."

"And said what? That I did want to be with you?" I demand. "That I just couldn't trust myself enough? That I—"

She leans forward and brings her mouth to mine. I have never been so profoundly glad to be forced to shut up.

I close my eyes, because even seeing her is too much right now.

I feel like a man who's been living on bread and water and is now overwhelmed by a feast. I feel like someone chained in the dark for so long that the light has become terrifying. My heart wants to beat its way out of my chest.

Her lips are soft, sliding against mine. I am lost in kiss after drowning kiss. My gloved fingers trace the skin of her cheek and the hollow of her throat until she moans into my mouth. My blood is boiling, pooling low in my gut.

She unknots my tie with quick fingers. When I pull back

to look at her, she grins and tugs the cloth free from my collar in a single motion.

I raise both eyebrows.

With a laugh Lila pushes herself off the floor and reaches out her gloved hand to haul me to my feet. "Come on," she says.

I stand up. Somehow my shirt has gotten untucked. Then we're kissing again, staggering up the stairs. She stops to kick off her boots, bracing herself against me and the wall. I shrug out of my jacket.

"Lila," I say, but that's all I can manage as she begins to unbutton my white dress shirt.

It falls to the floor of the hallway.

We lurch into my bedroom, where I imagined her a thousand times, where I thought I had lost her forever. Those memories seem blurred now, hard to count as important beside the vividness of her cool leather-clad hand brushing over the hard planes of my stomach and the corded muscles of my arms. I suck in my breath.

She steps away to bite the end of her glove, pulling it off her hand that way. When she drops it, my gaze tracks its fall.

I catch her bare hand and kiss her fingers, which makes her stare at me, wide-eyed. I bite down on the heel of her hand, and she groans.

When I pull off my own gloves, my hands are shaking. The taste of her skin is on my tongue. I feel feverish.

If I have to die tomorrow when the Feds come for me, then this is the last request of my heart. This. The sight of lashes brushing her cheek as her eyes flutter closed. The pulse in her throat. Her breath in my mouth. This.

I have been with girls I cared about and girls I didn't. But I have never been with a girl I loved more than anything else in all the world. I am staggered by it, overwhelmed with the desire to get everything right.

My mouth dips low to trace the scar on her neck. Her nails dig into my back.

Lila breaks away to yank her shirt over her head, and throws it onto the floor. Her bra is blue and covered in lace butterflies. Then she comes back into my arms again, her lips opening, her skin impossibly soft and warm. When I run my bare hands over it, her body arches against me.

She starts to unbuckle my belt with fumbling fingers.

"Are you sure?" I say, pulling away.

In answer she steps back, reaches around, and unclasps her bra, tosses it in the direction of her shirt.

"*Lila,*" I say helplessly.

"Cassel, if you make me talk about this, I will kill you. I will literally kill you. I will strangle you with your own tie."

"I think that tie's downstairs," I say, fighting to remember why in the world I wanted to talk as she comes forward to kiss me again. Her fingers thread through my hair, tugging my mouth down to hers.

A few short steps and we sprawl backward onto the bed, knocking pillows to the floor.

"Do you have anything?" She's speaking against my shoulder, her bare chest against mine. I shudder with each word and force myself to focus.

It still takes me a moment to realize what she means. "In my wallet."

"You know I haven't done this a lot." There's a tremble in her voice, as if she's suddenly nervous. "Like, once before."

"We can stop," I say, stilling my hands. I take an unsteady breath. "We should—"

"If you stop," she says, "I will also kill you."

So I don't.

CHAPTER THIRTEEN

I WAKE UP WITH SUN-
light streaming in through the dirty windowpane. I reach
out my bare fingers, expecting them to brush warm skin,
but they close on a tangle of bedsheets instead. She's
already gone.

I didn't stop loving you, Cassel.

My skin is alive with the memory of her hands. I stretch,
bones all down my spine popping languorously. My head
feels clearer than I can ever remember.

I grin up at the cracked plaster of my ceiling and picture her creeping out of the room while I'm sleeping, hesitating to kiss me good-bye, not leaving a note or any other
normal-person thing. Of course not. She wouldn't want to

seem sentimental. She'd dress in the bathroom and splash water on her face. Carry her boots and run across the lawn in stocking feet. Sneak back into that fancy penthouse apartment before her criminal mastermind of a father could realize that his daughter spent the night at a boy's house. At my house.

I can't stop grinning.

She loves me.

I guess I can die happy.

I head into my parents' room and dig around, find a beat-up leather duffel bag into which I stuff a couple of T-shirts and my least favorite pair of jeans. No point in packing anything I like, since I have no idea where Yulikova is taking me or whether I'll ever see any of this stuff again. I stash my wallet and identification under my mattress.

My objectives are simple—figure out if Yulikova's going to double-cross me, do the job so Patton can't hurt my mother, and come home.

After that I guess we'll see. I didn't sign any papers, so I'm not an official member of the LMD. I can still get out if I want. At least I think I can. This is the federal government we're talking about, not some crime family with blood oaths and slashed throats.

Of course, even if I'm not an agent, I'll still have to deal with everyone else who's looking for someone with my particular talents.

I imagine for a moment being on my own after high school, living in New York, waiting tables and meeting Lila for espressos late at night. No one would need to know what I am. No one would need to know what I can do. We'd go back to my tiny apartment, drink cheap wine, watch black-and-white movies, and complain about our jobs. She could tell me about gang wars and all the new things that fell off trucks, and I could—

I shake my head at myself.

Before I get too involved in fantasies about an impossible future, I better show up for detention. Otherwise I'm not even going to graduate from Wallingford.

Glancing at the clock on my phone, I see that I have about a half hour. That gives me time to go back to my dorm, pick up Sam, and figure out what we're going to say on Mina's behalf. Barely enough time, but still.

I'm walking out to my car, duffel bag over one shoulder, when my phone rings.

It's Barron. I flip it open. "Hey," I say, surprised.

His voice is carefully neutral. "I did some digging."

I stop, leaning against the front of my Benz, keys still in my hand. "What kind of digging?"

"After what you said about the Patton job, I persuaded one of my friends to let me use her ID card and rifle through some files. You were right. It's a setup, Cassel. You're supposed to get pinched."

I feel cold all over. "They want to arrest me?"

He laughs. "The really hysterical part is that they're getting you to turn Patton into a toaster or whatever to cover their own screwup. They could go in, guns blazing, if they weren't the reason Patton's so unstable in the first place. This is their mess."

I look out at the lawn. The leaves have almost all fallen, leaving behind barren trunks of trees, their black branches reaching for the sky like the long fingers of endless hands. "What do you mean?"

"Patton's aides called the Feds once they realized Mom had worked him. If she hadn't been so sloppy, you wouldn't be in the lurch."

"She didn't have time to do a better job," I say. "Anyway, politics isn't exactly her thing."

"Yeah, well, my point is that I read the reports and they tell a fabulous tale of fuckupitude. After the aides call the Feds, they bring in a state-sanctioned emotion worker to "fix" Patton. But, see, the government is full of hyperbathygammic idiots who have been taught not to use their powers unless they really have to, so the emotion worker agent they sent in didn't exactly have a deft touch.

"He works Patton to hate and fear Mom, thinking that strong emotions are the only way to negate what she did. But instead Patton gets completely unhinged. Like, no hinge in sight. All violent outbursts and crying jags."

I shudder, thinking about what it would be like to be made to feel two contradictory things at the same time. It's worse when I realize that's what I was asking Daneca to do to Lila. Love and indifference warring together. I don't know what might have happened. Thinking about it is like looking down into the deep ravine you somehow missed stepping into in the dark.

Barron goes on. "Now, the backbone of getting proposition two passed is having workers who are also upstanding citizens endorse it. Prominent members of the community coming forward and submitting themselves for voluntary testing makes the rest of us look bad, but it makes the program look good. Safe. Humane. Problem was, Patton decided that now was the time to be crazy. He got everyone with a positive HBG test fired.

"Then he started asking federal employees to get tested. He managed to put a lot of pressure on them. He wanted the federal units with hyperbathygammic agents disbanded."

"Like the LMD," I say, thinking of Yulikova and Agent Jones. "But he's got no authority over them."

"I told you this was a comedy of errors," says Barron. "Sure, he can't do a thing to make that happen. But he can threaten to embarrass them by telling the press how they worked him against his will. So, in all their wisdom, what do you think Team Good does?"

"I have no idea," I say. Another call makes my phone buzz, but I ignore it.

"They send *another* worker so that he can fix the first botched job on Patton's brain."

I laugh. "I bet that went real well."

"Oh, yeah. Patton *killed him*. That's how well it went."

"Killed him?" Since this is Barron, it's possible he's embellishing the truth, if not outright lying. But the story he's telling adds up in a way that the story Yulikova told me doesn't. Barron's story is messy, full of coincidences and mistakes. As a liar myself, I know that the hallmark of lies is that they are simple and straightforward. They are reality the way we wish it was.

"Yeah," Barron says. "The agent's name was Eric Lawrence. Married. Two kids. Patton strangled him when he figured out that Agent Lawrence was trying to work him. Amazing, right? So they have a homicidal governor on their hands and the higher-ups tell them they need to clean up the mess before there's a huge scandal."

I take a deep breath and let it out slowly. "So after I transform Patton, what? They arrest me, I guess. I have a motive, because of Mom. Then I'd get put in jail. What's the use of that if they want me to work for them? I can't work for them in prison—or at least whatever I could do would be pretty limited. Transform other inmates. Make cigarettes into bars of gold."

"That's the brilliant part, Cassel," Barron says. "You're not getting it. Not only would they have a scapegoat, but once you become a criminal who is no longer protected by an immunity deal, you'd have a lot fewer civil liberties. They could control you. Totally. They'd have exactly the weapon they want."

"Did you find out where this is going to take place?" I ask, and open the car door. I feel numb.

"Monday speech out near Carney, on the site of a former internment camp. They'll pitch tents by the memorial. The Feds have got the security sewn up, but who cares, Cassel? You're obviously not going."

I have to go, though. If I don't go, Patton gets away with it and Mom doesn't. I might not think my mother is a good person, but she's better than him.

And I don't want the Feds to get away with it either.

"Yes, I am," I say. "Look, thanks for doing this. I know you didn't have to, and it really helps, knowing exactly what I'm getting into."

"Fine, go. But just show up and screw it up. What are they going to do, give you a good scolding? Mistakes happen. You screw up everything anyway."

"They'll just set me up again," I say.

"Now you'll be looking for it."

"I was *already* looking for it," I say. "I still didn't see what was going on. Besides, someone *should* stop Patton. I have a chance."

"Sure," he says. "Someone should. Someone who's not being *set up*. Someone who's *not you*."

"If I don't go along with this, the Feds are threatening to go after Mom. And that's the best we can hope for—because Patton will kill her. He's already tried once."

"He did what? What do you mean?"

"She got shot and she didn't want us to know. I would have told you, but the last time we talked, you hung up on me abruptly."

He ignores the rest of what I've said. "Is she okay?"

"I think so." I belt myself into the driver's seat. Then, sighing, I turn on the ignition. "But look, we have to do something."

"*We* aren't doing anything. I've done all I'm going to do, looking through those files. I'm looking out for myself. Try it sometime."

"I have a plan." The vent floods the car with cold air. I crank up the heat and rest my head against the wheel. "Or, well, not a *plan* exactly, but the beginnings of one. All I need you to do is stall Patton. Find out where he's going to be on Monday and keep him there so he's late to his speech. For Mom's sake. You don't even have to visit me in jail."

"Do something for me, then," he says, after a pause.

The chances of me pulling this off and getting away with it are so bad that I'm actually not that concerned about whatever evil scheme my brother will try to involve me in next.

It's kind of freeing.

"Fine. I'll owe you a favor. But after. I don't have time right now." I look at the clock on the dashboard. "In fact, I don't have any time. I have to get to Wallingford. I'm already late."

"Call me after your school thing," Barron says, and hangs up. I toss the phone onto the passenger seat and pull out of the driveway, wishing that the only plan I've got didn't depend on putting my faith in two of the people I trust least in the world—Barron and myself.

It's ten after ten when I pull into the Wallingford parking lot. There's no time to go to my room, so I grab for my phone as I'm crossing the lawn, figuring I'll call Sam and get him to bring the photos of Wharton. But as I start thinking about the pictures, I have that awful feeling that there's something I've overlooked. In the diner I said that I thought Mina must have intended for us to *see* the pictures, but she didn't just let us see them. She made sure that we had copies.

Cold dread works its way up my spine. She wanted

someone else to blackmail Wharton. Someone to claim they took photographs and they want money. But we don't have to really do it. We just have to *seem like we're doing it.*

Stupid, stupid. I am so stupid. As I am thinking that, the phone rings in my hands. It's Daneca.

"Hey," I say. "I can't really talk. I'm so late to detention, and if I get another demerit—"

She sobs, liquid and awful, and I bite off whatever I was planning to say next. "What happened?" I ask.

"Sam found out," she says, choking out the words. "That I was seeing your brother. We were in the library together this morning, studying. Everything was just normal. I don't know, I wanted to see him—and figure out if there was still anything between us, if I felt—"

"Uh-huh," I say, crossing the green, hoping that Wharton is still in his office. Hoping that I'm wrong about Mina's plans. Hoping that Sam is somewhere burning those photos, even though I'm pretty sure he's too busy being devastated, and even if he wasn't, he has no reason to think we're in trouble. "Maybe he'll get over it."

It's pointless to think about the fact that neither of them getting over things is what broke them up in the first place. He's going to be furious with her and doubly furious at me for not telling him about Barron. Which, predictably, I deserve.

"No, *listen.* I left the room for a minute, and when I got back— Well, Barron must have texted me. And Sam read it—and read the other ones too. He started screaming at me. It was really ugly."

I pause. "Are you okay?"

"I don't know." She sounds like she's trying to fight back more tears. "Sam's always been so gentle—sweet. I just never thought he could be that angry. He scared me."

"Did he hurt you?" I am pushing open the doors of the administrative building, trying to think.

"No—nothing like that."

I head for the steps. No one's in any of the offices. My footfalls are loud in the hallways. The only sounds I can hear are the ones I'm making. Everyone's home for the weekend. My heart starts to race. Wharton's gone, and Mina has probably already told him that Sam and I are blackmailing him. He'll toss our room, and if he does, he's going to *find the pictures* . . . and, oh God, the gun. He's going to find the gun.

"Sam threw his books across the room, and then he got really cold, really distant," Daneca is saying, although it's hard to focus on her words. "It was like something just switched off inside him. He told me that he was supposed to meet you and he didn't care if you didn't show. He said that he'd take care of things, for once. He said he had a—"

"Wait. What?" I ask, snapping to attention. *"What did he say he had?"*

A shot rings through the stairwell from the floor above me, echoing through the empty building.

I don't know what I expect to see when I burst into Wharton's office, but it's not Sam and the Headmaster grappling on the antique oriental rug. Wharton is crawling across the floor, toward a gun that seems to have skittered away from both of them, while Sam's trying to pin him down.

I go for the gun.

Wharton looks at me dazedly when I swing the barrel in his direction. His white hair is sticking up all over the place. Sam slumps bonelessly, with a moan. That's when I realize that the red stain surrounding Sam isn't part of the pattern of the carpet.

"You shot him," I say to Wharton, in disbelief.

"I'm sorry," Sam gets out between locked teeth. "I screwed up, Cassel. I really screwed up."

"You're going to be fine, Sam," I say.

"Mr. Sharpe, you are *twenty minutes late* for your detention," Dean Wharton says from the floor. I wonder if he's in shock. "If you don't want to be in more trouble than you already are, I suggest that you give me that gun."

"You're kidding me, right? I'm calling an ambulance." I cross to Wharton's burled wood desk. The photos of Mina are there, on top of the other papers.

"No!" Wharton says, pushing himself to his feet. He lunges for the phone cord and pulls it out of the wall with a violent jerk. He's breathing hard, looking at me with glazed eyes. "I forbid it. I absolutely forbid it. You don't understand. If the board finds out about this— Well, you just don't understand the difficult position that will put me in."

"I can imagine," I say, pulling out my cell with one hand. I can't quite work out how to dial and keep the gun trained on him at the same time.

Wharton staggers toward me. "You can't call anyone. Put that phone down."

"You shot him!" I yell. "Stay back or I'll shoot you!"

Sam moans again. "It really hurts, Cassel. It really hurts."

"This can't be happening," Wharton says. Then he looks at me again. "I'll tell them that you did it! I'll say that you both came here to rob me and you two got into an argument, and then you shot him."

"I should know who shot me," says Sam. He winces as he puts pressure on his leg. "I'm not going to say it was Cassel."

"That won't matter. Whose gun is that, Mr. Sharpe?" Wharton says. "Yours, I'll wager."

"Nope," I say. "I stole it."

He gives me a sudden blank look. He is used to good boys in tidy uniforms who only play at being trouble-makers before doing what they're told, and the sudden suspicion that I'm nothing like that seems to disorient him. Then his mouth twists. "That's right. Everyone knows your background. Who are they going to believe—you or me? I am a respectable member of the community."

"Not when they see the pictures of you and Mina Lange. That's pretty sketchy stuff. You're not going to look good. You're sick, right? Brain starting to go. First you forget small things, then bigger ones, and the doctor gives you the news that it only gets worse from here. Time to resign from Wallingford. Not much you can do legally—but *illegally*— Well, now we're talking. You can buy children, little girls like Mina, and she can't cure you because it's degenerative, but she can give you the next best thing.

"So you don't get any worse and she starts getting sick. At first you rationalize it. She's young. She'll get better. So she misses some classes? That's nothing for her to be upset about. After all, you've gotten her a scholarship to Wallingford, a prestigious prep school, so that you could have her on hand whenever you needed her.

"When she told you we had the pictures, you probably were willing to pay. But then when Sam comes in here, he says something that makes you realize the money is for Mina. And that puts you in a tough spot. If she goes, you get sick again. And if anyone sees the pictures, you lose your job. You can't have that, so you go for the gun."

Wharton looks toward the desk as though he wants to make a mad grab for the photos. Sweat is beading on his forehead. "She was in on it?"

"She *orchestrated* this. She took those pictures. The only thing she didn't expect was someone to actually try to help her. Sam did, because he's a good guy. See what it got him. Now I am making this call and you're not going to stop me."

"No," Wharton says.

I glance at Sam. He looks very pale. I wonder how much blood he's already lost.

"Look, I don't care about Mina or the money or you losing your mind," I say. "Take the photos. Keep your secret. Tell the ambulance people whatever you want when they come. But he's really hurt."

"Okay. Let me think. You must know someone," the dean says in a low, pleading voice. "The kind of doctor who won't report a shooting."

"You want me to call a *mob doctor*?"

The eagerness on his face is exaggerated, manic. "Please. Please. I'll give you anything. You can both graduate with a 4.0. You can blow off all your classes. If you make this go away, as far as I'm concerned, you can do whatever you want."

"And no more demerits," says Sam weakly.

"Are you sure?" I ask Sam. "This doctor's not going to have all the stuff that a real hospital—"

"Cassel, *think about it*," Sam says. "If an ambulance comes, we're all in trouble. We all lose."

I hesitate.

"My parents," he says. "I can't—they can't find out." I look at him for a long moment and then remember that Sam was the one who brought a gun into the dean's office and threatened him with it. Normal parents probably frown on that kind of thing. I bet judges don't like it either. This isn't a zero-sum game for the dean, Sam, and me. There's plenty of trouble to go around.

With a sigh I flick the safety on, shove the gun into my pocket, and make the call.

The doctor with the crooked teeth arrives a half hour later. His answering service never asked for a name from me and never gave one for him, either. In my head I am still calling him Dr. Doctor.

He's wearing a similar outfit to the one I saw him in the last time—sweatshirt and jeans. I notice he's got on sneakers with no socks and there's a scab of some kind on his ankle. His cheeks look more sunken than I remember, and he's smoking a cigarette. I wonder how old he is. He looks like he's maybe in his thirties with a full head of unruly curls and the scruff of a man who can't be bothered to shave every day. The only thing that indicates he's a doctor at all is the black bag he's carrying.

I've elevated Sam's leg and padded it with my T-shirt. I am sitting on the floor, applying pressure. Dean Wharton wrapped Sam in my coat to stop him from shivering. We've done our awful best, and I am feeling like the worst friend in the world for not insisting we take him immediately to the hospital, whatever the consequences.

"You got a bathroom?" the doctor says, glancing around.

"Through those doors and down the hall," says Dean Wharton, frowning at the doctor's cigarette disapprovingly, still apparently trying to stay in control of the situation. "This is a no smoking building."

The doctor gives him an incredulous look. "I've got to scrub in. Clear off the desk while I'm gone. We're going to have to get the patient up there. And get some more lights. I need to see what I'm doing."

"Do you trust that man?" Dean Wharton asks me as he lifts stacks of papers and shoves them into his filing cabinet haphazardly.

"No," I say.

Sam makes a choked sound.

"I didn't mean it that way," I say. "You're going to be fine. I'm just pissed off. Mostly at myself—no, scratch that, mostly at Wharton."

The dean drags a floor lamp to his now clear desk and flips it on. He manages to position a couple of other lights on the bookshelves, tilting their flexible necks to point bulbs at the table, like faces all turned toward a performance.

"Help me get him up," I say.

"Don't lift me," Sam says, slurring the words slightly. "I can hop."

This seems like a terrible idea, but I am not arguing with a wounded man. Putting his arm around my neck, I haul him up. He makes a low sound in the back of his throat, like he's biting back a scream. His gloved fingers dig into my bare arm. His face contorts with pain and concentration, his eyes closing tightly.

"Don't put any weight on it," I remind him.

"Screw you," he says through gritted teeth, which I take to mean that he's doing okay.

We move across the room, his body half-slumped on mine. My T-shirt slides off his leg, and blood seeps sluggishly from the hole as he climbs up onto the desk.

"Lie down," I say, reaching for the shirt. I have no idea how clean anything is, but I try to mop up the worst of the blood and reapply pressure.

Wharton stands back, watching us with what looks like a mixture of distaste and terror. Possibly he's mourning the ruination of his desk.

The doctor comes back into the room, his cigarette gone. He's got on what looks like a plastic poncho and gloves. His hair has been pulled back with a bandana.

Sam moans. "What—what is he going to do?"

"I am going to need an assistant for this," the doctor says, looking at me. "You okay with blood?"

I nod.

"You're lucky. My last job wasn't too far from here. Sometimes I can get pretty backed up."

"I bet," I say. I wish he would stop talking.

He nods. "So . . . I need the money. It's going to be five hundred up front, like my answering service said. Maybe more, depending on how things go, but I'll need to have that now."

I look over at Wharton, and he fusses around with one of the drawers in his desk. He must be used to paying other people in cash, because he unlocks some section inside a lower part and counts out a wad of bills.

"Here's a grand," the dean says, his hand shaking as he holds out the cash. "Let's make sure things go well. No complications, do you understand?"

"Money soaks up germs. It's dirty stuff. You take it, kid," Dr. Doctor says. "Put it in my bag. And take out the bottle of iodine. Then, before you do anything else, I want you to go wash your hands."

"My gloves?" I ask.

"Your *hands*," he tells me. "You're going to wear a pair of plastic gloves. Those are ruined."

In the bathroom I scrub furiously. My hands. My arms. He's right about my leather gloves. They are so sodden with blood that my hands were stained red underneath. I splash water onto my face for good measure. Bare to the waist, I feel like I should try to cover up somehow, but there's nothing to cover up with. My T-shirt is a disgusting mess. My coat is still on the floor of the other room.

I return to the dean's office to find the doctor has his bag open. It's a mess of bottles, cloths, and clamps. He's taking out sharp, scary metal instruments and laying them out on a side table he's dragged over. I put on a pair of thin plastic gloves and get out the iodine.

"Cassel," Sam says faintly. "I'm going to be okay, right?"

I nod. "I swear."

"Tell Daneca I'm sorry." Tears are welling up in the corners of his eyes. "Tell my mom—"

"Shut up, Sam," I say fiercely. "I said you were going to be fine."

The doctor grunts. "Get me one of the swabs, soak it in the iodine, and wipe off the bullet hole."

"But—," I say, not sure how to proceed.

"Cut off his pants." He sounds exasperated, and I can see that he's taking out a brown vial and a large needle.

I try to keep my hand steady as I take out the scissors from the kit and slice open Sam's cargo pants. The material rips wide, to his thigh, and I see the actual wound, just above his knee, small and welling with blood.

When my fingers touch his skin, brushing it with brown medicine, he twitches.

"It's fine, Sam," I say.

Across the room Wharton sits down heavily in a chair and puts his head in his hands.

The doctor walks over to Sam, holding up a syringe. He

taps it, like he's trying to get the air out. "This is morphine. It should help with the pain."

Sam's eyes go wide.

"You're going to need to be sedated for this," the doctor says.

Sam swallows and, visibly steeling himself, nods.

The doctor sticks the needle into a vein in Sam's arm. He makes a sound that's half moan and half swallow.

"Do you think she really likes him?" Sam asks. I know who he means. Barron. And I don't know the answer, not really.

The doctor looks at me, then back at Sam.

"No," I say. "But maybe you shouldn't worry about that now."

"Distracting—" Sam's eyes roll back in his head, his body going limp. I wonder if he's dreaming.

"Now you've got to hold him down," the doctor says. "While I dig out the bullet."

"What?" I say. "Hold him how?"

"Just keep him from moving too much. I need his leg to stay steady." He looks across the room at Dean Wharton. "You. Come over here. I need someone to hand me forceps and a scalpel when I ask for them. Put on these gloves."

The dean stands and crosses the room dazedly.

I move to the other side of the desk and put one hand on Sam's stomach and the other on his thigh, leaning my weight against them. He turns his head and groans, although he remains out of it. I let go immediately, stepping back.

"*Hold him.* He won't remember this," the doctor says, which doesn't comfort me even a little. There's lots of stuff

I don't remember, but that doesn't mean it didn't happen.

I put my hands back in place.

Dr. Doctor leans in and presses around the wound. Sam moans again and tries to shift position. I don't let him. "He's going to stay semiconscious. It's safer that way, but it means you've really got to stop him from moving. I think the bullet's still in there."

"What does that mean?" Dean Wharton asks.

"It means we've got to get it out," says the doctor. "Give me the scalpel."

I turn my head at the moment the point of the knife sinks into Sam's skin. He writhes under my hands, squirming blindly, forcing me to put my full weight against him. When I look again, the doctor has cut a deep slice. Blood is welling up out of it.

"Retractor," the doctor says, and Wharton hands it over.

"Hemostat," the doctor says.

"What's that?" Wharton asks.

"The silver thing with the curved tip. Take your time. It's not my emergency."

I shoot the doctor my filthiest glare, but he isn't looking. He's pushing an instrument into Sam's leg. Sam moans, low, and jerks slightly.

"Shhh," I say. "It's almost over. It's almost over."

Blood sprays out of the leg suddenly, hitting my chest and face. I stagger back, shocked, and Sam nearly jerks off the table.

"Hold him, you idiot!" the doctor shouts.

I grab Sam's leg, slamming myself down onto it. The

blood pulses along with his heart, rising and falling. There is so much blood. It's in my eyelashes, smeared over my stomach. It's all I can smell and all I can taste.

"When I say hold him, I'm not joking! Do you want your friend to die? *Hold him.* I have to find the vessel I nicked. Where is that hemostat?"

Sam's skin looks clammy. His mouth looks bluish. I turn my head away from the surgery, my fingers digging into his muscles, holding him down as firmly as I can. I grit my teeth and try not to watch the doctor tie off the artery or watch him root out the bullet or start stitching up the wound with black string. I hang on and watch the rise and fall of Sam's chest, reminding myself that so long as he's breathing and moaning and shifting, so long as he's in pain, he's alive.

After, I slump on the floor and listen to the doctor give Dean Wharton instructions. My whole body hurts, my muscles sore from fighting Sam's.

"He's going to have to take antibiotics for two weeks. Otherwise he's at serious risk for infection," the doctor says, taping the gauze in place and wadding up his bloody poncho. "I can't write him a prescription, but this is enough for the first week. My answering service will contact whichever one of you called about getting more antibiotics."

"I understand," the dean is saying.

I understand too. Dr. Doctor can't write a prescription because he's had his license revoked. That's why he's acting as a concierge doctor for Zacharov and for us.

"And if you need a cleanup service for in here, I know some very discreet people."

"That would be very much appreciated."

They sound like two civilized men, discussing civilized things. They are two men of the world, a man of medicine and a man of letters. They probably don't think of themselves as criminals, no matter what they've done.

As the doctor walks out the door, I take my phone out of my pocket.

"What are you doing?" Dean Wharton demands.

"I'm calling his girlfriend," I say. "Someone's going to have to stay with him tonight. It can't be me, and he wouldn't want it to be you."

"You have somewhere more important to be?"

I look up at Wharton. I'm exhausted. And I hate that I can't stay, when this is all my fault in the first place. My gun. My dumb joke with Mina, the finger in my pocket that made it seem like bringing a gun was the right move. *It can't be me.*

"I absolutely forbid you to call another student, Mr. Sharpe. This situation is chaotic enough as it is."

"Bite me," I say, my gloved fingers leaving sticky brown marks behind when I tap the keys.

"Did you find him?" Daneca says, instead of "hello." "Is he all right?"

The connection isn't very good. She seems scratchy and far away.

"Can you come to Dean Wharton's office?" I ask. "Because if you can, I think you should come now. Sam could really use you. It would really help if you came right now. But don't panic. Please just don't panic and please come now."

She says she will in a bewildered tone that makes me think I must sound very strange. Everything feels empty.

"You should go," I tell Dean Wharton.

By the time Daneca arrives, he's already gone.

She looks around the room, at the blood-soaked carpet, and the lamps on the bookshelves, at Sam lying on Wharton's massive desk, unconscious. She looks at his leg and at me, sitting on the floor without a shirt on.

"What happened?" she asks, walking over to Sam and touching his cheek lightly with her glove.

"Sam got—he got shot." She looks scared. "A doctor came and fixed him. When he wakes up, I know he'll want you there."

"Are you okay?" she asks. I have no idea what she means. Of course I'm all right. I'm not the one lying on a desk.

I stagger to my feet and pick up my coat.

I nod. "But I have to go, okay? Dean Wharton knows about this." I gesture vaguely, mostly toward his carpet. "I don't think we can move Sam until he wakes up. It's what—about noon now?"

"It's two in the afternoon."

"Right," I say, glancing toward the windows. Dean Wharton drew the blinds, I remember. Not that I would be able to tell the time by the amount of sunlight. "I can't—"

"Cassel, what's going on? What happened? Does where you're going have to do with Sam?"

I start to laugh, and Daneca looks even more worried. "Actually," I say, "it's totally unrelated."

"Cassel—," she says.

I look at Sam, lying on the desk, and think of my mother in Zacharov's house, nursing her own gunshot wound. I close my eyes.

At the end of a criminal's life, it's always the small mistake, the coincidence, the lark. The time we got too comfortable, the time we slipped up, the time someone aimed a little to the left.

I've heard Grandad's war stories a thousand times. How they finally got Mo. How Mandy almost got away. How Charlie fell.

Birth to grave, we know it'll be us one day. Our tragedy is that we forget it might be someone else first.

CHAPTER FOURTEEN

I AM SHAKING WHEN I
walk out of Wharton's office, trembling with such force that
I'm afraid I'll stumble as I make my way down the stairs.
Sam's blood is staining my skin, soaking through my pants.
I force myself to walk across the quad, hunched over so that
my coat hides the worst of it. Most students are gone on the
weekends, and I am careful not to take any of the paths, and
to veer away if I see anyone. I stick to the shadows of trees
and darkness.

Once I make it to my dorm hall, I head straight for the
communal bathroom. I see myself in the mirror. There is a
smear of red across my jaw, and for a moment, as I try to
wipe it and only smear it wider, I feel like I am looking at a

stranger, someone older with hollow cheekbones and lips curled in a mean scowl. A madman fresh from a murder. A sicko. A killer.

I don't think he likes me much.

Despite the scowl on his face, his eyes are black and wet, as if he's about to start crying.

I don't like him much either.

My stomach lurches. I have barely enough time to make it into one of the stalls before I start to retch. I haven't eaten anything, so it's mostly sour bile. On my knees on the cold tile, choking, the wave of anger and self-loathing that sweeps over me is so towering and vast, I cannot imagine how there will be anything of me that's not carried away with it. I feel like there's nothing left. No fight in me.

I have to focus. Yulikova will be here in a couple more hours, and there's stuff I need to take care of, things that need to happen before I can go with her. Arrangements. Last details and instructions.

But I'm frozen with horror at everything that has happened and everything in front of me. All I can think of is blood and the guttural, raw sound of Sam moaning in agony.

I better get used to it.

I take a shower so hot that my skin feels sunburned when I get out. Then I dress for my date with the Feds—crappy T-shirt that got chewed up by one of the dryers, my leather jacket, and a new pair of gloves. The bloody clothes I run under the tap until they're less foul, then wrap them in a plastic bag. Even though it's a risk, I keep my phone, turning off the ringer and tucking it into my sock.

I shove a bunch of other things into my jacket—things I plan on transferring to the duffel I left in the car. Index cards and a pen. Styling gel and a comb. A few pictures of Patton that I print out with Sam's crappy ink-jet and then fold. A beaten-up detective paperback.

Then I walk to the corner store, dumping the plastic bag of bloody clothes into the garbage can outside. Mr. Gazonas smiles at me, like he always does.

"How's your little blond girlfriend?" he asks. "I hope you're taking her someplace nice on a Saturday night."

I grin and get myself a cup of coffee and a ham and cheese sandwich. "I'll tell her it was your idea."

"You do that," he says as he gives me my change.

I hope I get to take Lila out some Saturday night. I hope I get a chance to see her again.

Trying not to think about that, I go back to the parking lot and force down my food, sitting in my parked car. Everything tastes like ashes and dust.

I listen to the radio, flipping through channels. I can't concentrate on what I'm listening to, and after a while I can't keep my eyes open either.

I wake to a tapping on the window. Agent Yulikova is standing beside the car, with Agent Jones and another woman I don't recognize beside them.

For a moment I wonder what would happen if I refused to get out. I wonder if they'd have to leave eventually. I wonder if they'd get one of those jaws of life and pop the top off my Benz like it was a tin can.

I open the car door and grab for my duffel.

"Have a nice rest?" Yulikova asks me. She's smiling sweetly, like she's the den mother of my Boy Scout troop instead of the lady who wants to send me up the river. She looks healthier than she did in the hospital. The cold has made her cheeks rosy.

I force a yawn. "You know me," I say. "Lazy as a bedbug."

"Well, come on. You can sleep in our car if you want."

"Sure," I say, locking the Benz.

Their car is predictably black—one of those huge Lincolns that you can spread out in. I do. And while I'm getting comfortable, I lean down to put my key into my bag and surreptitiously lift out my cell. Then, leaning back, I palm my phone into the pocket of the car door.

The last place anyone is going to look for contraband is in their own vehicle.

"So, you have something to turn in?" Yulikova says. She's in the back with me. The other two agents are up front.

The gun. Oh, no, the gun. I left it in Wharton's office, under the desk.

She must see it in my face, the flash of horror.

"Did something happen?" she asks.

"I forgot it," I say. "I'm so sorry. If you let me out, I'll go get it."

"No," she says, exchanging a look with the other female agent. "No, that's all right, Cassel. We can get it when we bring you back. Why don't you tell us where it is."

"If you want me to get it—," I say.

She sighs. "No, that's fine."

"Are you going to tell me what's going on now?" I ask. "I'd really feel a lot more comfortable if I was in on the plan."

"We're going to tell you everything. Honest," she says. "It's very simple and straightforward. Governor Patton is going to give a press conference, and when it's over, we'd like you to use your gift to change him into—well, into a living thing that can be contained."

"Do you have a preference?"

She gives me a look, like she's trying to gauge whether or not I'm testing her. "We'll leave that up to you and whatever is going to be easier, but it's imperative that he doesn't get away."

"If it's all the same, I'll turn him into a big dog, I guess. Maybe one of those fancy hounds with the pointy faces— salukis, right? No, *borzois*. Some guy my mother used to know had those." His name was Clyde Austin. He hit me in the head with a bottle. I leave those details out. "Or maybe a big beetle. You could keep him in a jar. Just remember to put in the airholes."

There is a sudden flicker of fear in Yulikova's eyes.

"You're upset. I can see that," she says, reaching out and touching her gloved hand to mine. It's an intimate, motherly gesture, and I have to force myself not to flinch. "You're always sarcastic when you're nervous. And I know this isn't easy for you, not knowing details, but you have to trust us. Being a government operative means always feeling a little bit in the dark. It's how we keep one another safe."

Her face is so kind. What she's saying is reasonable. She seems truthful, too—she's got no obvious tells that would indicate otherwise. The thought nags me that Barron could have made up everything he told me about the content of the files. That would be profoundly awful and totally plausible.

I nod. "I guess I'm used to relying on myself."

"When you first came to us, I knew you were going to be a special case. Not just because of your power but because of where you were from. We seldom have significant contact with boys like you and Barron. The average LMD recruit is a kid who's been living on the street, either because they left home or because they were forced out. Sometimes a family contacts us with a child who they think might be a worker, and we bring them into the program."

"Nonworker families, you mean?" I ask. "Are they scared—the parents?"

"Usually," she says. "Sometimes the situation is so potentially violent that we have to remove the child. We have two schools in the country for worker children under the age of ten."

"Military schools," I say.

She nods. "There are worse things, Cassel. Do you know how many worker children are murdered by their own parents? The statistics are one thing, but I've seen the bones, heard the terrified excuses. We'll get a report of a kid who might be a worker, but when we get to the town, the girl will be staying with "relatives," whom no one has any reliable contact information for and who don't have a phone. The boy will have transferred to another school, only there's no record of where that might be. They're usually dead."

I don't have anything to say to that.

"And then there are the neglected children, the abused children, the kids who are raised to think their only choice is becoming a criminal." She sighs. "You're wondering why I'm telling you all this."

"Because that's what you're used to—not kids like me, with mothers like mine and brothers like mine."

She nods, glancing toward the front of the car, where Agent Jones is sitting. "I'm not used to being thought of as the enemy."

I blink at her. "That's not what I think."

She laughs. "Oh, I so wish for a lie detector test right now, Cassel! And the worst part is that I realize it's at least partially our fault. We only know about you because you had no other choice but to turn yourself in—and now with your mother being in a lot of potential trouble, well, let's just say that our loyalties are not in alignment. We've had to make deals, you and I, which isn't how I want us to proceed. I want us to be on the same page, especially going into such an important mission."

She lets me chew that over for a while. Eventually the car stops in front of a Marriott. It's one of the innocuous massive box hotels that are perfect for keeping track of someone in, because every floor leads to one central lobby. Pick a high enough floor, and all you need is someone posted outside the room and maybe another person by the stairs and another by the elevator. That's three people—exactly the number in the car with me right now.

"Okay," I say as Agent Jones kills the engine. "After all, I am entirely in your hands."

Yulikova smiles. "And we're in yours."

I grab my duffel, they take navy overnight bags and briefcases out of the trunk, and we head for the main entrance. I feel like I am going to a very dull sleepover.

"Wait here," Yulikova says, and leaves me standing in the lobby with the nameless female agent while Yalikova and Jones check us in.

I sit on the arm of a beige chair and stick out my free hand. "Cassel Sharpe."

She regards me with all the suspicion that Jones usually does. Her short ginger hair is pulled back into a low pony-tail, and her navy suit matches her overnight bag. Sensible beige pumps. Panty hose, for God's sake. Tiny gold hoops in her ears complete the effect of a person with no tells and no inner life. I can't even tell her age; it could be anywhere between late twenties and late thirties.

"Cassandra Brennan."

I blink several times, but when she reaches out her hand, I take it and we shake.

"I see why they gave you this job," I say finally. "Brennan family, huh? Yulikova said she hadn't worked with *many* people who come from worker families. She didn't say she'd worked with *none*."

"It's a common enough name," she says.

Then Yulikova comes back and we head to the elevators.

My room is part of a suite, attached to the rooms where

Yulikova, Jones, and Brennan will be sleeping. Of course, I'm not given my own key. My door, predictably, does not exit into the hallway but opens onto the main room, where there's a crappy couch, a television, and a mini fridge.

I dump my duffel in my bedroom and head back out into the central room. Agent Jones is watching me, as if I'm about to pull some kind of ninja move and escape through the air vent.

"You want something from the vending machine, you ask one of us to accompany you. Otherwise you won't be able to reenter the room—the doors lock automatically," he says, like I've never been in a hotel before. Jones is about as subtle as a two-by-four to the face.

"Hey," I say. "Where's that partner of yours? Hunt, wasn't it?"

"Promoted up the chain," he says tersely.

I grin. "Give him my felicitations."

Jones looks like he wants to slug me, which is only subtly different from his usual way of looking at me like I'm a slug.

"Are you hungry?" Yulikova asks me, interrupting our little conversation. "Did you have dinner?"

I think of the remains of the sandwich moldering in my car. The thought of eating still fills me with a vague queasiness, but I don't want them to notice.

"I didn't," I say. "But I am eager to hear some specifics about what happens next."

"Perfect," Yulikova says. "Why don't you wash up, and Agent Brennan can go out and get us some food. There has to be a Chinese place around here. Then we'll talk. Cassel, is there anything you don't like?"

"I like everything," I say, and walk into my room.

Jones follows. "Can I have a look at that bag?"

"Go right ahead." I sit down on the bed.

He smiles thinly. "It's just procedure."

My duffel seems to bore him after he feels around the lining and looks at my pictures and blank index cards. "Have to pat you down too," he says.

I stand up and think of my cell phone in the pocket of their car door. It's hard not to smile, but I remind myself that congratulating myself on my own cleverness is a good way to get caught.

He leaves, and I waste some time reading my paperback. It contains the unlikely reveal that the detective and the murderer he's been tracking are actually the same person. I am incredulous at how long it took him to figure that out. I got it a lot faster when it was me.

A little while later I hear the far door to the suite open and some conversation. Then someone knocks on my door.

By the time I emerge, Brennan is passing out paper plates. The smell of grease makes my mouth water. I thought I wasn't hungry, but I am suddenly ravenous.

"Did we get hot mustard?" I ask, and Jones passes a couple of packets in my direction.

As we eat, Yulikova puts a map on the table. It's of an open area, a park. "Like I said in the car, this is a very straightforward plan. Complications are to be avoided. We wouldn't allow you to be part of an operation we weren't very confident in, Cassel. We understand that you're inexperienced.

"Governor Patton is giving a press conference on the site of one of the former worker internment camps. He'd like to position proposition two as helping workers, but he'd also like to subtly remind everyone to be afraid."

She takes out a ballpoint pen from her jacket and marks an *X* on a clearing. "You'll be here the whole time, in one of the trailers. The only real danger is that you're going to be bored."

I smile and take another bite of my kung pao chicken. I get a hot pepper and try to ignore my burning tongue.

"They're going to build a stage there." She touches the page. "And a trailer for Patton to get dressed in will go here. Over this way are a few other trailers for his staff to work out of. We've managed to get one that we're assured can be kept secure."

"So I'm going to be by myself?"

She smiles. "We'll have people everywhere outside, posing as local police. We also have a few people in Patton's security detail. You'll be in good hands."

Which makes sense, sort of. But it also makes sense that if I'm alone in the room and I come out and attack Patton, I'll look like I was acting alone. The Feds will be off the hook.

"What about security cameras?" I ask.

Agent Brennan raises her eyebrows.

"Because it's outdoors, there aren't any," Yulikova says, "but what we need to worry about are press cameras." She makes a blue dot in front of where she marked the stage.

"The press pit is here, but there will be vans parked in the lot over there, where our vehicles will be too. If you stay in the trailer, you should be out of sight."

I nod.

Agent Jones serves himself another pile of sesame chicken and rice, squirting sauce over the whole thing.

"Governor Patton is going to make a brief speech, and then he's going to answer questions from reporters," Yulikova says. "You're going to slip into one of the trailers and stay there until Governor Patton takes the stage. We have a monitor set up so that you can watch the local news. They're broadcasting the event live."

"What's the speech supposed to be about?"

Yulikova coughs discreetly. "Senator Raeburn has attacked Patton in the press. This is supposed to be his chance to redirect the conversation—and to reach out to the rest of the country. If proposition two passes in New Jersey, other states will start drafting similar legislation."

"Okay, so I wait until Patton leaves the stage. Then what? Do I count to three and jump out at him?"

"We have a uniform for you. You'll have a clipboard and headset mic. You'll look like one of the crew backstage. And we have a specially formulated black ink that covers your hand. It looks like you're wearing a glove, but your fingers will remain bare."

"Clever." I am eager to see that stuff. My grandfather would be happy to know that the government really has been holding out on us in terms of secret cool toys. Too bad I can't tell him.

"While Patton is giving his speech, you will move to his dressing room and wait for him there. When he comes in, well, it's a pretty tight space. It shouldn't be too difficult to get your hands on him. We'll be able to communicate with you through the headset, so if you have any questions or want to know the position of the governor, we will be able to give you all the support you need."

I nod again. It's not a terrible plan. It's a lot less complicated than Philip's whole lurk-around-the-bathroom-all-night scheme for killing Zacharov. It's also eerily similar. I guess transformation work assassinations all have a certain pattern.

"So, okay. Governor Patton's a borzoi. Everyone's freaking out. Now what? What's my exit strategy? I have a minute or two—maybe less—before the blowback hits. His bodyguards are right outside."

She makes a circle on the paper where the trailer is. "Figure the confrontation happens here."

Agent Brennan leans forward to see the mark.

"The bodyguard who's in our employ—the man who's going to be on the left—will explain that Patton doesn't want to be disturbed. Patton will doubtless be in great distress, but—"

"Doubtless," I say.

No one ever laughs at this stuff.

"We believe his erratic behavior makes it likely that our agent will be able to explain away the scuffle and the sounds that follow. When you're ready, let us know through the headset and we'll get you both out of there."

"I won't be able to go right away," I say. Agent Jones starts to speak, and I hold up a gloved hand, shaking my head. "No, I mean I *can't*. The blowback makes it so that I will be shifting shape. You might be able to move me a short distance, but it's going to be complicated, and I won't be able to help."

They look at one another.

"I've seen him do it before," Jones says. "As much as I hate to say it, he's right. We're going to have to stall for time."

Yulikova and Agent Brennan are both eyeing me speculatively.

"It's that bad?" Agent Brennan asks. "I mean—"

I shrug. "I don't know. I'm not really looking. Sometimes I don't really have anything to look *with*, if you know what I'm saying."

She blanches. I think I may have successfully freaked out my first FBI agent.

Go me.

"All right," Yulikova says, "we'll change the plan. We'll wait out Cassel's blowback and *then* get him out. We'll have a car standing by."

I grin. "I'll need a leash."

Agent Jones gives me an evaluating look.

"For Patton. And a collar. Can we get a really embarrassing one?"

His nostrils flare.

"That's very practical thinking." Yulikova seems sincere and calm, but Jones's jumpiness is getting on my nerves. It might just be that he gets like this before missions, but it is driving me up the wall.

"And that's it," Yulikova says, reaching for another egg roll. "The whole thing. Any questions, Cassel? Any questions, anyone?"

"Where will you all be?" I touch the map, pushing it a little toward her.

"Back here," she says, her gloved finger tapping against the table, indicating a vague place distantly in front of the stage. "There's a van we can use as a command center where Patton won't be threatened by our presence. He's requested all his own security, so we can't be too obvious. But we will be there, Cassel. Very close by."

Very close by, but not anywhere I'll know about. Great.

"What if I need to find you?" I ask. "What if the monitor isn't working or the headset shorts out?"

"Let me give you some very good advice that was once given to me. Sometimes on missions things go wrong. When that happens, you have two choices: Keep going because the thing that went wrong wasn't important, or abort the mission. You've got to go with your gut. If the monitor goes out, just stay in the room and do nothing. If it doesn't feel right, do nothing."

That is good advice—and it's not the kind that seems useful to give someone that you want to get caught. I look at Yulikova, drinking her diet soda and chewing her food. I think of my brother. Am I really trying to decide which of them is more worthy of my trust?

"Okay," I say, and pick up the map. "Can I keep this? I want to make sure I know the layout."

"You act like you've done this before," Agent Brennan says.

"I come from a long line of grifters," I say. "I've pulled a con or two."

She snorts, shaking her head. Jones glowers at both of us. Yulikova cracks open her fortune cookie and holds up the fortune. Printed across the ribbon of paper in block letters are the words: "You will be invited to an exciting event."

I turn in shortly after that.

Looking at the hotel phone by my bed, I itch to call Daneca and find out how Sam's doing. Even knowing that it's probably bugged, I am tempted. But he should be resting, and I don't even know if he'll want to talk to me.

Any mention of him being shot would have the Feds making all the wrong guesses and asking too many questions. One more thing no one can afford.

I shouldn't call Lila, either, even though last night seems more dream than real. Just thinking of her as I sit on the scratchy hotel comforter, remembering the slide of her skin on mine, the way she laughed, the curve of her mouth—it feels risky. As though even the memory of her will give the Feds something they can use against me.

Now that she knows I'm working with the agency, I wonder what she'll do with that information. I wonder what she'll expect me to do.

I get into bed and try to sleep, my thoughts careening between Lila and Sam. I hear her laugh and see his blood, feel her bare hands and hear his scream. On and on until everyone's laughing and everyone's screaming all the way down into my dreams.

The next morning I stumble out into the main room.

Agent Jones is there, sitting on the couch and drinking a mug of room service coffee. He glowers in my direction in the manner of a man who has taken a shift that started many hours ago. I bet the three of them traded off all night, to make sure I didn't skip out.

I find another cup and pour myself some coffee. It's terrible.

"Hey," I say, thinking suddenly of my mother and a hotel nothing like this one. "Can you really cook meth in a hotel coffeepot?"

"Sure," he says, looking into his cup thoughtfully.

Guess Mom was right about one thing.

After I take a shower and get dressed, the rest of them are there, ordering breakfast. The whole day stretches in front of us with very little to do. Jones wants to watch a basketball game on the big plasma television, so I spend the afternoon playing cards with Yulikova and Brennan at the table. First we gamble for candy from the vending machine, then for spare change, then for choice of which film we rent.

I pick *The Thin Man*. I need a laugh.

CHAPTER FIFTEEN

MONDAY MORNING I wake up not remembering where I am. Then it all comes rushing back—the hotel, the Feds, the assassination.

Adrenaline hits my bloodstream with such force that I kick off the covers and stand, pace the room with no idea where I am going. Corralling myself into the bathroom, I avoid my own gaze in the mirror. I am nearly sick with nerves, doubled over by them.

I don't know whether to believe Barron or not. I don't know if I'm being set up. I don't know who the good guys are anymore.

I thought that the people I grew up around—mostly criminals—were different from regular people. Certainly different from cops, from federal agents with their shiny badges. I thought grifters and con men were just born bad. I thought there was some inner flaw in us. Something corrupt that meant that we'd never be like other people—that the best we could do is ape them.

But now I wonder—what if everyone is pretty much the same and it's just a thousand small choices that add up to the person you are? No good or evil, no black and white, no inner demons or angels whispering the right answers in our ears like it's some cosmic SAT test. Just us, hour by hour, minute by minute, day by day, making the best choices we can.

The thought is horrifying. If that's true, then there's no right choice. There's just choice.

I stand there in front of the mirror, trying to figure out what to do. I stand there for a long time.

When I get it together enough to go out into the main room, I find Yulikova and Jones already dressed. Brennan isn't with them.

I drink crappy gray room service coffee and eat some eggs.

"I've got your props," Yulikova says, disappearing into her room. She comes back with a paintbrush, a small tube of what looks like oil paint, a brown hoodie, a lanyard with an ID tag hanging from it, and a headset.

"Huh." I turn the ID tag over in my hands. The name George Parker is on it, underneath a blurred picture that could pass for me. It's a good piece of identification. The photo is forgettable and would be useless on a wanted poster or blasted across the Internet. "Nice."

"This is *our job*," she says wryly.

"Sorry." She's right. I have been thinking of them as amateurs, honest and upright government employees trying to pull off a scam they're unused to—but I keep forgetting, this is what they do. They con criminals, and maybe they're conning me.

"I'll need you to take off your gloves," she says. "This stuff takes a long time to dry, so if you need to do any last preparations, do them now."

"She means go take a piss," Agent Jones says.

I shoulder on the hoodie and zip it up, then go into the bedroom, where I fold the pictures of Patton up and shove them into the back pocket of my jeans. I put the comb in the other pocket, with the index cards. The pen and hair gel I stick into the front pocket of the hoodie, along with my car keys.

I walk back out to the table and take off my gloves, spreading my fingers out on the pressed wood of the table as I sit.

Yulikova glances at my face and then back at my hands. She picks up my right hand with her gloved fingers and draws it closer to her, turning it palm up.

Jones is watching us, readiness in every line of his body. If I grabbed for the bare skin of her throat, he'd be out of his chair and on us in seconds.

If I grabbed for her throat, he'd be too late. I bet he knows it too.

She uncaps the tube and squirts cold black gel onto the back of my hand. She doesn't look flustered at all, just calm and efficient. If she thinks of me as anything more danger-ous than just another worker kid she's training, she doesn't show it.

The bristles of the brush tickle—I'm not used to any-thing touching my hands so directly—but the paint cov-ers my skin thoroughly, drying to a dull leathery sheen. Yulikova is careful to ink everything, even the pads of my fingers, and I am careful not to move, no matter how much I want to laugh.

"Okay," she says, capping the tube. "As soon as that dries, we'll be ready to go. You can relax now."

I study her face. "You promise that the charges against my mother will be dropped after this, right?"

"It's the least we can do," she says. There is nothing in her expression that gives me any reason not to believe her, but her words aren't exactly a guarantee.

If she's lying, I know what I have to do. But if she's not, then I will have thrown away everything for nothing. It's an impossible choice. The only chance I have is to rattle her into revealing something. "What if I don't want to join the LMD? I mean, after this operation. What if I decide I'm not cut out for federal agenting?"

That makes her stop in the process of cleaning off the brush in a cup of water. "That would be very difficult for me. My superiors are interested in you. I'm sure you can imagine. A transformation worker is very rare. In fact . . ."

She brings out a stack of familiar papers. The con-tracts. "I was going to wait to do this later, when we had a few minutes alone, but I think now is the time. My bosses would feel a lot more comfortable if you would go ahead and sign."

"I thought we agreed to wait until I graduated."

"This operation has forced my hand."

I nod. "I see."

She leans back and pushes her gloved fingers through her mop of gray hair. She must not have gotten all the paint off her glove, because some of it smears like soot over her bangs. "I can understand if you have doubts. Go ahead and think about them, but remember why you first talked about joining us. We can keep you from becoming a prize to be fought over by rival crime families. We can protect you."

"Who's going to protect me from you, though?"

"From *us*? Your family are some of the worst—," Jones starts, but Yulikova stops his words with a wave of her hand.

"Cassel, this is a real step forward for you. I'm glad you're asking me this—I'm glad you're being honest."

I don't say anything. I am holding my breath, without really knowing why.

"Of course you feel this way. Listen, I know you're conflicted. And I know you want to do the right thing. So we'll keep talking and keep being honest. For my part, I am telling you honestly that if you walk away from the LMD now, my bosses won't be happy with your decision and they won't be happy with me."

I stand up, flexing my fingers, looking for cracks in the faux gloves. They move like a second skin.

"Is this about Lila Zacharov?" Yulikova asks. "The reason you're hesitating?"

"No!" I say, and then close my eyes for a long moment, counting my breaths. I didn't rattle Yulikova. She rattled me.

"We always knew you two had a close relationship." She has tilted her head and is studying my reaction. "She seems like a nice girl."

I snort.

"Okay, Cassel. She seems like a very ruthless girl whom you like very much. And she also seems like she wouldn't want you working for the government. But this decision is yours, and you should make it. You and your brother are a lot safer here. She'll come around if she really cares about you."

"I don't want to talk about her," I say.

Yulikova sighs. "All right. We don't have to, but you need to tell me whether you're going to sign."

There is something reassuring about the stack of paperwork. If they were just going to throw me in prison, they wouldn't need me to agree to anything. They'd have all the bargaining power once I was behind bars.

I pick up the lanyard and hang it around my neck. Then I grab the headset off the table. I'm not going to be able to figure anything out this way—we could talk forever and Yulikova would never slip up, never reveal anything by mistake.

"The Zacharovs are a crime family, Cassel. They'll use you up and spit you out if you let them. And her, too. She's going to have to do things for them that will change her."

"I said I didn't want to talk about it."

Agent Jones stands up and looks at his watch. "It's almost time to go."

I glance toward the bedroom. "Should I pack up my things?"

Jones shakes his head. "We'll come back here tonight before we drop you off at Wallingford. Let you sleep off the blowback and wash off that paint."

"Thanks," I say.

He grunts.

All of that sounds possible. I might really be coming back to this room, Yulikova and Jones might really be federal agents trying to figure out how to deal with a kid whose criminal past and valuable skill make him both an asset and a liability. They might really not be planning on double-crossing me.

Time to go all in, one way or the other. Time to decide what I want to believe.

You pays your money and you takes your chance.

"Okay," I say, sighing. "Give me the papers." I take the pen out of my hoodie and sign on the dotted line, with a flourish.

Agent Jones's eyebrows go up. I grin.

Yulikova walks over and looks at the papers, tracing one gloved finger just under my name. She puts the other hand on my shoulder. "We're going to take good care of you, Cassel. I promise. Welcome to the Licensed Minority Division."

Promises, promises. I put away the pen. Now that the final decision is made, I feel better. Lighter. The burden of it is removed from my shoulders.

We head out. In the elevator I ask, "Where's Agent Brennan?"

"Already there," is Jones's response. "Setting things up for us."

We cut through the lobby and go out to the car. When I get in, I make sure to take the same side that I rode in on the way here. As I fumble with my seat belt, I grab my cell phone out of the side well in the door and shove it into my pocket.

"You want to stop for a breakfast burrito or something?" Jones asks.

Last meal. I think it but don't say the words aloud.

"Not hungry," I say.

I look out the tinted window at the highway and silently go over all the things I am going to have to do once we arrive at the press conference. I list them all to myself and then list them all again.

"It's going to be over soon," Yulikova says.

That's true. It's all going to be over soon.

They let me out into the memorial park by myself. I squint against the bright sunlight. I keep my head down as I pass through security, holding up my ID tag. A woman with a clipboard tells me that there's a courtesy table with coffee and doughnuts for volunteers.

There is a big stage with a blue curtain covering the back. Someone is rigging a mic up to an impressive-looking lectern with the seal of New Jersey on it. A roped VIP section is being set up to one side of the press pit. A couple other people are stacking speakers under the stage, which is fronted by a shorter curtain, this one white.

Behind that is the area where the trailers are, arranged in a semicircle around several tables where volunteers are arranging stacks of leaflets, signage, and T-shirts. Then there's the far table, with the food on it. Several people are milling around there, talking and laughing. Most of them are wearing headsets like mine.

Yulikova did her homework. The layout is just like the map. I pass by the trailer that Governor Patton's supposed to use and head into the one that Yulikova marked for me. Inside is a gray sofa, a dressing table, a small bathroom, and a television mounted high on the wall, tuned to a news channel that's promising a live broadcast of the speech. Two newscasters are talking to each other. Below them is the closed-captioning of what they're saying, slightly off and on a delay, based on my limited lipreading skills.

I check my phone. It's seven forty in the morning. Patton's speech isn't until nine. I have a little time.

I depress the flimsy lock on the doorknob, then rattle the door a little. It seems to hold, but I don't trust the lock. I could probably pick it blindfolded.

There's a crackle in the headphones, and then Agent Brennan's voice. "Cassel? Are you in?"

"Yeah, everything's perfect here," I say into the mouthpiece. "Never better. How about you?"

She laughs. "Don't get cocky, kid."

"Duly noted. I guess I just watch TV and wait."

"You do that. I'll check with you in fifteen minutes."

I take off the headset and rest it on the table. It's hell to just sit here and do nothing, especially when I have so much to do. I want to get started, but I also know that they're going to be paying attention now. Later they'll get bored. For now I take out the index cards and pen and amuse myself by figuring out where in the room a camera could be hidden. Not that I am sure there is one. But I figure that if I stick to being as paranoid as possible, I can't go wrong.

Finally I hear the headset crackle again. "Anything to report?"

"Nada," I say, picking it up and speaking into the mic. "All good."

It's nearly eight. An hour isn't a lot of time.

"I'll check in with you in another fifteen," she says.

"Make it twenty," I say, hopefully just as casually. Then I find the switch on the headset and turn it off. Since they didn't specifically tell me not to do that, I figure that even though they probably won't be happy, they probably won't come looking for me either.

If they've got some kind of GPS tracking thing on me, it's in the ID tag, the hoodie, or the headset. I'm betting it's not the ID tag, since it has to be scanned. I take off the hoodie and leave it on the table. Then I go into the bathroom and turn on the taps to muffle any sounds.

I strip off my clothes. I fold them and rest them on the small table with the towels and antibacterial glove soap. I take out and unfold my pictures. Then, naked, I crouch down on my knees and rest my bare hands on my thighs. The floor is cold. I dig my fingers into my skin.

I concentrate on everything I learned over the past week, every detail I know. I concentrate on the photos in front of me and the videos I saw. I bring Governor Patton into my mind's eye. Then I become him.

It hurts. I can feel everything shift, bones crack, sinews pull, flesh reshape itself. I try very hard not to scream. I mostly succeed.

Just as I'm starting to stand up, the blowback hits.

My skin feels like it's cracking open, my legs melting. My head feels like it's the wrong shape and my eyes are at first closed, then wide, seeing everything through a thousand different lenses, as though I am covered in unblinking eyes. Everything is so bright, and all the different textures of pain unfold around me, pulling me under.

It's so much worse than I remembered.

I don't know how much time passes before I'm able to move again. It feels like a while. The sink's flooded, splashing over onto the floor. I wobble to my feet and turn the taps, grabbing for my clothes. The T-shirt and boxers fit badly. I can't get into the jeans at all.

I look at myself in the mirror, at my bald head and lined face. It's jarring. It's him. With my comb and gel I groom the few silver hairs on my head to be just like in the photos.

My hands are shaking.

When I was a kid, I wanted to be a transformation worker because it was rare. It was special. If you were one, *you* were special. That's all I knew. I never really thought about the actual power much. And then, when I figured out that I *was one*, I still didn't really understand. I mean, I knew it was unique and powerful and cool. I knew it was dangerous. I knew it was rare. But I still didn't really comprehend why it scared powerful people so deeply. Why they wanted me on their side so much.

Now I know why people are afraid of transformation workers. Now I know why they want to control me. Now I get it.

I can walk into someone's house, kiss their wife, sit down at their table, and eat their dinner. I can lift a passport at an airport, and in twenty minutes it will seem like it's mine. I can be a blackbird staring in the window. I can be a cat creeping along a ledge. I can go anywhere I want and do the worst things I can imagine, with nothing to ever connect me to those crimes. Today I might look like me, but tomorrow I could look like you. I could *be* you.

Hell, I'm scared of myself right now.

Holding my phone in one hand and my index cards in the other, edging past where I guess cameras might be so as not to be caught on film, I walk out of the trailer.

People turn their heads, wide-eyed, at Governor Patton in his underwear, standing in the open air. "Wrong damn trailer," I growl, and push open the door to Patton's.

There, just like I hoped, hangs the suit I ordered from Bergdorf Goodman, zipped up in a cloth storage bag and tailored to his measurements. A new pair of shoes and socks and a fresh white shirt, still in plastic. A silk tie is hanging around the hanger holding the suit.

Other than that the trailer looks a lot like mine. Couch, dressing area. Television monitor.

Seconds later an assistant comes in the door without knocking. She looks panicked. "I'm so sorry. We didn't realize you had arrived. They're ready for you in makeup, Governor. No one saw you come in, and I didn't— Well, I'll let you finish getting ready."

I glance at my phone. It's eight thirty. I lost about half an hour being unconscious and missed checking in with Agent Brennan on top of it. "Come back and get me in ten minutes," I say, trying to keep my voice inflections as like his as I can. I watched all those videos and I practiced, but it's not easy to sound entirely unlike yourself. "I have to finish getting dressed."

When she leaves, I call Barron.

Please, I say to the universe, to whatever's listening. *Please pick up the phone. I'm trusting you. Pick up the phone.*

"Hey, little brother," Barron says, and I slump onto the couch with relief. Until that moment I wasn't sure he would come through. "One government drone to another, how are you doing?"

"Just tell me you're actually—," I start.

"Oh, I am. Oh, *definitely*. I'm here with him now. I was just explaining how our mother's a federal agent and how this was all a government conspiracy."

"Oh," I say. "Uh, good."

"He already knew most of it." I can hear the grin in his voice. "I'm just filling in details. But go ahead and let everyone know that Governor Patton is going to need to delay that press conference by a half hour, okay?"

I guess that if you tell a compulsive liar to stall a guy who's completely paranoid, then wild conspiracy theories are the way he's going to do it. I should be glad that

Barron isn't explaining how the governor of Virginia is aiming a laser at the moon and they all need to proceed to underground bunkers immediately. I grin too. "I can definitely do that."

Hanging up, I grab the suit pants and shove my foot into the leg hole. They're nicer clothes than I've ever worn before. Everything about them feels expensive.

By the time the assistant comes back, I'm tying my tie and ready to go to makeup.

You might wonder what I'm doing. I kind of wonder that myself. But someone has to stop Patton, and this is my chance.

There are tons of people on the governor's support staff, but luckily, most of them are still at his mansion, waiting for the real Patton to leave. I only have to deal with the ones who came ahead. I sit on a director's chair outside and let a girl with short, spiky hair spray foundation on my borrowed face. People ask me a lot of questions about interviews and meetings that I can't answer. Someone brings me a coffee with cream and sugar that I don't drink. Once, a judge calls, asking to talk to me. I shake my head.

"After the speech," I say, and study my mostly blank index cards.

"There's a federal agent here," one of my aides tells me. "She says there could be a security breach."

"I'd expect them to try to pull a trick like that. No—I'm going on. They can't stop me," I say. "I want one of our security officers to make sure she doesn't disrupt me when I'm onstage. We're going out live, right?"

The aide nods.

"Perfect." I don't know what Yulikova and the rest of them suspect or don't, but in a few minutes it won't matter.

That's when Agent Brennan comes around the side of the trailer I'm supposed to be in, holding up her badge.

"Governor," she says.

I stand and do the only thing I can think of. I walk up onto the stage, in front of the small crowd of supporters waving signs and the larger crowd of press correspondents with video cameras pointed at me. It might not be that many people, but it's enough. I freeze.

My heart thumps in my chest. I can't believe I am really doing this.

It's too late to stop.

I clear my throat and reshuffle my index cards, walking until I'm standing behind the lectern. I can see Yulikova, talking frantically into a radio.

"Fellow citizens, distinguished guests, members of the press, thank you all for extending me the courtesy of your attendance today. We stand on the very spot where hundreds of New Jersey citizens were detained after the ban passed, during a dark period in our nation's history—and we stand here looking ahead to legislation that, if it passes, may again take us in directions we don't anticipate."

There is applause, but it's cautious. This isn't the tone that the real Patton would take. He'd probably say some crap about how testing workers will keep them safe. He'd talk about what a glorious day we are at the dawn of.

But today I'm the one with the microphone. I toss my index cards over my shoulder and smile at my audience. I clear my throat. "It was my plan to read a short prepared statement and take questions, but I am going to diverge from my usual procedure. Today is not a day for politics as usual. Today I plan to speak to you from the heart."

I lean against the lectern and take a deep breath. "I've killed *a lot of people*. And when I say 'a lot,' I mean—really—a lot. I've lied, too, but honestly, after hearing about the killing, I doubt you care about a little lying. I know what you're asking yourself. Does he mean he killed people directly or merely that he ordered their deaths? Ladies and gentlemen, I'm here to tell you—I mean both."

I look out at the reporters. They're whispering back and forth. Cameras flash. Signs sag.

"For example, I killed Eric Lawrence, of Toms River, New Jersey, with my own hands. Gloved hands, mind you. I'm not some kind of pervert. But I did strangle him. You can read the police report—well, you could have if I hadn't suppressed it.

"Now you might ask yourself, why would I do such a thing? And what does this have to do with my crusade against workers? And what in the world made me say any of this out loud, no less in public? Well, let me tell you about a very special lady in my life. You know how sometimes you meet a girl and you go a little crazy?"

I point at a tall guy in the front. "*You* know what I mean, don't you? Well, I want to come clean with regard to Shandra Singer. I might have exaggerated some things there. If your girlfriend breaks up with you, sometimes you get upset—and you might be tempted to phone her up twelve times in a row to beg her to take you back . . . or maybe spray paint something obscene on her car . . . or *maybe* you frame her for a massive conspiracy . . . and try to have her gunned down in the middle of the street. . . . And if you're really upset, maybe you try to wipe out all workers in the state.

"The more you love her, the crazier you get. My love was great. My crimes were greater.

"I'm not here asking for forgiveness. I don't expect forgiveness. In fact, I expect a media circus of a trial followed by a lengthy incarceration.

"But I tell you this today because you, my fellow citizens, deserve my honesty. Hey, better late than never—and I've got to say, it does feel really good to get it all off my chest. So in summary, I killed people. You probably shouldn't put too much stock in other stuff I said before right now, and—oh, yeah. Proposition two is a terrible idea that I supported mostly to distract you from my other crimes.

"So, any questions?"

For a long moment there is only silence.

"Okay, then," I say. "Thank you. God bless America, and God bless the great state of New Jersey."

I stumble off the stage. There are people with clipboards and aides in suits all staring at me as if they're afraid to approach me. I smile and give them the thumbs-up sign.

257

"Good speech, huh?" I say.

"Governor," one of them says, heading in my direction. "We have to discuss—"

"Not now," I tell him, still smiling. "Have my car brought around, please."

He opens his mouth to say something—maybe that he has no idea where my car *is*, since it's probably still with the real Patton—when my arm is jerked behind me and I nearly lose my balance. I yelp as metal comes down on my wrist. Handcuffs.

"You're under arrest." It's Jones in his sharp black federal agent suit. *"Governor."*

Cameras flash. Reporters are streaming toward us.

I can't help it. I start to laugh. I think about what I just did, and I laugh even harder.

Agent Jones marches me away from the crowd of shouting people, to a cleared spot of street where police cars and television vans are parked. A few of the cops come over to try to push back the rush of news cameras and paparazzi.

"You really dug your own grave," he mutters. "And I'm going to bury you in it."

"Say that louder," I tell him, under my breath. "I dare you."

He gets me to a car, opens the door, and pushes me inside. Then I feel something go over my head, and I look down. Three of the amulets I made—the ones that prevent transformation, the ones I gave to Yulikova—are hanging around my neck.

Before I can say anything, the door slams.

Agent Jones gets into the driver's seat and guns the

engine. Flashes go off through the window as we start to pull away from the crowd.

I lean back, letting my muscles relax as much as possible. The cuffs are too tight to get out of, but I'm not worried. Not anymore. They can't arrest me—not for this, not when now they can arrest Patton without difficulty. Simple lies are always better than a complicated truth.

Explaining that the Patton on television, the one that confessed, wasn't really Patton, but the real Patton *had* actually committed those crimes, is too confusing.

They might scream at me, they might not want me to be a member of the LMD anymore, but they'll eventually have to admit that I solved the problem. I took down Patton. Not the way that they wanted, but no one got hurt, and that has to be worth something.

"Where's Yulikova?" I ask. "Are we going back to the hotel?"

"No hotel," Jones says.

"Want to tell me where we are going?" I ask.

He doesn't say anything, just keeps driving for a few more moments.

"Come on," I say. "I'm *sorry*. But I had some information that there was a plan to set me up for working Patton. You can deny it if you want to—and maybe my information was wrong—but I got cold feet. Look, I know I shouldn't have done what I did, but—"

He pulls abruptly onto the shoulder of the road. Cars are whizzing by us on one side, and there is a dark patch of trees on the other.

I stop talking.

He gets out and comes around to open my door. When he does, he's pointing a gun at me.

"Get out," he says. "Slowly."

I don't move. "What's going on?"

"Right now!" he yells.

I'm cuffed; I don't have a lot of choices. I slide out of the car. He pushes me around to the back and pops the trunk.

"Uh," I say.

Then he undoes the top two buttons on my shirt, so that he can push the amulets against my skin. When he buttons everything up and tightens my tie, the charms are trapped underneath. Now I have no chance of shaking them off.

"Get in," he says, indicating the trunk. There's not much in there. A spare tire and a first aid kit. A length of rope.

I don't even bother to tell him no, I just run. Even with my hands cuffed behind me, I think I can maybe make it.

I crash down the hill, sliding more than anything else. The dress shoes are awful, and my body is heavy and unfamiliar. I'm not used to the way it moves. I keep losing my balance, expecting my legs to be longer. I slip, and my suit pants slide on the muddy grass. Then I'm up again and heading for the trees.

I'm moving way too slow.

Jones comes down hard against my back, tackling me to the ground. I struggle, but it's no use. I feel the cold muzzle of the gun against my temple and his knee against the hollow of my back.

"You're as cowardly as a goddamn weasel. You know that? A *weasel*. That's what you are."

"You don't know me," I say, spitting blood onto the dirt.

I can't help it. I start to laugh. "And you obviously don't know much about weasels, either."

His fist slams into my side, and I nearly black out from the pain. Someday I am going to learn to keep my mouth shut.

"Get up."

I do. We walk back to the car like that. I don't crack any more jokes.

When we get there, he shoves me against the trunk.

"In," he says. "Now."

"I'm sorry," I say. "Patton's fine. He's alive. Whatever you think I did—"

The gun clicks once, ominously close to my ear.

I let him shove me into the trunk. He takes rope and knots it around my legs, connecting that to the chain of the handcuffs in back—tight, so that I can barely move. No more running for me.

Then I hear the rip of duct tape and feel it wrap my hands in two separate sticky cocoons. He's taping something against my palms, something heavy—stones. When he's done, he rolls me over, so that I'm looking at him and the highway beyond. Every time a car barrels past, I think that maybe someone will stop, but no one does.

"I knew you were too much of a wild card when we brought you in. You're too dangerous. You'll never be loyal. I tried to tell Yulikova, but she wouldn't listen."

"I'm sorry," I say, a little desperate. "I'll tell her. I'll tell her you're right. Just let her know where we are."

He laughs. "Nope. But, then, you're not Cassel Sharpe anymore, are you? You're Governor Patton."

"Okay," I say, fear making me babble. "Agent Jones, you're one of the good guys. You're supposed to be better than this. You're a *federal agent*. Look, I'll go back. I'll confess. You can lock me up."

"You should have just let us frame you," Jones says, cutting off a length of silvery duct tape with an army knife. "If no one has any control—if you're out there, free to make deals with anyone—how's that going to be? It's only a matter of time before some foreign government or some corporation makes you a deal. And then you will be the dangerous weapon we let slip through our fingers. Better to just take you out of the equation."

It barely registers that I was right, that they were setting me up.

"But I signed the—"

He brings the tape down over my mouth. I try to spit and turn my head, but he gets it on, tight across my lips. For a moment I forget I can breathe through my nose and I panic, trying to suck in air.

"And while you were making your little speech, I had an idea. I called up some very bad people who are real eager to meet you. I think you know Ivan Zacharov, don't you? Turns out he's willing to pay a lot of money for the pleasure of personally murdering a certain governor." He grins. "Bad luck for you, Cassel."

As the trunk lid comes down, plunging me into darkness, and then the car starts to move, I wonder if I've ever had any other kind.

CHAPTER SIXTEEN

THE AIR GETS WARM
fast in the trunk, and the oil and gasoline fumes make me
want to gag. Worse, every bump in the road sends me sliding around, banging against metal. I try to brace with my
feet, but as soon as we turn a corner or hit a pothole, my
head or arms or back smacks into one of the sides. The
way I'm tied, I can't even curl against the blow.

All told, this is a pretty bad way to spend the last hours
of my life.

I try to think through my options, but they're dis-
mal. I can't transform, not with three amulets around
my neck. And since I can't touch my own skin with my

hands, even if I somehow managed to rip the amulets off, I'm not sure I could change myself anyway.

One thing I have to say for Agent Jones—he is thorough.

I hear the moment that we pull off the highway. The noise of traffic dims. Gravel under the tires sounds almost like heavy rain.

A few minutes later the engine gutters out and a car door slams. I hear voices, too distant and low to be recognized.

By the time Agent Jones opens up the trunk, I am wild-eyed with panic. The cold air rushes in, and I start struggling against my bonds, even though there's no way that I am going to do anything but hurt myself.

He just watches me squirm.

Then he pulls out his knife and saws through the rope. I can finally extend my legs. I do so slowly, my knees hurting from being bent too long.

"Out," he says. I struggle to sit up. He has to help me onto my feet.

We are outside, underneath a massive industrial structure, with huge iron framing pieces holding up a tower that looms above us, spewing fire into the cloudy late morning sky. Plumes of smoke rise to blot out the shining steel bridges leading to New York. It looks like it's about to rain.

I turn my head and see that maybe ten feet away from me is another sleek black car, this one with Zacharov leaning against it, smoking a cigar. Stanley is standing next to him, screwing a silencer onto a very large black gun.

Then, just as I am sure nothing about this can get worse, the passenger door opens and Lila steps out.

She's got on a black pencil skirt with a gray belted coat and calf-high leather boots. Sunglasses cover her eyes, and her mouth is painted the color of old blood. She's got a briefcase in her gray gloved hands.

I have no way to signal her. Her only glance in my direction is cold and perfunctory.

I shake my head *No, no, no.* Agent Jones just laughs dryly. "Here he is, just like I promised. But I never want to see his body again. Do you understand?"

Lila sets down the suitcase next to her father. "I have your money," she tells Jones.

"Good," says Agent Jones. "Let's get started."

Zacharov nods, blowing a cloud of smoke that spirals up and away from him, like the plumes from one of the buildings. "What guarantee do I have that you aren't going to try to pin it on my organization? Your offer came as a real surprise. We don't make so many deals with representatives of the government."

"This is just me. One man, doing what I think is right." Agent Jones shrugs his shoulders. "Your guarantee is that I'm here. I'm going to watch you gun him down. My hands might be clean, but we're both responsible for his death. Neither one of us wants an investigation. Forensics might find a way to place me at the scene. If I rat on you, I'll go down for kidnapping at the very least. I'll hold up my end of the bargain."

Zacharov nods slowly.

"You got cold feet?" Jones asks. "You get to be a worker hero, and eliminate a guy who has been gunning for you lately."

"That was a misunderstanding," Zacharov says.

"You mean that you haven't been sheltering Shandra Singer? My mistake." Agent Jones doesn't even attempt to disguise his sarcasm.

"We don't have *cold feet*," says Zacharov.

"I'll do it," Lila says. Then she looks at Stanley, pointing to the gun. "Give me that."

I widen my eyes, pleading silently. I move my foot in the dirt, hoping I can spell something out fast. *M*, I try to manage, upside down, so she can read it. *ME*, I want it to say.

Agent Jones clocks me on the side of the head with the butt of his gun, hard enough to make the world shift out of focus. I feel like my brain is actually rattling around in my skull. I fall onto my stomach, hands still cuffed behind my back. I didn't even see that he'd drawn a weapon.

I lie there, gasping.

"It's so unexpectedly nice to see him squirming in the dirt," Zacharov says, walking over to me and bending down to pat my cheek with one gloved hand. "Governor, did you really think that no one could touch you?"

I shake my head, not sure what that's supposed to convey. *Please*, I think. *Please ask me something you need answered. Please rip off the tape. Please.*

Lila steps forward with the gun held at her side. She looks at me for a long moment.

Please.

Zacharov rises to his feet. His black coat swirls around him like a cape.

"Get him up," he tells Agent Jones. "A man should be on his feet when he dies—even this man."

Lila's blond hair blows gently around her face, a halo of gold. She takes off her sunglasses. I'm glad. I want to look into her eyes one last time. Blue and green. The colors of the sea.

A girl like that, Grandad said, perfumes herself with ozone and metal filings. She wears trouble like a crown. If she ever falls in love, she'll fall like a comet, burning the sky as she goes.

At least it's you pulling the trigger. I wish I could say that, if nothing else.

"Are you sure?" Zacharov asks her.

She nods, touching a gloved finger to her throat, almost unconsciously. "I took my marks. I'll take the heat."

"You'll have to go into hiding until we're sure it won't be traced to you," Zacharov says.

Lila nods again. "It'll be worth it."

Ruthless. That's my girl.

Agent Jones pulls me to my feet. I stagger unsteadily, like a drunk. I want to cry out, but the tape smothers the sound.

The gun in her hand wavers.

I take one last look and then close my eyes so tightly that they're wet at the corners. So tightly that spots dance in the blackness of my vision.

I wish I could tell her good-bye.

I expect the gunshot to be the loudest thing in the world, but I forgot about the silencer. All I hear is a gasp.

Lila is leaning over me, pulling off her gloves so that she can get a fingernail under the corner of the duct tape. She rips it off my mouth. I am looking up at the late morning sky, so grateful to be alive that I am barely conscious of the pain.

"I'm me," I say, babbling. "Cassel. I swear it's me—"

I don't even remember falling, but I am lying on the gravel. Agent Jones is beside me, unmoving. Blood pools in the dirt. His blood, as bright as paint. I try to roll onto my side. Is he dead?

"I know." She touches the side of my face with bare fingers.

"How?" I say. "How did you— When?"

"You are such a jackass," she says. "Do you think I don't watch television? I heard your insane speech. Of course I knew it was you. You told me about Patton."

"Oh," I say. "That. Of course."

Stanley pats down Jones and unlocks my cuffs. As soon as they're off and the duct tape is pulled away, taking skin and stone and ink with it, I rip at my collar, pulling off the amulets and throwing them onto the ground.

All I want is to get out of this body.

For the first time the pain of the blowback feels like a release.

I wake up on an unfamiliar couch, with a blanket slung over me. I start to sit up, and realize that Zacharov's sitting on the other side of the room, in a shallow pool of light, reading.

The glare of the bulb is giving his face the hard lines of a sculpture. A study of a crime boss in repose.

He looks up and smiles. "Feeling better?"

"I guess so," I say, as formally as I can manage from a mostly prone position. My voice creaks. "Yeah."

I sit upright, smoothing out the wrinkled mess of my suit. It doesn't fit anymore, my arms and legs too long for the sleeves and pants, the body of it hanging off me like extra skin.

"Lila's upstairs," he says. "Helping your mother pack. You can take Shandra home."

"But I didn't find the diamond—"

He puts down the book. "I don't hand out compliments easily, but what you did—it was impressive." He chuckles. "You single-handedly torpedoed a piece of legislation I've been working toward ending for a long while, and you eliminated a political enemy of mine. We're square, Cassel."

"Square?" I echo, because I can't quite believe it. "But I—"

"Of course, if you do find the diamond, I would really appreciate your returning it to me. I can't believe your mother *lost* it."

"That's because you've never been to our house," I say, which isn't exactly true. He was in the kitchen once—and maybe he was there other times I didn't know about. "You and my mother have had quite a history." After the words come out of my mouth, I realize that whatever he says next isn't something I want to hear.

He looks faintly amused. "There's something about her— Cassel, I have met many evil men and women in my life. I have made deals with them, drank with them. I have done things that I myself have difficulty reconciling— terrible things. But I have never known anyone like your mother. She is a person without limits—or if she has any, she hasn't found them yet. She never needs to reconcile anything."

He says this thoughtfully, admiringly. I look at the glass on the side table next to him and wonder how much he's had to drink.

"She fascinated me when we were younger—I met her through your grandfather. We—she and I—never much liked each other, except when we did. But— Whatever she said to you about what was between her and me, I want you to know that I always respected your father. He was as honest as any criminal can hope to be."

I'm not sure I want to hear this, but suddenly it becomes clear why he's telling me: He doesn't want me to be angry on my father's behalf even though he knows I know he slept with my mother. I clear my throat. "Look, I don't pretend to understand—I don't *want* to understand. That's your business and her business."

He nods. "Good."

"I think my dad took it from her," I say. "I think that's why it's gone. He had it."

Zacharov looks at me oddly.

"The diamond," I say, realizing I wasn't making any sense. "I think my dad took the diamond from my mom and replaced it with a fake. So that she never knew it was gone."

"Cassel, stealing the Resurrection Diamond is like stealing the *Mona Lisa*. If you have a buyer lined up, then you might get something close to its real value, but otherwise you steal it because you're an art lover or just to show the world that you *can*. You can't fence it. There would be too much attention. You would have to cut it into pieces, and then it would only fetch a fraction of its worth. For that, you might as well steal a handful of white diamonds at any jewelry store in town."

"You could ransom it," I say, thinking of my mother and her crazy plan to get money.

"But your father didn't," Zacharov says. "If he had it. Although he would have had it for only a couple of months."

I give him a long look.

He snorts. "You aren't seriously asking yourself if I caused your father to have a car accident, are you? I think you know me better than that. If I'd killed a man who I knew had stolen from me, I would have made him an example. No one would have failed to know who was responsible for a death like that. But I never suspected your father. He was a small-time operator, not greedy. Your mother I considered, but dismissed. Wrongly, as it turns out."

"Maybe he knew he was going to die," I say. "Maybe he really believed the stone would keep him alive. Like Rasputin. Like you."

"I can't think of anyone who didn't like your father— and if he was really afraid, surely he would have gone to

Desi." Desi, my granddad. It jolts me to hear his first name; I forget he has one.

"I guess we'll never know," I say.

We regard each other for a long moment. I wonder whether he sees my father or my mother when he looks at me. Then his gaze seems to focus on something else.

I turn. Lila's on the stairs in her pencil skirt and boots, with a filmy white shirt. She smiles down at us, her mouth curved upward on one side, turning the expression wry.

"Can I have Cassel for a minute?"

I start toward the stairs.

"Bring him back in one piece," her father calls after her.

Lila's bedroom is at once exactly what I should have expected and nothing like I imagined. I was in her dorm room at Wallingford, and I guess I figured this room would be a somewhat nicer version of that one. I didn't take into account the wealth of her family and their love of imported furniture.

The room is huge. On one end a very long light green velvet daybed rests next to a mirrored dressing table. The shining surface is littered with lots of brushes and open pots of makeup. Several satiny ottomans sit on the floor nearby.

On the other end, beside the window, there's a massive ornate mirror, the silvering faded in some spots, showing its age. Near that is her bed. The headboard looks old and French, carved from some light wood. The whole thing is piled with more satin—a bedspread and pale yellow pillows. An overstuffed bookshelf works as her side table, covered in piles of books and a big golden lamp. A huge gilt chandelier swings from the ceiling, glittering with crystals.

It's an old-fashioned starlet's room. The only incongruous thing is the gun holster hanging from one side of her dressing table. Well, that and me.

I catch sight of myself in the mirror. My black hair is tangled, like I just got out of bed. There's a bruise on the side of my mouth and a lump at my temple.

She leads me in and then stops, like she's not sure what to do next.

"Are you okay?" I ask, moving to sit on the daybed. I feel ridiculous in the remains of Patton's suit, but I don't have any other clothes here. I shrug off the jacket.

She raises her brows. "You want to know if *I'm* okay?"

"You shot someone," I say. "And you ran out on me before that, when we— I don't know. I thought maybe you were upset."

"I *am* upset." She doesn't speak for a long moment. Then she starts pacing the floor. "I can't believe you made that speech. I can't believe you almost died."

"You saved my life."

"I did! *I absolutely did!*" she says, pointing at me accusingly with a gloved finger. "And what if I hadn't? What if I wasn't there—if I hadn't figured out it was you? What if that federal agent thought there was someone with a bigger grudge against Patton than my dad?"

"I—" I suck in a breath and let it out slowly. "I guess I'd be ... dead."

"Exactly. You can't go around making plans that have

you getting killed as a by-product. Eventually one of them is going to *work*."

"Lila, I swear I didn't know. I thought I would get in trouble, but I didn't have any idea about Agent Jones. He just snapped." I don't talk about how scared I was. I don't tell her that I thought I was going to die. "None of that was part of my plan."

"You keep talking, but you're not making any sense. Of course you upset someone in the government. You *pretended to be the governor of New Jersey* and *confessed to a bunch of crimes*."

I can't help the small smile that's playing at the corners of my mouth. "So," I say, "how did it go over?"

She shakes her head, but she's smiling too. "Big. It's being broadcast on all the channels. They say proposition two will never pass now. Happy?"

I am struck by a sudden thought. "If he'd been assassinated, though . . ."

She frowns. "I guess you're right. It would have passed easily."

"Look," I say, standing and walking to her. "*You're* right. No more crazy schemes or lunatic plans. Really, really. I'll be good."

She's studying me, clearly trying to decide if I'm telling the truth. I curl my fingers around her small shoulders and hope she doesn't push me away when I bring my mouth down to hers.

She makes a soft sound and reaches up to fist her hand in my hair, pulling it roughly. The kiss is frantic, bruising. I can taste her lipstick, feel her teeth, am drinking down the panting sobs of her breath.

"I'm okay," I tell her, speaking against her mouth, echoing her own words, my arms coming around her to hold her tightly against me. "I'm right here."

She tucks her head against my neck. Her voice is so soft that I can barely make out the words. "I shot a federal agent, Cassel. I'm going to have to go away for a while. Until things cool down."

"What do you mean?" I ask, dread making me stupid. I want to pretend I misheard her.

"It's not going to be forever. Six months, maybe a year. By the time you graduate, probably things will have blown over and I'll be able to come back. But it means that—well, I don't know where that leaves us. I don't need any promises. It's not like we're even—"

"But you shouldn't have to go," I say. "It was because of me. It's *my* fault."

She slides out of my arms, walks to the dressing table and dabs at her eyes with a tissue. "You're not the only one who can make sacrifices, Cassel."

When she turns around, I can see the shadows of the mascara she's wiped away.

"I'll say good-bye before I go," she tells me, looking at the floor, at the ornate pattern of what is probably a ridiculously expensive rug. Then she glances at me.

I ought to say something about how I'll miss her or about how a couple of months is nothing, but I am silenced by rage so terrible that it locks my throat. *It's not fair*, I want to scream at the universe. I just found out she loves me. Everything was just beginning, everything was perfect, and now it's snatched away again.

It hurts too much, I want to shout. I'm tired of hurting.

Since I know that those are not okay things to say, I manage to say nothing.

The silence is broken by a knock on the door. After a moment my mother comes in and tells me that it's time to go.

Stanley drives us home.

CHAPTER SEVENTEEN

WHEN I GET UP THE
next morning, Barron is downstairs frying eggs. Mom is sitting in her dressing gown, drinking coffee out of a chipped porcelain mug. Her mass of black hair is twisted up into ringlets and clipped like that, with a bright scarf to keep it all in place.

She's smoking a cigarette, tapping the ashes into a blue glass tray.

"There are some things I will definitely miss," she's saying. "I mean, no one likes being held prisoner, but if you are going to be locked up, you might as well— Oh, hello, dear. Good morning."

I yawn and stretch, reaching my arms toward the ceiling.

It feels truly wonderful to be back in my own clothes, back in my own body. My jeans are comfortable, old and worn. I can't face putting on a uniform right now.

Barron hands me a cup of coffee.

"Black, like your soul," he says with a grin. He's got on dark slacks and wing-tip shoes. His hair is rakishly disheveled. He appears not to have a care in the world.

"We're out of milk," Mom informs me.

I take a deep and grateful gulp. "I can run out and get some."

"Would you?" Mom smiles and touches my hair, pushing it back from my forehead. I let her, but I grit my teeth. Her bare fingers brush my skin. I am thankful when none of my amulets crack. "Do you know what the Turkish say about coffee? It should be black as hell, strong as death, and sweet as love. Isn't that beautiful? My grandfather told me that when I was a little girl, and I never forgot it. Unfortunately, I still like my milk."

"Maybe he was from there," Barron says, turning back to the eggs. Which is possible. Our grandfather has passed down lots of different stories to explain our perpetually tanned skin, from the one about being descended from an Indian maharaja to the one about runaway slaves to something about Julius Caesar. Turkish, I never heard. Yet.

"Or maybe he read it in a book," I say. "Or maybe he just ate a box of Turkish delight and that's what it said on the back."

"Such a cynic," my mother says, picking up her plate,

scraping the toast crusts into the trash, and putting it in the sink. "You boys play nice. I'm going to go get dressed."

She brushes by us, and I hear her footfalls on the stairs. I take another sip of coffee. "Thanks," I say. "For delaying Patton. Just—thanks."

Barron nods. "Heard on the radio that they arrested him. He had a lot to say about conspiracies that I take credit for personally. It was good stuff. Of course, after that speech, everyone has to realize that he's bonkers. I don't know where you got all that—"

I grin. "Oh, come on. It was some fine rhetoric."

"Yeah, you're like a modern day Abraham Lincoln." He sets a plate of eggs and toast in front of me. "'Let my people go.'"

"That's *Moses*." I grab for the pepper mill. "Well, my years on the debate team finally paid off, I guess."

"Yeah," he says. "You're the hero of the hour."

I shrug.

"So what happens now?" he asks.

I shake my head. I can't tell Barron what happened after I got off the stage, how Agent Jones tried to kill me and is now dead, how Lila is leaving town. To him it must seem like a large-scale prank, a joke I played on Yulikova.

"I think I'm done with the Feds. Hopefully they're done with me, too," I say. "How about you?"

"Are you kidding? I love being a G-man. I'm in for the long haul. I'm going to be so corrupt that I'll be a legend down in Carney." He grins, sitting across from me at the table and stealing a piece of toast off my plate. "Also, you owe me one."

I nod. "Sure," I say, with a feeling of dread. "And I fully intend to pay up. Just tell me."

He looks toward the door and then back at me. "I want you to tell Daneca what I did for you. That I helped. That I did something good."

"Okay," I say, frowning. There must be a catch. "That's it?"

He nods. "Yeah, just tell her. Make her understand that I didn't have to do it, but I did it anyway."

I snort. "Whatever, Barron."

"I'm serious. You owe me a favor, and that's what I want." His expression is one I don't often see him wear. He looks oddly diffident, as though he's waiting for me to say something really cruel.

I shake my head. "No problem. That's easily done."

He smiles, his usual easy, careless grin, and grabs for the marmalade. I toss back the rest of my cup.

"I'm going to get Mom's milk," I say. "Can I take your car?"

"Sure," he says, pointing to the closet near the door. "Keys are in the pocket of my coat."

I pat down my jeans and realize my wallet is upstairs, under the mattress, where I left it for safekeeping before I went off with the Feds. "Can I borrow five bucks, too?"

He rolls his eyes. "Go ahead."

I find his leather jacket and root around in the inside pocket, eventually coming up with both keys and wallet. I flip open the wallet and am in the process of taking out money, when I see Daneca's picture in one of the plastic sleeves.

I slide it out with the cash and then leave quickly, slamming the door in my haste.

After I get to the store, I sit in the parking lot, staring at the picture. Daneca's sitting on a park bench, her hair blowing in a light wind. She's smiling at the camera in a way that I've never seen her smile before—not at me and not at Sam. She looks lit up from the inside, shining with a happiness so vast that it's impossible to ignore.

On the back is the distinctive scrawl of my brother's handwriting: "This is Daneca Wasserman. She is your girlfriend and you love her."

I look at it and look at it, trying to decipher some meaning behind it other than the obvious—that it's true. I never knew Barron could feel that way about anyone.

But she isn't his girlfriend anymore. She dumped him.

Leaning against the hood of the car, I take one last glance at the photo before I rip it into pieces. I throw those into the trash can outside the store, nothing more than colored confetti on top of discarded wrappers and soda bottles. Then I go inside and buy a pint of milk.

I tell myself that he meant to throw out Daneca's picture, that he just forgot. I tell myself I got rid of it for his own good. His memory is full of holes, and an outdated reminder would just be confusing. He might forget that they broke up, and embarrass himself. I tell myself that they would have never worked out, not in the long run, and he'll be happier if he forgets her.

I tell myself that I did it for him, but I know that's not true.

I want Sam and Daneca to be happy together, like they were before. I did it for myself. I did it to get what I want.

Maybe I should regret that, but I can't. Sometimes you do the bad thing and hope for the good result.

There is a black car idling next to the driveway when I return.

I pull past it, park, and get out. As I start toward the house, the passenger-side door opens and Yulikova steps onto the grass. She's got on a tan suit with her signature chunky necklaces. I wonder how many of the stones are charms.

I walk a little ways toward her but stop, so that she has to close the distance on her own.

"Hello, Cassel," she says. "We've got some things to talk about. Why don't you get into the car?"

I hold up the milk. "Sorry," I say. "But I'm a little busy right now."

"What you did—you can't think there are no consequences." I'm not sure if she means the speech or something worse, but I don't much care.

"You set me up," I say. "One big con. You can't blame me because I turned out not to be gullible enough. You can't blame the mark. That's not how it works. Have some respect for the nature of the game."

She's quiet for a long moment. "How did you find out?"

"Does it really matter?"

"I never meant to betray your trust. It was for your safety as much as anything else that I agreed we should implement—"

I hold up one gloved hand. "Just spare me the justifications. I thought you were the good guys, but there are no good guys."

"That's not true." She looks honestly upset, but then, I've learned that I can't read her. The problem with a really excellent liar is that you have to just assume they're always lying. "You would never have spent a single night in jail. We weren't going to lock you up, Cassel. My superiors felt that we needed a little leverage over you, that's all. You haven't exactly been trustworthy yourself."

"You were supposed to be better than me," I say. "Anyway, that's done."

"You think you know the truth, but there are more factors in play than you're aware of. You don't understand the larger picture. You can't. You don't know what chaos you've created."

"Because you wanted to get rid of Patton, but you also wanted proposition two to pass. So you decided to make a martyr out of him. Two birds, one stone."

"It's not about what I want," she says. "It's bigger than that."

"I think we're done here."

"You know that's not possible. More people are aware of you now, people high up in the government. And everyone is very eager to meet you. Especially my boss."

"That and a dollar will almost buy me a cup of coffee."

"You signed a contract, Cassel. That's binding."

"Did I?" I say, smirking. "I think you should check again. I'm pretty sure you're going to find out that I never signed anything. My name is nowhere. My name is gone." *Thank you, Sam*, I think. I would have never thought a disappearing-ink pen could come in so handy.

Her irritation shows on her face for once. I feel oddly

triumphant. She clears her throat. "Where's Agent Jones?"

She says it like that's her trump card.

I shrug. "Beats me. Did you lose him? I hope you find him, even though— Let's face it, he and I were never close."

"You're not this person," she says, waving her hand in the air to indicate me. I don't know what she was expecting. Clearly she's frustrated by my reaction. "You're not this— this *cold*. You care about making the world a better place. Snap out of it, Cassel, before it's too late."

"I've got to go," I say, jerking my head toward the house.

"Your mother could be brought up on charges," she says.

Fury makes my mouth curl. I don't care if she sees it. "So could you. I hear you used a worker kid to frame a governor. You can ruin my life, but you'll have to destroy your own to do it. I promise you that."

"Cassel," she says, her voice rising several decibels. "I am the least of your worries. Do you think that if you were in China you would be free?"

"Oh, give me a break," I say.

"Right now you're a bigger problem than Patton was, and you saw how my superiors handled that problem. The only way this can be over is if you—"

"*This is never going to be over,*" I shout. "Someone will always be after me. There's always consequences. Well, *BRING IT.* I am done with being afraid, and I am done with you."

With that, I stalk back to the house. But on the porch I hesitate. I look back at Yulikova. I wait until she walks back to the gleaming black car, gets in, and is driven away. Then I sit down on the stoop.

I stare out at the yard for a long time, not really thinking about anything, mostly just shaking with anger and adrenaline.

The government is big, bigger than any one person can game. They can come after the people I care about, they can come for me, they can do something that I haven't thought of yet. They could make their move now or a year from now. And I'm going to have to be ready. Always and forever ready, unless I want to give up everything I have and everyone I love.

Like, they could go after Lila, who shot and killed someone in cold blood. If they ever managed to figure that out, to charge her with Agent Jones's murder, I would do anything to keep her free.

Or they could go after Barron, who works for them.

Or—

As I'm thinking, I realize I am looking out at our old barn. No one's gone in there in years. It's full of old furniture, rusted tools, and a bunch of stuff my parents stole and then didn't want.

It's where my dad taught me how to pick locks. He kept all his equipment out there, including the supersecure box. I vividly recall my father, cigarillo resting in one corner of his mouth as he worked, oiling the gears of a lock. My memory adds in the spool pins, the mortis sets, and the bolts.

I remember that no one could get into that box. Even knowing there was candy inside, we were still hopeless.

The barn is the one place that Grandad and I didn't clean out.

I leave the milk on the stoop and walk over to the big, worn double doors, then lift the latch. The last time I was inside was in a dream. It feels dreamlike now, dust rising up with my footfalls, the only light coming through gaps in the planks, and windowpanes shaded gray with cobwebs and dirt.

It smells like rotten wood and animal habitation. Most of the furniture is covered with moth-eaten blankets, giving everything a ghostly appearance. I spot a garbage bag filled with plastic bags, and several worn cardboard boxes overstuffed with milk glass. There's an old safe—so rusted that the door is ossified open. Inside I find only a pile of pennies, greenish and stuck together.

Dad's worktable is covered with a cloth too. Pulling it back with a single sweep of my hand, I see the piled mess of his tools—a vise, cylinder remover, sesame decoder, hammer with interchangeable heads, the supersecure box, a bundle of twine, and a bunch of rusted picks.

If my father had the Resurrection Diamond, if he wanted to keep it, if he *couldn't* sell it, then I can picture him tucking it away where no outsider would think to look and no family member was skilled enough to get into. I cast about for a few minutes and then do what I never would have thought to do as a kid.

I clamp the box in the vise. Then I plug in a reciprocating saw and slice it open.

Metal filings are scattered across the floor, curled in glittering piles, by the time I'm done. The box is destroyed, the top cut completely off.

There's no diamond inside, just a bunch of papers and a

very old half-melted lollipop. I would have been extremely disappointed, had I ever managed to open it as a kid.

I'm disappointed now.

I unfold the papers, and a photo falls out into my hands. A bunch of very blond boys standing in front of a huge house—one of those old-money Cape Cod mansions with a widow's walk and columns, looking right onto the ocean. I turn it over and see three names in a spidery hand I don't recognize: "Charles, Philip, Anne." Guess one of them wasn't a boy after all.

For a moment I wonder if I'm looking at the research for an old con. Then I unfold another piece of paper. It's a birth certificate for a Philip Raeburn.

Not Sharpe, a name I always knew was as fake as the prize in a Cracker Jack box. Raeburn. My dad's real last name. The one he gave up, the one he hid from us.

Cassel Raeburn. I try it out in my head, but it sounds ridiculous.

There's a newspaper clipping too, one about how Philip Raeburn died in a boating accident off the shore of the Hamptons at the age of seventeen. A ridiculously expensive way to die.

The Raeburns could afford to buy anything. Certainly they could afford to buy a stolen diamond.

The door creaks open, and I turn around, startled.

"I found the milk by the door. What are you doing out here?" Barron asks. "And—what did you do to Dad's lockbox?"

"Look," I say, holding up the lollipop. "There really was candy in there. Go figure, right?"

Barron gapes at me with the horrified expression of someone realizing that he might be the stable brother after all.

I am back at Wallingford just after dinner. My hall master, Mr. Pascoli, gives me an odd look when I try to hand him the note my mother wrote me.

"You're fine, Cassel. The dean already explained that you might be out for a few days."

"Oh," I say. "Right." I'd nearly forgotten about the deal Dean Wharton made with Sam and me. There was so much about to happen back then that taking advantage of it was a dim hope. Now that I am at Wallingford again, though, I wonder what I can really get away with.

I wonder if I could stay in bed and just sleep until I wasn't tired anymore, for instance.

Probably not.

I don't know what I expect when I walk into my room, but it's not Sam, lying on the bed, his left leg wrapped with gauze. Daneca is sitting beside him and they're playing what appears to be a very intense game of gin rummy.

Clearly Sam is already getting away with having a girl in our dorm room. I admire his gumption.

"Hey," I say, leaning against the door frame.

"What happened to you?" Daneca asks. "We were worried."

"*I* was worried," I say, looking at Sam. "Are you okay? I mean—your leg."

"It still hurts." He lowers it gingerly to the floor. "I have a cane for right now, but I might have a limp, the doctor said. It might not go away."

"That quack? I hope you got a second opinion." The wash of guilt I feel makes the words come out harsher than I intend.

"We did the right thing," Sam says, taking a deep breath. There is a seriousness in his face that I don't remember being there before. Pain shows. "I don't regret it. I almost ruined my whole future. I guess I took it for granted before—everything. The good college, the good job. I thought what you were doing seemed so exciting."

"I'm sorry," I say, and I am. I am very, very sorry if that's what he thought.

"No," he says. "Don't be. I was stupid. And you saved me from getting into a lot of trouble."

I look over at Daneca. Sam is always too generous, but I can trust her to tell me if she thinks I've done something wrong. "I never wanted you—I never wanted either of you to get hurt because of me."

"Cassel," Daneca says, in the exasperated affectionate tone she reserves for us when we're being complete idiots. "You can't blame yourself for Mina Lange. She's not some-one you brought into our lives. She goes to school here, remember? You didn't make this happen. And you can't blame yourself for—for whatever else you're thinking of. We're your friends."

"That might be your first mistake," I say, half under my breath.

Sam laughs. "In a good mood, are we?"

"Did you see?" Daneca asks me. "Proposition two isn't going to pass. And Patton resigned. Well, he was arrested, so I guess he had to. You must have seen it. He even admitted that your mother hadn't done anything wrong."

I think about telling Daneca the truth. Of all the people I know, she's the one who would be the most proud of me. But it feels unfair to get them involved—no matter what they say, especially since this is something far bigger and more dangerous than anything I've been in the middle of before.

"You know me," I say, shaking my head. "I'm not much for politics."

She looks at me slyly. "Too bad you didn't see it, because if I am made valedictorian of our class, I'd love to have help writing my speech, and Patton's is the perfect model. It sets the exact right tone. But I guess if you really don't care about that kind of thing—"

"You want to tell everyone that today's the day you speak from your heart and confess all your crimes? Because I didn't think you had all that much to confess."

"So you did see it!" Sam says.

"You're a liar, Cassel Sharpe," Daneca says, but there's no heat in it. "A lying liar who lies."

"I guess I heard someone talking about it somewhere." I smile up at the ceiling. "What do you want? A leopard can't change his spots."

"If the leopard was a *transformation worker*, he could," Sam says.

I get the sense that maybe I don't have to say anything.

They appear to have put a theory together on their own.

Daneca grins at Sam.

I try not to think of the photo in Barron's wallet or of the way she was smiling at my brother in the picture. I especially try not to compare it to her smile now.

"Deal me in next go-around," I say. "What are we playing for?"

"The sheer joy of victory," Sam tells me. "What else?"

"Oh," Daneca says, and gets up. "Before I forget." She walks over to her bag and pulls out a bundled T-shirt. She unknots it and pushes back the cloth. Gage's gun is there, oiled and gleaming. "I got this out of Wharton's office before the cleaners came."

I stare at the old Beretta. It's small, and as silvery as the scales of a fish. It shines under the light of the desk lamp.

"Get rid of it," Sam says. "For real, this time."

The next day it starts to snow. The flakes float down, coating the trees in a thin powder, making the grass sparkle with ice.

I walk from statistics to Developing World Ethics to English. Everything seems bizarrely normal.

Then I see Mina Lange, hurrying to class, wearing a black beret dusted white.

"You," I say, stepping in front of her. "You got Sam shot."

She looks at me with wide eyes.

"You're a terrible con artist. And you aren't a very nice person. I almost feel sorry for you. I have no idea what happened to your parents. I have no idea how you wound up stuck curing Wharton, with no end in sight and no way out and no friends you trust enough to let help you. I can't even say that I wouldn't have done what you did. But Sam almost died because of you, and for that I will never forgive you."

Her eyes fill with tears. "I didn't mean—"

"Don't even try it." I reach into my jacket and give her Yulikova's business card and the wrapped T-shirt bundle. "I can't promise you anything, but if you really want to get out, take this. There's a death worker, a kid named Gage, who wants his gun back. You give it to him, and I bet he'd be willing to help you out. Teach you how to be on your own, get work, and not be beholden to anyone. Or you can call the number on the card. Yulikova will make you a trainee in her program. She's looking for the gun too. She'll help you too, more or less."

Mina stares at the card, turning it over in her hand, holding the bundle against her chest, and I walk away before she can thank me. The last thing I want is her gratitude.

Giving her that choice is my own personal revenge.

The rest of the day goes about as well as any day. I make another mug in ceramics that doesn't blow up. Track is canceled because of the weather. Dinner is a somewhat gummy mushroom risotto, haricots verts, and a brownie.

Sam and I do our homework, flopped on our beds, throwing wadded-up pieces of paper at each other.

It snows even harder while we sleep, and in the morning we have to fight our way to class through a volley of snowballs. Everyone arrives with ice melting in their hair.

The debate club has a meeting in the afternoon, so I go to that and doodle in my notebook. Through sheer lack of attention I wind up stuck with the topic Why Violent Video Games Are Bad for America's Youth. I try to argue my way out of it, but it's impossible to debate the whole debate team.

I am crossing the quad, heading back to my room, when my phone rings. It's Lila.

"I'm in the parking lot," she says and hangs up.

I trudge through the snow. The landscape is hushed, quiet. In the distance there is only the sound of cars moving through slush.

Her Jaguar is idling near the pile of snow the plow built at one end of the lot. She's sitting on the hood, in her gray coat. The black hat she's wearing has an incongruously cute pom-pom at the top. Strands of gold hair blow in the wind.

"Hey," I say, walking closer. My voice sounds rough, like I haven't spoken in years.

Lila slides off the car and comes sweetly into my arms. She smells like cordite and some kind of flowery perfume. She's not wearing makeup and her eyes have a slight puffy redness that makes me think of tears. "I told you I'd say good-bye." Her voice is almost a whisper.

"I don't want you to go," I murmur into her hair.

She pulls back a little and twines her arms around my neck, drawing my mouth down to hers. "Tell me you'll miss me."

I kiss her instead of speaking, my hands sliding up to knot in her hair. Everything is quiet. There is only the taste of her tongue and the swell of her lower lip, the curve of her jaw. There is only the sharp shuddering gasp of her breath.

There are no words for how much I will miss her, but I try to kiss her so that she'll know. I try to kiss her to tell her the whole story of my love, the way that I dreamed of her when she was dead, the way that every other girl seemed like a mirror that showed me her face. The way my skin ached for her. The way that kissing her made me feel like I was drowning and like I was being saved all at the same time. I hope she can taste all that, bittersweet, on my tongue.

It's thrilling to realize that I'm allowed this at last, that for this moment she's mine.

Then she takes an unsteady step back. Her eyes shine with unsaid things; her mouth is ruddy from being pressed against mine. She bends down and picks up her hat. "I've got to—"

She's got to go and I've got to let her.

"Yeah," I say, curling my hands at my sides to keep from grabbing for her. "Sorry." I shouldn't already feel the loss of her so acutely, when she's not yet gone. I have had to let her go so many times, surely practice ought to make this easier.

We walk to her car together. The snow crunches under my feet. I look back at the bleak brick dorms.

"I'll be here," I say. "When you get back."

She nods, smiling a little, like she's humoring me. I don't think she realizes just how long I've been waiting, how long I will wait for her still. Finally she meets my gaze and smiles. "Just don't forget me, Cassel."

"Never," I say.

I couldn't if I tried.

Believe me, once upon a time, I tried.

She gets into the car and closes the driver's side door

with a slam. I can tell it costs her something to act casual, to give me that last little wave and grin, to put her car into gear and start to pull out of the lot.

That's when it hits me. In a single moment everything becomes suddenly, gloriously clear. I have a choice other than this one.

"Wait!" I yell, legging it over and knocking on the window.

She hits the brakes.

"I'm coming with you," I say as she rolls the window down. I'm grinning like a fool. "Take me with you."

"What?" Her face looks blank, like she's not sure she's hearing me right. "You can't. What about graduating? And your family? And your whole life?"

For years Wallingford has been my refuge, proof that I could be a regular guy—or that I could pretend well enough that no one could tell the difference. But I don't need that anymore. I'm okay with being a con artist and a grifter. With being a worker. With having friends who will hopefully forgive me for taking off on a mad road trip. With being in love.

"I don't care." I get in on the passenger side, slamming the door on everything else. "I want to be with you."

I can't stop smiling.

She looks at me for a long moment, and then starts to laugh. "You're running away with me with your book bag and the clothes on your back? I could wait for you to go to your dorm—or we could stop by your house. Don't you need to get anything?"

I shake my head. "Nope. Nothing I can't steal."

"What about telling someone? Sam?"

"I'll call from the road." I hit the knob on the radio, filling the car with music.

"Don't you even want to know where we're going?" She's looking at me like I'm a painting she's managed to steal but will never be allowed to keep. She sounds exasperated and oddly fragile.

I look out the window, staring out at the snow-covered landscape as the car starts to move. Maybe we'll go north and see my father's family, maybe we'll try to find her father's diamond. It doesn't matter.

"Nah," I say.

"You're crazy." She's laughing again. "You know that, right, Cassel? Crazy."

"We've spent a lot of time doing what we're supposed to do," I say. "I think we should start doing what we want. And this is what I want. You're what I want. You're what I've always wanted."

"Well, good," she says, tucking a lock of spun-gold hair behind her ear and leaning back in her seat. Her smile is all teeth. "Because there's no turning back now."

Her gloved hand turns the wheel sharply, and I feel the giddy rush that comes only at the end of things, that comes when, despite everything, I realize that we actually got away with it.

The big score.

ACKNOWLEDGMENTS

Several books were really helpful in creating the world of the curse workers. In particular, David W. Maurer's *The Big Con*; Robert B. Cialdini's *Influence: The Psychology of Persuasion*; Kent Walker and Mark Schone's *Son of a Grifter*; and Karl Taro Greenfeld's *Speed Tribes*.

I am deeply indebted to many people for their insight into this book. Thanks to Cassandra Clare, Sarah Rees Brennan, Josh Lewis, and Robin Wasserman for looking at many, many permutations of scenes and for their suggestions on two scenes in particular. Thanks to Delia Sherman, Ellen Kushner, Maureen Johnson, and Paolo Bacigalupi for the many helpful suggestions and general cheerleading while we were in Mexico. Thank you to Justine Larbalestier and Steve Berman for their detailed notes and focus on getting the details just right. Thank you to Libba Bray for letting me talk the whole end through with her. Thanks to Dr. Elka Cloke and Dr. Eric Churchill for their medical expertise and generosity. Thanks to Sarah Smith, Gavin Grant, and Kelly Link for helping me polish the whole book to a shine.

Most of all I have to thank my agent, Barry Goldblatt, for all his sincere support; my editor, Karen Wojtyla, for pushing me to make these books far better and for the care she took with all aspects of the series; and my husband, Theo, who gave me lots of insight into private schools and scams and who once again let me read the whole book to him out loud.